ACCOLADES

He's Fine...But Is He Saved?

"We've all been there. Praying, hoping and wishing Mr. Right Now could somehow become 'Mr. Right.' *He's Fine . . . But Is He Saved?* captivated me from the very first page. I couldn't wait until the end! This is the book that every young and adult woman must buy for herself and a friend or two. Read it together. You'll loooove it!"
  MARINA WOODS -Founder, The GOOD GIRL Book Club™ and Editor In Chief www.goodgirlbookclubonline.com

"Looks don't mean a thang, he's only a fine devil if he ain't got Jesus! Fiction comes to life in this book as it becomes a voice of single women and their challenges with finding true love and happiness."
  TY ADAMS -Author of bestselling **Single, Saved, and Having Sex**

"This is a book that will grab your attention, challenge your motives, and move you to reach for the expectations of God in finding the right relationship."
  PASTOR LOUIS SMITH -Author of bestseller **Sexual Sins of the Bible**

"Fun, refreshing, and exciting! *He's Fine . . . But is He Saved?* is a realistic, contemporary novel that proves how, in the midst of all the drama, God truly holds the outcome."
  ED GRAY -Author of **40 Days to a Life of G.O.L.D.** (God-Ordained Life Development)

"Awesome! *He's Fine . . . But is He Saved?* is an intriguing and exciting novel that superbly unveils the glorious plans God has for our love lives."
  GILLIS TRIPLETT -Author of **Why People Choose The Wrong Mate**

"I've watched Kim over the time she has been working on this novel. I have seen very few people as dedicated to her dream as she has been. Kim is a gifted writer. Her style of writing draws you in and keeps you engaged. She has worked hard to bring this novel into being. I congratulate her on a job well done."
  REBECCA OSAIGBOVO -Author of **Chosen Vessels** and **It's Not About You -It's About God**

He's FINE... But is He SAVED?

A NOVEL

KIMBERLEY BROOKS

DRIVEN ENTERPRISES

HE'S FINE...BUT IS HE SAVED?
published by Driven Enterprises

©2004 Kimberley Brooks

International Standard Book Number: 0-9760390-0-1

Library of Congress Catalog Card No.: 2004095731

Cover photography: Andy Greenwell
Author Photo: Victor A. Toliva
Cover Design: LaTanya Terry
Printed by Sheridan Books, Ann Arbor, MI

"You Are so Beautiful," written by Billy Preston and Bruce Fisher, Copyright © 1972 by Billy Preston. Copyright renewed.

All Scripture quotations are taken from
The Holy Bible, King James Version

Driven Enterprises
P. O. Box 231133
Detroit, MI 48223-1133
Visit our website at www.kimontheweb.com

I dedicate this book to God.

Acknowledgments

First, I would like to thank my Heavenly Father, the Almighty God. In Him I live, move, and have my being. Words cannot express my gratitude. From now until eternity, Jesus will always be my Lord.

I would like to thank my family: my wonderful mother, Lutricia Brooks,who has always been a blessing to me, my encouraging father, Lawrence L. Brooks, who has always had faith in me, my amazing sister, Kelley A.Thompson, who has always been there for me, her amicable husband, Rickey Thompson, and my awesome nephew, Sean. I would like to thank my beautiful aunt, Henrietta Spiller *(thanks for all the books over the years!)*, my admirable uncle, Owsley G. Spiller, my loving uncle, John H. Clark Jr., and my terrific cousins, Karen A. Spiller and Donna L. Spiller.

Thank you, the entire Brooks family, down south and beyond: Grandmother Alfreda Brooks (Madear), Aunt Barbara and family, Uncle Eugene and family, Aunt Launtenia and family, and Uncle Ernest Tony and family. I love you all.

To Bishop Keith A. Butler, founder of Word of Faith International Christian Center: Thank you for teaching me the unadulterated Word of God, along with your wife, Minister Deborah L. Butler. Thank you, Pastor Keith A. Butler II, the first to teach me how to be a young, enthusiastic, single saint *(Y.E.S.S. to the Lord!)*, his wife, Minister Tiffany Butler, and their daughter, Alexis. Thank you, Minister MiChelle Butler, and Minister Kristina Butler.

A special thank you goes out to my entire Word of Faith family.

Thank you, my closest friends: my best friend and confidante, Tonya L. Myers Esq., my "consultant" and a major source of encouragement, LaKeisha A. Monts, and a faithful supporter and friend, Ivy Mitchell.

Thank you to the following who have helped turn a vision into a reality: my editor, Debra Griffin, my interior layout and book cover designer, LaTanya Terry, my web designer, Dornique Jefferson, my proofreader, Kimberly Alsup, my makeup artist for the cover models, Jessica Hernandez, my photographers: Andy Greenwell for the cover, and Victor A. Toliva for the author photo, Sheryl Stokes, Chantelle Stokes, and all of the book cover models: Lamont Nash, Ashlee McLemore, Joy Sorce, and LaKeysha McLaurin.

Thank you, those who initially offered feedback, or knowledge about their expertise: Tinelda Williamson, Tianna Reid, Tristina Thornton, Danielle Chaney, Amy Sanders, Harold McDuffie II, Daniel Livingston Jr., Carl Williams, Greta Newman, and Ramona Ward.

Thank you Nicolé Moore, Matthew Afful, Ifeoma Obianwu, Llewellyn Jones, Gloria Jones, Joerina Harrington, The Myers Family, The Monts Family, and Pastor Joel E. Gregory and family.

Thank you, those in the industry who willingly shared insight and encouragement: Jacquelin Thomas, Victoria Christopher Murray, Rebecca Osaigbovo, Pastor Louis Smith, Stephanie Perry Moore, Ty Adams, Ed Gray, Terrence Wilson, Michael Baisden, and Gillis Triplett.

Thank you, American Christian Writers/Detroit, Marina Woods of The Good Girl Book Club, and Charis Hunt of Ministry Marketing Solutions.

To Pam Perry of MMS, *Soul Source*, and ACW/Detroit: Thank you for all you've done, and for showing me the ropes of the industry. You are a living example of the scripture that states, "My little children, let us not love in word, neither in tongue; but in deed and in truth." (1 John 3:18)

Finally, thank you, reader, for partaking of my debut novel. May God bless you richly, and may He forever keep you in His care.

THE WOMEN

Michelle Williamson

Sandra A. Moore

Elizabeth Coleman

Contents

Chapter 1

Flirting

"HE FIIIIIIINE," SANDY SANG ACROSS THE restaurant table and ran her tiny, cream-colored hand through her short black tresses. She was referring to some stranger seated at the bar.

Sandy, Liz, and I were enjoying Sunday brunch on a chilly afternoon in April at one of Detroit's finest restaurants downtown. The soothing jazz sounds coming from the black, baby grand increased my enjoyment as I swayed with the music.

We single ladies are celebrating the fact that we're "big girls now." We're all in our early-to-late twenties, graduated from different colleges, and have fairly decent jobs. We can afford to splurge once in a while.

I snapped back into the reality of Sandy's comment and

looked around to make sure no one else heard her remark. "Who fine?" I asked and then looked back down at my jambalaya.

I tell you. Sandy can be so obvious at times. One day I'm going to teach her young, twenty-three-year-old self how to do things with class, or at least learn how to use codes so that the whole restaurant doesn't know we're checking a brotha out.

"What man are you talking about now?" retorted Liz. Liz is twenty-seven, two years older than I am. She has never approved of Sandy's flirtatious ways.

I watched Liz play with her house salad. Her meal selection is a result of her trying to lose weight. In the past three months, Liz went from a size ten to a size sixteen. I believe a lot of her weight gain has to do with having to put up with her single mother's wild antics at home. Next to praying, Liz's favorite thing to do when something is bothering her is eat. However, she still looks good with her flawless caramel-colored skin and shoulder length, black micro-zillions that are half braided, half loose.

Liz and I have always had lunch together after church. Then four months ago, the Lord reunited Sandy and me, former high school classmates, one day at the grocery store. We exchanged numbers, and I invited her to church. That following Sunday, dressed in four inch heels and a short and tight jean dress with rhinestones, Sandy responded to the altar call. I walked down the aisle with her and she, in tears, got saved. I haven't been able to get rid of Sandy since that day. Now the Lord has given me a spiritual assignment to be her spiritual guide and friend.

I don't mind too much, I guess, even though sometimes I do have to remind Liz, my best friend of five years now, that Sandy is still young in the Lord. Sandy's behavior can be quite unpredictable at times, especially when it comes to her interactions with the opposite sex.

"Him, at the bar," Sandy whispered loudly while pointing toward the bar with her fork. I peeked at the

bar section and saw an older white gentleman wearing a
hideous toupee, an older black woman wearing a tight red
dress holding a glass of mimosa, and a black man who
looked to be in his late twenties.

He was dark-skinned with a bald head, had thick juicy
lips, and enough muscles to make Tyrese look bad. The
black muscle shirt he wore proved he was built, and his tan
pants hugged his thighs.

I must admit, the brotha was fine. As Sandy kept flirting
with him with her dark brown eyes, the man responded by
looking over at her with hungry eyes of his own and a sexy
smile.

"Give me a break," Liz said after sneaking a glance at
the man and then snapping her neck. "You just got out of
church not even an hour ago, and here you are flirting with
some man. Ghetto."

"The Bible doesn't say that anything is wrong with
flirting, right Mickey?" Sandy dipped her shrimp in its
cocktail sauce and took a bite while keeping her eyes on the
good-looking stranger. She kept her left hand positioned
underneath her shrimp so she wouldn't get any sauce on
her white, form-fitted dress that perfectly complimented her
small, size four frame.

Sandy is one of the smallest girlfriends I have, although
she eats all the time and should weigh 300 pounds. It must
be in her genes.

"Her name is Michelle," Liz corrected Sandy for the
umpteenth time. Liz hates when Sandy calls me "Mickey."
I've gotten pretty used to it myself.

"And besides," Liz continued, "the Bible says 'he
that findeth a wife, findeth a good thing,' not she that is
desperate throws herself at a man so she can catch one."

Sandy rolled her eyes at Liz. I lightly kicked Liz under the
table. Liz looked at me innocently as if to say, "What did I
say?"

I've had enough of those two. I love my best friend and
all, and Liz is called to be an evangelist and just graduated

from ministry school last year, but she still has room for improvement when it comes to having patience with people who are recently born again. Sandy is a rare and difficult case, I agree, but we still have to work with her and be a godly example.

Our waiter came over with a bottle of Merlot in his hand. *Who ordered that?*

"Compliments of the gentleman," said the attractive waiter. He pointed toward the man Sandy had been flirting with all along. The man looked over and winked at Sandy. Sandy beamed as she realized that the kind stranger had bought a bottle of red wine for our whole table.

"Thanks anyway, sir, but we don't drink," Liz blurted.

"Oh, no?" The waiter asked.

Sandy's facial expression grew dim as she gave Liz the evil eye.

"No, we don't," I co-signed.

Dejected, Sandy put her hand on her head and didn't say a word.

"What, do *you* want the wine?" I asked her.

"No," Sandy said with a sigh.

"Well, then, what's wrong?" I asked.

"Nothing. I guess. I mean, that was nice of him to send it over. What if he paid a lot of money for it?"

"We would have still sent it back, and he would have just wasted his money," Liz interjected.

"But he didn't have to go to all the trouble and buy it for us," Sandy whined.

"If we turn it down, then the waiter just takes it back unpaid for. Isn't that right?" I asked the waiter.

The waiter nodded and said, "That's right, ma'am."

"That's fine then. You can take it back," I instructed.

The handsome waiter tugged on his tuxedo jacket and departed with the bottle.

I looked over at Sandy's frowning face and assured her, "That may have been a nice gesture, but you have to remember something, Sandy: we don't drink."

"I know. At least, I don't anymore," Sandy said with lowered eyes.

"Look," I said. "I know you probably didn't want to appear to be rude by turning down that man's bottle of wine, but we have to set the standard. We don't drink, and that's that."

"He shouldn't have assumed that we did anyway," Liz added, folding her arms.

Sandy didn't say another word but continued to eat her food and sip her water. She glanced toward the bar and saw that the man's spot was now vacant. Maybe we did offend him by not accepting his bottle of wine. Oh well.

"Excuse me, is this seat taken?" asked a deep voice behind Sandy. Sandy turned around, looked way up, and saw her dream man, whom she thought had gotten away. I didn't realize he was so tall; he looked about 6'4". He made a motion to sit in the seat right beside Sandy.

"No, this seat isn't taken," Sandy said with renewed joy.

"Well, good. Mind if I sit here?" he asked Sandy, ignoring Liz and me.

"No, no! Go right ahead, have a seat." Sandy beamed as she pulled out his chair for him. That girl still has a lot to learn.

"I'm Dustin, Dustin Richmond," he said as he took his seat and reached his hand out towards Sandy.

Sandy shook his hand softly and said, "Nice to meet you, Dustin. I'm Sandra A. Moore."

"Nice to meet you as well, Sandra A. Moore," he said and then turned her hand over and kissed it ever so lightly. Sandy grinned.

Dustin released Sandy's hand and said to me, "And you are?"

"Michelle Williamson," I said confidently without extending my hand. He wasn't about to kiss my hand. No telling where his lips had been.

"And you?" He looked at an agitated Elizabeth Coleman. I could tell already that Liz didn't like this brotha.

"Liz," she replied with clutched teeth and folded arms. I could also tell that Liz wasn't too pleased with Mr. "God's Gift to Women" inviting himself over to dine with us. Sandy, on the other hand, was elated.

"Excuse me for one moment," Dustin said. He took his silver flip cell phone from off his hip and proceeded to press buttons. I should have known this man was just another brotha who thought he was all that, trying to show off and be rude with his cell phone. He prolly was just calling his momma.

Dustin looked over at a now disappointed Sandy and said, "Excuse me while I phone my father; he told me to call him the minute I fell in love."

Sandy's wrinkled face mustered up a huge Kool-Aid grin. I had to chuckle at that one myself. The brotha was smooth. Dustin closed his phone, returned it to his hip, and got comfortable in his chair.

"Did you ladies get the bottle of Merlot I sent over?" Dustin looked around the table for it.

"Yes, we did get it, Dustin," Sandy said, "but we sent it back." She lowered her eyes.

"Oh, really? Why did you do that?"

"Because we don't drink, Dustin," Liz blurted.

"Oh, I'm sorry. I didn't know."

"Don't be; that was nice of you, though," Sandy said while lightly patting his hand.

"A woman that doesn't drink," Dustin said while looking deep into Sandy's eyes. "I think I've hit a gold mine," he added with a charming smile.

Sandy smiled in return.

Dustin continued, "In all seriousness, Sandra, I must admit I have never laid my eyes on a woman as beautiful as you."

How original. However, I could tell Sandy was eating it all up because her Kool-Aid grin never went away.

"Maybe you haven't," Sandy said with sheer confidence.

"But you know what? I think I have though, because I

think it *was* you."

"Excuse me?" Sandy said, confused.

"I think I've seen you somewhere before."

"Don't they all say that," Liz whispered to me.

I poked Liz in her side.

"No, I have; I really have."

Sandy looked perplexed. Surely she would have remembered bumping into a brotha looking as fine as Dustin Richmond. She shrugged her shoulders and said, "Maybe you have."

"You know what, maybe you have seen Sandy before!" Liz chimed suddenly in an unusually loud tone. "Have you ever been to our church, 'Hype for Jesus,' over there on 8 mile?"

Here we go. I should have known. A church commercial advertisement from Liz.

"Ya'll go to 'Hype'? That big church with all those young people, and that young pastor, Pastor Wilkins? Isn't he like, eighteen or something?" Dustin asked.

"No, he's not eighteen. He's twenty-seven. He just looks young for his age. And the church isn't that big, compared to a lot of these churches around here. We have about three thousand members, and the church is about seven years old," I said.

"Yeah, that's Hype. Three thousand people? That's big to me. As a matter of fact, my brother-in-law goes there, and I think I went there with him one time."

"Well, maybe that's where you've seen me before!" Sandy made an attempt to regain Dustin's attention and divert the conversation back to her favorite subject-herself.

"Maybe it is. Do you have a church home, Mr. Richmond?" Liz asked. In a minute I could sense that Liz was about to pull out one of our church's business cards.

"No, I don't," Dustin said honestly, giving Liz his full attention. Sandy sighed and sat back in her chair.

"Have you ever confessed Jesus Christ as your personal Lord and Savior?" Liz asked.

"No, I guess I haven't," Dustin admitted. "I mean, don't get me wrong, I believe in God and everything. I was baptized when I was four."

That was my cue. I reached behind my chair, grabbed my brown purse, and pulled out my small black Bible. Liz and I like to catch people off guard and witness to them about Jesus. One time I ministered to a man that was initially trying to holla at me at the gym.

I scooted my seat over to Dustin and showed him Romans 10:8-10, which talks about how as long as you confess Jesus Christ as your Lord and Savior and believe in your heart that God raised Him from the dead, then you shall be saved. Dustin, taken aback at first, eventually listened intently as I showed him other scriptures which talked about man's need for a Savior and how, if he were the only person on earth, God still would've sent His Son, Jesus, to die for him.

"So are you ready to receive salvation?" I asked at the end of my miniature sermon.

Puzzled, Dustin said, "Excuse me?"

"Just repeat after me: Dear Father God..."

After a brief pause Liz repeated with Dustin, *"Dear Father God . . . "*

"I now take Jesus . . ."

"I now take Jesus . . . "

"as my personal Lord and Savior . . ."

"as my personal Lord and Savior. . ."

Dustin completed the sinner's prayer right there at the restaurant. He didn't seem really sure of what just happened, so I explained to him that he was now born again, and though he looked the same on the outside, on the inside Jesus had come to live in his heart and that he was now saved. Hallelujah!

Afterward, sure enough, Liz pulled out one of Hype's business cards that detailed the service times. Dustin rose up delighted yet a bit embarrassed; he shook hands with all of us and excused himself from our table.

After he left, Liz and I talked about how God would grow Dustin up in the Lord and use him mightily for the kingdom of God. We all bowed our heads and grabbed hands as Liz prayed that the Lord would continuously lead and guide Dustin on the path towards God's perfect will for his life.

Yes, we were all glad that the Lord decided to use us to minister to a fine brotha on this chilly Sunday afternoon. Now he can add some substance to his good looks, and I'm sure one day he'll make a fine catch for a virtuous bride. I peeked at Sandy and noticed that she looked solemn; she remained quiet during the rest of the afternoon. What in the world was wrong with her?

Chapter 2

Frustration

"LORD, WHY COULDN'T *HE* BEEN SAVED?!"
Sandy screamed in frustration once she got home from
the restaurant. She knew she was home alone because her
grandmother, Madear, normally played bridge with her
girlfriends on Sundays.

"I can't believe it! The brotha was fine!" Sandy yelled
out loud, "Fine, smart, I mean, the brotha had it going
on! Except, he wasn't *saved*! Where are all the fine, saved
brothas at? Ones that we don't have to end up witnessing to
by the end of the conversation?"

Sandy waited to hear a response from her cry in the air,
but she heard nothing. So she just threw her small pink
purse on Madear's brown-plastic couch, plopped on the
couch herself, grabbed the remote, and turned on the T.V.

Sandy was watching videos when the telephone rang. She grabbed the cordless phone and couldn't believe whose voice she heard.

It was Mark, her ex, the one she broke up with just a month after she got saved, the one she considered her first love, and the first and only one she'd ever slept with.

"Mark, is that you?" asked an anxious Sandy.

"It's me, baby girl; how ya been?"

Sandy really knew it was Mark when he called her "baby girl." She used to love when he called her that. She also used to love how they spent at least three times a week having hot, passionate sex in her bedroom when Madear was out working part-time at Daisy's Gift Shop. Once Sandy got saved they still had sex, but she eventually felt guilty and, after much encouragement from Michelle, broke up with him.

Mark complied and didn't bother her anymore. However, today, three months after Sandy told him that she no longer wanted him in her life because she was now totally committed to God, Mark was calling again.

"I been good; how you been?" asked Sandy.

"I been a'ight. I been out of town for the last month visiting my older brother in Chicago. That's why I hadn't talked to you for a while. But man, did I miss hearing your sweet voice."

Sandy was surprised. Mark was never the type to talk about "missing" anything, and he never would offer any explanation as to why he hadn't kept in touch. She figured maybe he was finally being sincere.

"I miss talking to you, too," Sandy crooned. She began to have flashbacks about the good times they shared together. Deep down, she really did miss him, and sometimes regretted breaking up with him.

"Hey, Sandy, baby girl, why don't you let me come on over there and we can watch some movies, just like old times?" Mark asked.

Sandy said nothing as she thought about Mark's request.

Maybe he has changed.

"So can I come over, or what?" asked Mark impatiently.

"I don't know . . . "

"Look," Mark continued, "I'm not going to do anything. I *promise* I'll keep my hands to myself. Besides, I been going to church now with my sister, and I kinda like it. The Word is tight, ya know?"

Sandy remembered that Mark's sister, Sheila, was called to the ministry, and had been praying for years that her little brother would finally give his life over to the Lord.

"Well," Sandy hesitated, "if you insist, but you can't stay too late, though."

"A'ight then," Mark said. "I'll see you later on, about eight o'clock?"

"Okay." Sandy hung up. She hopped off the couch, jumped up and down, and sang, "My baby coming over! My baby coming over!"

She rushed to the bathroom and fixed her short, black hair with her fingers. Sandy put on a fresh coat of glossy pink lipstick and black eyeliner.

"I can't believe my boo is coming over!" Sandy squealed. "And he saved now. He saved! He could very well be the answer to my prayers. Praise the Lord!"

Out of the bathroom, Sandy headed to her bedroom to figure out what to wear. She tore off her white dress and pulled out her tight pink baby tee and dark blue designer jeans from her dresser drawer. Sandy looked at herself in the full-length mirror on her closet door; she loved the way her jeans made her plump behind look. It was rather large compared to her tiny frame, and she considered it one of her greatest assets. "Lookin' good, girl," Sandy proclaimed.

She was so excited that she wanted to call Michelle, but she didn't want Michelle to talk her into not letting Mark come over. Besides, Sandy felt she could trust him now; she knew deep down in her heart that things had changed.

At 8:05, the doorbell rang. Sandy looked through the peephole and saw her ex-boyfriend and first love carrying a small white bag. When Sandy saw his 5'6", caramel-complexioned self smile at her with those adorable, signature dimples of his, she almost melted. Sandy was only 5'2", and everybody always said they made the cutest couple.

"What's up, baby girl?" Mark said when Sandy opened the door. He gave her the biggest, most affectionate hug she had received in what seemed like forever. She loved the feel of his broad shoulders engulfing her tiny frame.

"Hey, Mark," Sandy crooned. He hugged her so tight that she almost didn't want to let go.

Once he finally let go, he stepped inside and looked around as if he hadn't been inside the house for years. He noticed the same old antique furniture, the same gold couch and love seat covered in plastic, and the same mustard-yellow carpet that looked like it hadn't been cleaned in years.

"Wow, it still looks good in here," he said.

"Thanks," answered Sandy.

"Where's Madear?"

"Oh, she's out playing bridge with the girls. You know how it is," Sandy said as they both headed to the living room. The plastic made a loud noise as Mark sat down on the sofa.

"Oh, yeah. She still be going out playing bridge with them old ladies on Sunday nights?" Mark removed his brown cap and placed it beside him, revealing his black curly hair that Sandy used to just love to play in. "Man, nothing's changed, has it?"

"No, I guess not," Sandy said as she took a seat beside Mark. Sandy feasted her eyes on the white object in Mark's hands. "What cha got in the bag? Did you bring a good movie?"

"No, I picked this up when I was out of town. I got it for you."

"Really, what is it?" Sandy snatched it right out of his hands.

"Dang, we're mighty anxious, aren't we?"

"Well, what is it?" Sandy repeated as she put her nose inside the bag. Mark barely bought her anything during the six months they had gone together.

"Check it out," he said with a sexy smirk that accentuated his thin, wet lips.

Sandy's eyes grew big as she pulled out a small, pocket-sized pink Bible with her name engraved in gold on the front of it: "Sandra A. Moore." She couldn't believe it. He bought her a *Bible*, and a small pink one at that, which was Sandy's all-time favorite color.

"I know how you and your girls like to witness to people and stuff, so I bought you a little Bible that you can probably keep in your purse."

How thoughtful and sincere. Glory to God; Mark had changed. Sandy was speechless. She hugged him and sang, "Mark, I looove it, thank you."

She hugged him so tight that Mark began to moan. "Hmmmm . . . I knew you would." His hand slid from rubbing her back to resting just above her behind.

After the hug, Sandy re-composed herself and got up to put one of her favorite movies, "Love and Basketball" in the DVD player. When Sandy bent over to put the movie in, Mark nearly went into a trance as he gazed at Sandy's behind.

As they watched the movie, Sandy purposely sat on the opposite end of the couch. She was so touched by Mark's gift that now she was really attracted to his little, cute self. She wanted to maintain control of herself by sitting as far away as possible. Mark eventually looked at Sandy hungrily and motioned her to come over to him. "I won't bite," he reminded her. His lips looked so inviting.

Sandy moved next to him and he placed his arm over her shoulders. Sandy's heart began to race as she laid her head on his shoulder, and the love scene in the movie didn't help the atmosphere at all.

Mark whispered in Sandy's ear, "You know what, Sandy,

I really miss you. I miss having you in my life." He stroked her hair. "I miss talking to you, I miss seeing you all the time, and just being in your presence."

"I know," Sandy whined. "I been missing you, too, boo. But I been having a lot of things on my mind lately. You know I'm living for God now, and things really have changed, fo'real. I'm not the same person anymore, Mark. I don't even know why I'm here sitting with you now. It seems . . . kind of awkward," Sandy admitted.

Mark lifted Sandy's chin, looked her right in the eyes, and responded, "It's not awkward; I love it. I love sitting here with you. I wish I could sit here with you all night. You may think things have changed, but they really haven't. I mean, you know the Lord, and I know Him now, too. And I know that by Him bringing you in my life when He did, and even by breaking us up, He was able to show me who He was, through you. You changed my life, Sandy. And I thank you for it." Sandy smiled at her ex, and he gently kissed her on her forehead.

Sandy closed her eyes.

The twenty-four-year-old man who would never admit that he ever did anything wrong is now thanking God that Sandy was in his life? The man that acted like a woman wasn't anything but a nice toy to play with, is now acting like this totally changed human being? Sandy could hardly believe it; she couldn't resist. She opened her glistening dark brown eyes, looked right at him, and whispered, "Thank you."

She shed a tear. And he kissed it, ever so lightly. Mark kissed her forehead, then her nose, and then her pink lips. Then they were going at it, kissing each other hungrily, and holding each other tightly, just like old times.

They kissed for about ten minutes straight before Mark's so called new "holy hands" began to roam. They roamed up Sandy's shirt, then they roamed to her waist, and they finally settled on the button of her jeans as he unbuttoned it.

Sandy started to think something wasn't right, but heck,

it sure felt right to her. She didn't want him to stop.

Just then, the telephone rang. It rang several times, and Mark ignored it, but Sandy didn't. After the fifth ring, Sandy got up and answered it.

"Hello," said Sandy, while buttoning her pants and fixing her shirt. "Oh, hey Mickey, what's up? What am I doing? Oh, just sitting here watching a movie." Sandy failed to mention that she was watching it with her ex.

"Earlier, at the restaurant? Oh, nothing was wrong. I'm straight. I'm sure."

Mark sat up, looking discouraged. He was aroused and ready to finish the deal, so he got up, put his whole body around Sandy, and started kissing her neck. "Stop," she said, giggling. "Oh nothing, Michelle. That was nobody."

"Nobody?" answered Mark, loud enough for Michelle to hear. "So I'm nobody now? How you doing, Michelle?" Mark sang loudly in the phone. Sandy attempted to shush him, but it didn't work.

"I'm in love with yo' girl, Michelle," Mark sang. Mark used to always use the "L" word loosely, so Sandy wasn't too moved by his last comment.

Sandy was a little upset that he was yelling in the phone like that so Michelle could hear him, though. Mark knew that Michelle was Sandy's "religious friend," and that Michelle was also probably a big reason why the two of them broke up.

"Huh?" Sandy answered on the phone. "Oh that's Mark; he just dropped by." She tried to sound casual. "What do you mean what is he doing over here? We just watching a movie."

Michelle wasn't buying it. "Giggling? I'm just giggling because Mark over here acting silly."

"Hey, Michelle, why don't you bring your little tight butt over here so we can have a threesome!"

"What?" Sandy screamed in disbelief and almost dropped the phone. "Boy get off me!" She shook Mark off of her. He always had a way of ruining a nice moment with some stupid comment.

"Michelle, I'ma call you back," Sandy said and hung up the phone. She turned to Mark. "Why you always gotta say something stupid?"

"Girl, you know I was just playing," he chided.

"No, you wasn't. The Word of God says out of the heart the mouth speaks, so what you said came from your mouth and was in your heart!" Sandy retorted.

"How you gon' tell me what the Word of God says?" Mark asked sounding half drunk. "You wasn't telling me what the Word of God was saying when I just had you lying on yo' back!"

Crushed, Sandy screamed, "Get out of here Mark! Just get out! You haven't changed a bit!" She was almost in tears.

"C'mon now, baby girl," Mark said as he eased closer to Sandy. "I'm sorry, baby. I'm just so happy to see you, that's all." He wrapped his arms around Sandy's neck while breathing hard in front of her.

"Get yo' hands off of me and get out of my face," Sandy commanded through clinched teeth. Mark ignored her plea.

"Leave me alone!" She screamed at the top of her lungs like a frightened child.

Mark didn't let go. "What if I said . . . no?"

Sandy was about ready to knee him in the groin and call the cops.

"You know you want it," Mark said. He grabbed Sandy's right hand and rubbed his chest with it. Tears streamed from Sandy's face; she couldn't believe he was treating her like some freak. Sandy snatched her hand away.

"You know you want some of this milk chocolate bar," Mark said, grinning. Now he really was sounding like his old self. "And guess what, baby? It wants you, too." He had such a silly grin on his face that Sandy just wanted to smack him.

"Now c'mon, baby girl," Mark insisted, pulling her closer and attempting to kiss her neck.

"Get away from me!" Sandy screamed in his ear. She pushed him with a burst of sudden strength and Mark flew two feet away. "Get away from me and get outta my house, now!" she demanded with tears streaming down her beet-red face. "I hate you Mark, I hate you! Get out, just get out!"

"Alright then," he said finally as he grabbed his jacket. "I can see when I'm not wanted." Mark opened the door then turned around and said, "If you ever want me for anything, baby girl, you know where to find me." He left and closed the door behind him.

Sandy fell on the couch and wept. She wept, and wept, and wept some more. "Why Lord, why?" she cried. "Why do I have to be so stupid?" She made pools of tears on the plastic couch until finally, she cried herself to sleep.

Sandy thought she heard the doorbell ring in a dream. However, it kept ringing and ringing, until finally it sounded as if someone was pounding on the door. Sandy jumped up and realized that somebody was knocking on the door. Afraid it was Mark again, she screamed, "Go away!"

But the voice on the opposite side of the door said, "Open the door, Sandy; it's me, Michelle."

Relieved, Sandy opened the door and threw her arms around Michelle's neck. "Oh Mickey, I'm so glad it's you. I was so stupid tonight. I let that punk Mark come over, thinking he was all changed and stuff, and he wasn't." Michelle closed the door behind her and the two of them sat on the couch as Michelle began to speak to her newly born-again friend.

"Sandy, I know you mean well. I know you have a heart for God. And I know you trust other people and have faith in them, but you just can't believe everything you hear."

"I know," Sandy said, "but he got me a Bible." She looked around for it. "Where'd it go? That punk took my Bible! I know it was here." She pointed at the glass coffee table. "Oh well, I didn't need to see it anyway; it would only remind me of him." Sandy sighed.

"Now Sandy, I know you feel bad about what just happened, but God loves you, and He doesn't want to see your feelings get hurt like this. He doesn't want you to keep running to this man while you sit back and have your emotions all messed up."

"I know, Michelle. I was just so naive, so dumb. I really thought he changed." Michelle handed Sandy a tissue. "I really did." Sandy wiped her nose.

"But even if he did, you know that two people who are attracted to each other, saved or unsaved, can't stand to be in a room alone together. I don't care how saved, sanctified, and filled with the Holy Ghost they are. The Word of God talks about avoiding even the appearance of evil. We are all still human, and we all can still miss it. I know I've missed it."

"Really, Mickey, *you've* missed it?"

"Hmm hmmm."

"Did you have sex?"

"No, but I did have sex before with a guy with all of our clothes on, if you know what I mean. And that's still wrong."

Sandy's eyes grew dim.

"But don't get into condemnation. We all make mistakes," Michelle reassured her. "All you have to do is repent, and God will honor your prayer and remember your sin no more. Spiritually speaking, God can restore that which was lost and make you pure again, just as if you were a virgin."

"Fo'real?" Sandy chimed.

"Hmm hmmm. The thing is, Sandy, when your heart is right before God, so much to the point that you would never willingly sin, He gives us 1 John 1:9." Michelle read from her pocket Bible: "If we confess our sins, He is faithful and just to forgive us our sins, and to cleanse us from all unrighteousness."

Sandy listened attentively.

"God loves us so much that He is a God of Grace. It was

His Grace and Mercy that caused Him to send Jesus when He did in order to save us, because we didn't deserve to be put back in fellowship with God."

"Praise the Lord," Sandy said with a renewed sense of hope.

"But I want you to know, Sandy, that even though God's Grace is sufficient, and that it is, we don't want to go around here taking God's Grace for granted. That's why He gives us His Word and He gives us His Wisdom, and He gives us spiritual common sense. That's why it's best not to give any place for the devil by creating an atmosphere where both you and another person of the opposite sex can be tempted. I'm sure as you and Mark were making out, that you knew on the inside that what you both were doing was wrong."

"Yeah, I knew," Sandy admitted. "I knew as soon as I laid my head on his shoulder that something wasn't right. And even as I was kissing him I felt like I shouldn't have been. But it just felt so good, and eventually, I gave in."

"Well, your sensing that something wasn't right was actually the Holy Spirit warning you about what not to do. That uncomfortable feeling at first was the Holy Ghost giving you a 'check' in your spirit, your human spirit, letting you know that it's best if you put on the brakes. But if you ignore that check and give in to the flesh, the more you give in, the more that check goes away. So don't let the flesh dominate, but most of all, keep yourself out of compromising situations."

"Thanks, Michelle. You're right. Thank God I have you as a friend. You're a blessing. Girl, I was so scared; I didn't know what was about to happen. Thank God that you called me when you did, and that you're here now." Sandy hugged her friend.

"Actually, I can't stay long. You know I have to get up at 6 a.m. to go to morning prayer at the church at 7 a.m. and then go to work," Michelle said as she hugged Sandy and headed toward the door. "Remember 1 John 1:9. Read it tonight, and do what it says. Talk to God about what happened tonight. He'll definitely listen and give you direction, and He won't condemn you. Just make sure you don't condemn yourself."

After Michelle left, Sandy retreated to the couch and grabbed her old large Bible from beneath the coffee table. She blew the dust off the top of it and turned to 1 John 1:9 to read it herself. She felt a little better after Michelle had stopped by, but she definitely felt like she needed to talk to her Father in Heaven about what happened.

Sandy prayed, "Lord, I'm sorry." All sorts of guilt rushed throughout her body. She cried, "I'm sorry, Lord. I didn't mean it. I didn't mean to be so stupid. Please forgive me, Lord." she wiped her tears with her hands. "Help me be strong, Lord."

Chapter 3

Why Me?

"THIS IS THE DAY THAT THE LORD HAS made; I will rejoice and be glad in it!" shouted Elizabeth as she woke up on a brisk Monday morning. Liz loved waking up to sunshine and the sound of birds singing outside her bedroom window, and she looked forward to each day as a day of new beginnings. Fortunately, Liz wasn't loud enough to wake her mother, who was surprisingly sound asleep in the only other bedroom in their home on the west side of Detroit. Liz's mother, Pauletta Coleman, often complained of Liz's "religious outbursts" that she so detests hearing at the crack of dawn. Normally, Ms. Coleman isn't home when Liz wakes up; she usually spends the night at some man's house, or with her "flava of the month," as Liz called them.

At twenty-seven, Liz would have preferred to live on her own and avoid the daily arguments she had with her mother about Christianity. Ms. Coleman had confessed Jesus Christ as her Lord and Savior right after high school, but she just viewed it as fire insurance and didn't think her salvation should dictate the way she chose to live her life. In addition, she constantly nagged Liz for not dating right now and had even accused her only child of being a lesbian.

Though Liz often grew weary of Ms. Coleman's constant criticisms and promiscuous ways, she believed God wanted her to live with her mother until He told her to leave. Pretty soon, Liz believed, as she continued to let her spiritual light shine, her mother would come to know the Truth, and the Truth would make her free.

"Cut out all that noise!" Ms. Coleman shouted from her bedroom down the hall, punctuating her statement with profanity.

Uh oh, I must have woke up the sleeping giant.

Liz hopped out of bed, showered, got dressed in her navy blue jumper dress and white shirt, and went to the kitchen to prepare her lunch. She made a salad with grilled chicken breast slices, which she had cooked the night before, and included an apple, a bag of pretzels, and a bottle of water.

Her mother, who was five feet tall and a size six, often criticized Liz for not being *at least* a size eight. "You can't get a man 'cause you gettin' too fat," Ms. Coleman would tell her. Little did Ms. Coleman know that Liz was content with not having a man right now, and that she was eating healthier so she could be healthier and feel good about herself, not so she could get a man. At her current size, Liz still had plenty men trying to talk to her. Liz wasn't even thinking about a man right now.

As Liz prepared her lunch, she smiled as she thought about her students at Bakersville Christian Academy. Liz loved being a second grade teacher there. She loved being able to sow into her students' lives by teaching them new things and being a positive role model. Liz graduated from college and earned her teaching certificate in English, and enjoyed teaching them how to read and write, among other things.

Before leaving the house, Liz spent time in prayer to get daily instruction from God. Liz retreated to her bedroom for privacy.

Liz thanked God for today, her home, and her mother, and she also thanked God that her mother, by faith, was fully committed to Christ, despite what it looked like on the outside. Even though it seemed the more Liz prayed, the more her mother rejected the things of God, Liz continued to pray for her.

Despite her prayers of victory, sometimes Liz had to admit that her flesh felt defeated, especially when her mother would come home at four in the morning from a bar or nightclub. Or when her mother didn't come home at all because she was out having a one-night stand with some greasy, grimy, no Jesus, and no job-having man. Liz often got on her mother about behaving so childishly.

Sometimes her mother made excuses for her wild behavior by saying, "I'm making up for lost time. When I had yo' butt twenty-seven years ago, my life had to stop. No partying, no gettin' my groove on, no nothing. And that sorry black man of mine, your father, left me at the altar for some chick when I was pregnant with you and didn't look back. Child support? He wouldn't even pay to get you a bag of diapers, let alone child support. And where is he now? Prolly in Bermuda somewhere with some dumb broad livin' it up. As if he ain't got a child here in Detroit, Michigan."

Ms. Coleman would go on and on. She called Dominic, Liz's father, every name under the sun, except the name that God gave him. Liz hated the fact that her mother swore so much. Whenever Ms. Coleman would go into another one of her swearing fits about her father, Liz would just lock herself in her room and pray in tongues.

Liz thought her mother slept around with several men

and then never talked to them again as a way of getting back at Dominic. Sometimes Ms. Coleman would have two or three men chasing her at one time. She did look extremely good for her age. After having Liz at eighteen, Ms. Coleman maintained her slim figure and looked decades younger than her current age of forty-five.

She thought it was so strange that Liz didn't have a man. But then again, Ms. Coleman also thought it absurd for a twenty-seven-year-old woman to spend most of her free time at church.

"What do you see in that church?" Ms. Coleman would ask. "You don't need the church; all you need is God."

After hearing comments like that from her mother, Liz thanked God everyday for her high school English teacher, Mrs. Nelson, who had brought Liz to the church where she got saved nine years ago.

Liz was now an active member of Hype for Jesus Church. She graduated from its three-year Bible school and discovered that she was called to be an evangelist. Last summer, Pastor Wilkins ordained her, and sometimes Liz went to different churches and high schools in the community to speak positive words of encouragement to other young people. She shared her testimony about growing up with no father in the home, which often lifted the spirits and hopes of other young people who were going through the same thing.

"Liiiiiiiz!" screamed her mother from her bedroom again, "Didn't I tell you I was trying to sleep!" Ms. Coleman then proceeded to cuss out her only child. Liz was so caught up in her morning prayer, praise, and worship that she had gotten a little louder than anticipated. "Sorry, Mom. I'll be more quiet." Liz said with a sigh.

Liz knelt down beside her bed, placed her face in her folded hands and prayed softly:

"Dear Lord, I come before You thanking You for Your Grace and Mercy and for Your Majesty. I thank You that Your Word says that it is Your will that none should perish but that all would come to the knowledge of the truth, and You are the Truth; You are the Way and the Life. No matter what it looks like, Father God, I'm going to stand on Your Word. I admit, sometimes it gets hard. Oftentimes I ask myself 'why am I here?' and, 'when can I be out on my own serving You every second of the day?' But then You remind me that You have me here for a reason.

"My mother needs me, Lord. She needs me so that she can see You. She needs me because I may be the only walking and talking Bible she ever encounters. But, Lord, why me? Why me? She always uses Your Name in vain. She stays out all night with these strange men. It's like talking to a brick wall sometimes. Why me, Lord?" Liz sat still and waited for the Lord's response. She had her notebook and pen ready to jot down all that He had to say.

To Liz's surprise, the Lord's response came in the form of three simple yet profound words. He spoke to her spirit and asked, "Why not you?"

Chapter 4

Are We Dating?

Bzzzzzzzz MAN DO I HATE THE SOUND of that alarm clock first thing in the morning. I've been meaning to change it to the gospel music station, but I'm afraid I'll just ignore it and sleep right through it. I turned over and saw that the clock read 6:00 a.m., which really meant it was 5:50 a.m., because I like to set all my clocks ten minutes fast to help me stay on time. Most of the time, though, it doesn't help. I hit the snooze button, rolled over, and got in another ten minutes of sleep.

Bzzzzzzzz There it goes again. Okay, Michelle, time to get up. Shoot, if only I hadn't stayed up extra late last night by going over to Sandy's. But, then again, I was only trying to help, I guess. I hit the snooze button a second time and closed my eyes.

Bzzzzzzzz Okay, now this time, I gotta get up. The clock read 6:20, which really meant it was 6:10, and I gotta get up and get dressed, so I can be ready to go to early morning prayer at church by 7 a.m. Besides, on this Monday morning, I had no idea what I was wearing.

I slowly crawled out of my twin-sized bed in my one-bedroom apartment, put on my black fuzzy house shoes, and headed toward my small closet. I've been living alone in the Lafayette Squares in downtown Detroit for the past year and a half. It's the first time I've been out of my parents' house. It didn't take long for me to get used to living alone, because even when I did live with them they were out of town most of the time. My father is a traveling pharmaceutical sales rep, and my mother is a retired nurse. Right now they're on a so-called business trip in Key West, Florida.

Hmmmmm. What am I going to wear today? I feel like something corporate yet boring, since it *is* Monday. Besides, I may have to conduct a new-hire orientation class, one of my many roles as a human resources representative at the corporate headquarters of an automotive supply company called Lazek. I've worked there for the past year and a half now; it was my first job upon earning my degree in human resources.

At Lazek, I'm responsible for conducting new-hire training classes, assisting in recruitment at the many big-name colleges in the state, and conducting exit interviews. Overall, I enjoy my job; however, it is only a stepping-stone to my ultimate goal, which is to work for myself as a human resources consultant for other major corporations. That way I can choose to get out of bed whenever I felt like it.

After I finally settled on a navy blue pantsuit, I went fumbling in my top dresser drawer for my matching navy blue bra and panty set and my navy blue stockings. Then I located my navy blue shoes and navy blue purse. I grabbed all of the essentials and headed to the bathroom, put on my shower cap, and hopped in the shower. I was a little upset that I had forgotten to wrap my hair up last night. I was just so tired after I came in last night. I normally take my showers in the evening, but now I have to deal with taking one in the morning and having to flat iron my black-and-brown-streaked shoulder length hair.

The shower revived me. I turned on my radio and sang right along with Fred Hammond as I got dressed, put on my makeup, and started flat-ironing my hair into its normal, wrapped style.

"Man, do I need a touch-up," I muttered as I noticed that the roots from my permed hair were starting to look a little nappy. Once I got dressed and beautified, I went to my small kitchen complete with yellow tile, a yellow stove, and yellow cabinets, popped a plain bagel in the toaster, and prepared a ham and cheese sandwich for lunch.

When I stepped inside my baby-blue Taurus the radio clock read 7:25, which meant that it was really 7:15.

I guess that system didn't work. Now I'm late for morning prayer. The church is another fifteen minutes away. Well, some prayer time is better than no prayer time, I guess.

Once inside Hype's sanctuary, I saw, as usual, a hundred fired-up saints praying out loud as Minister Anderson, one of the young male ministers on staff, led everyone in prayer. They prayed for the nation, they prayed for other believers, and they interceded for the lost.

I scooted around several people walking around praying out loud in tongues and finally found my usual spot in the corner. I laid my journal and Bible down on the chair and remained standing to pray along with the rest. I like being in the corner because I can pray with fewer distractions. This way, I felt like it was all about me and God, and no one else.

For some reason, this morning was different. As I prayed fervently before God in my corner, I couldn't help but notice someone walking around and praying especially loud, and walking as if he was going to walk right inside my corner, but then he would turn abruptly and go the other way. I probably wouldn't have noticed him if he didn't have on a bright orange fitted T-shirt that showed off his obvious muscular build.

He headed my way again, and then whipped around the corner, leaving me only to peek at his back, but I noticed that his physique looked mighty familiar. As I caught a good glimpse of him coming around the corner a third time, I saw that it was none other than Pierre Dupree.

Not Pierre.

I felt like a huge weight had been dropped inside my stomach.

What is he doing here? He hadn't been to morning prayer in several months, eight, to be exact. I grew angry and felt a pain shoot through my heart just from looking at him, because seeing his tall and extremely handsome self only reminded me of the past.

Pierre was the one I mentioned to Sandy last night, the one I didn't necessarily "date," but did everything else with him, sexually, without going "all the way." It had only been eight months since Pierre dumped me, and to this day, when I see him, I still have to cast down bitter thoughts, wild imaginations, and fond memories of our past relationship, if one would even call it that.

 I met Pierre a little over a year ago. I noticed his tall, fine, brown-skinned self, with his hazel eyes, close haircut, and neatly trimmed goatee for the first time one day at morning prayer, and the very next day he came right over to my corner and asked me my name and how long I been a member of Hype.

"Four years," I remember saying while looking at him with batting eyelids. I was so geeked that a fine brotha like Pierre was interested in knowing who I was; I had to maintain my composure by remaining cool and confident and not sounding all giddy.

After that first meeting, Pierre would make up any excuse to come over to my corner each morning after prayer and start having small talk about the weather, or whether or not I enjoyed the last church service. Sometimes, even directly after Sunday service or after Thursday night service, Pierre would just come over and say "hi" or just make sure that I saw him staring at me.

I must admit, I was a little excited that this fine brotha was definitely checking me out. At the time, he was a saved woman's dream. I found out through my sources that besides regularly attending church, he served in children's church as a children's leader in the room with the six-to-nine-year olds. I also learned that he was thirty-two and had never been married or had kids, and he made good money working for himself.

Pierre was definitely Hype's most sought-after bachelor; it seemed as if every single woman in the church between the ages of eighteen and forty-five wanted to somehow get his attention.

One night in March, after Thursday night service, exactly a month after he initially introduced himself to me at morning prayer, Pierre spotted me talking to a female associate and her sister in the lobby. Pierre waved at me and then winked with his sexy, hazel, almond-shaped eyes. I felt like melting right where I was standing. As he made his way over, the two ladies I was conversing with politely excused themselves and headed toward the restroom, as if they knew that they didn't want to intrude on a possible divine hook-up.

"Hello Michelle," Pierre said in his signature baritone voice. "You look extremely beautiful today, as always."

I felt like just leaping into his arms.

"Why thank you, Pierre," I replied with a grin. I avoided looking into his eyes for fear of giving away how I was extremely attracted to him.

"What are you doing after service tonight?" He asked.

"Nothing, really. I don't have any plans." I wondered if I

just sounded too desperate, like I didn't have a life. I tried to fix it by asking, "Why, what's going on tonight?"

"Oh, I was just wondering if you wanted to grab a bite to eat. Are you hungry?"

"A little, but not really." Actually, I was so hungry I could bite Pierre's head off and have it for dinner. I prayed that my stomach wouldn't growl after I made that statement.

"Well, did you want to go to *Friday's* to grab something to eat? I'm hungry myself, and it would be my honor and privilege if I could dine with a beautiful woman of God like you."

That did it. I was hooked.

"Why thank you, Pierre, you are so sweet. I would be honored to dine with you tonight as well."

"Good. I'll go pull my ride around to the back, and you can pull your car around, and we can follow each other to the restaurant."

Okay . . . that's weird.

It sounded like this brotha didn't have any problems taking on the leadership role, but why all the secrecy?

But, then again, I forgot at this church, some people think if they see two people hopping in the same car, they're about to be engaged or something. He probably just wanted to not give some of the nosy churchgoers something to talk about. I mean, we were just going to grab a bite to eat, right? Two single, consenting, hungry adults who just decide to grab a bite after service. That's not a real date, is it?

"Why don't I just meet you at the restaurant?" I suggested.

"Sounds good to me," Pierre said with a boy-next-door grin. It should be against the law for a brotha to look that fine.

As I hopped into my faithful Taurus and began driving to the restaurant, I pondered about whether or not I made the right decision.

"Okay, Lord, what do you think?" I asked out loud. "Am I doing the right thing by going out to dinner with this man? He seems like a nice guy; he comes to morning prayer almost every day, and he serves in the church." No reply.

"I don't know, Lord. I know that whoever I go out with is really supposed to be somebody I would consider learning more about for the purpose of marriage, and right now, I don't really know this guy. Am I wrong for going out with him now? I mean, should I have told him, not now, maybe later? He doesn't even have my phone number yet and here we are going out. Should I pay for my own meal? Or would that insult him? Should I not have accepted his offer to go out, making it seem like I don't have a life and am available all the time? Lord, you're going to have to help me on this one." I waited for a response and still heard nothing. I just couldn't stop thinking about how fine this brotha was.

I thanked God for favor as I pulled into the restaurant's parking lot and immediately spotted another car pulling out just as I was pulling in. Once parked, I pulled down my car visor and began re-applying my dark-red lipstick when I suddenly began having second thoughts again.

"What am I doing?" I said out loud with a sigh. After about ten more seconds, I finally went inside.

Pierre greeted me with a huge smile, like one he would give an old friend he hadn't seen in ages.

"Hey, Michelle, glad you made it!" Pierre sang and then pulled something from behind him, half dozen yellow roses. "For you," he said.

How in the world did he get those roses and still manage to beat me to the restaurant? Or maybe he bought them last night and just knew I was going to accept his dinner offer tonight? Whatever the case, I must admit, the brotha was smooth.

"Thank you; they're beautiful," I replied with a smile. "It's crowded tonight," I commented as I saw a number of people waiting around to be seated. "I hope we can get a table."

"Don't worry," Pierre replied. "They already have a table ready for us." I looked at him with sheer awe as he stuck his arm out to escort me to our table. "They know me around here," he concluded.

This brotha definitely had it going on. I wondered what he did for a living and how he had so many connections. Maybe he just made dinner reservations in advance, or maybe he just comes here a lot and he knows the owner. Or maybe he comes here a lot with a different woman every week. I need to stop speculating so much; I'm beginning to sound a bit ridiculous.

Pierre escorted me to a table for two near a window and made it a point to pull out my chair as I sat down. *A true gentleman; another plus.*

Pierre sat across from me, looked directly into my eyes and said, "You look very lovely tonight, Michelle."

This brotha acted like I went home and changed or something, as if he didn't just see me at church fifteen minutes ago.

"Thank you," I replied. "You are too kind. You told me after service tonight that I looked nice, and you're still complimenting me. You are just too sweet."

"No, *you're* sweet," Pierre corrected me, "and still beautiful."

I felt my brown skin turn pink. "Stop, Pierre, you're making me blush."

"I'm serious, Michelle. I just call 'em as I see 'em. And the main thing that attracted-"

Attracted? My facial expression gave away my initial shock.

"Yes, attracted me to you is that you're not just beautiful on the outside, you're beautiful on the inside as well."

This brotha is pretty bold and up-front, which is a character quality I've always admired in a man. Most men are either super shy or just simply afraid to verbally express how they honestly feel about a woman. Like they're afraid to drop their guard first or something. But not this brotha, no, no. Here it is, our first time out, and he's just laying it all out. I was impressed. Pierre grew silent and looked at me as if he was waiting for some type of a heartfelt response.

"Pierre, I don't know what to say." I didn't sound too eloquent.

"You don't have to say anything, just be. Be yourself, Michelle. I like it that way."

Just then a gum-smacking, eyes-rolling young girl came to our table.

"Ya'll ready to ordah?"

I was so caught up in Pierre's compliments that I hadn't even looked at the menu. I normally order chicken fingers or dessert when Liz and I come here after church. I didn't want to seem like a pig in front of Pierre, so I ordered my usual. Also, I wasn't sure if I was paying for the meal or if he planned on paying, so I decided against causing a brotha to go broke tonight, even though I heard my stomach squealing something terrible. I cleared my throat to cover up the sound of my stomach growling.

"And for you, sir?" The waitress smiled when she spoke to Pierre. It was funny how her broken English suddenly turned perfect as the teeny-bopper eyed the man I was dining with.

"I'll have the New York Strip meal with the grilled chicken caesar salad."

I underestimated Pierre. He must carry much bank in order to order steak. Maybe I should have ordered the shrimp combo. Whoever made up the stupid rule that women have to order first in a restaurant, anyway?

As the waitress made her departure, Pierre put on his investigative hat and started drilling me with twenty questions.

"So, Michelle, besides going to church, what else do you like to do?"

"Oh, I like to do a lot of things. I like reading, and going skating, and mainly hanging out with family and friends." I hoped that answer didn't sound too generic, but it was the truth. I'm not that deep.

"What do you do for a living?" he asked.

"Right now I'm an hr rep-excuse me-a human resources

representative for an automotive supply company called Lazek. There I speak mainly with new hires and conduct introductory training courses, among other responsibilities that I have."

"Interesting. Do you like what you do for a living?"

I felt like I was being interviewed by Barbara Walters instead of enjoying dinner with an attractive man of God from church.

"Actually, I do like my work, very much." I smiled proudly.

"What do you like about it?" Pierre probed.

This man never stops.

"Well, let's see. I love people. I love interacting with new hires. I love the fact that I am usually the first person they see on their first day on the job, so I am able to talk to them and ease them of a lot of the first-day-on-the-job-jitters that they may have."

"I see."

"I also love traveling to different colleges around the state, conducting initial weeder-type interviews with several candidates and then making recommendations to different hiring managers about who should be invited to corporate headquarters for a second interview."

"Interesting."

"Yup, that's about it. I just love helping people."

"It sounds like you have a sincere passion for what you do."

Sincere passion? I don't know about all that.

Pierre leaned over on the table, looked me right in the eye, and asked, "Do you dream of excelling in your position, Michelle? Do you see yourself going up the success ladder within the corporation?"

Is this man some kind of a career counselor?

"Actually, my ultimate goal is to be an hr consultant and work for myself," I admitted.

"Aha!" Pierre pronounced loudly with a bang on the table, causing a few heads in the restaurant to turn in our direction, "so you *are* about self-empowerment!"

I had to laugh at that one. "Well, I guess I am." This man was too much. "And what do you do, Pierre?"

"What do I do?" Pierre said with a chuckle.

Drum roll, please.

"Well, I do a number of things."

"Such as . . . "

"Well . . . I'm a financial consultant. I also own my own e-commerce business."

"You do both?"

"Yes, I do both, and quite well, I might add."

Cocky now, aren't we?

"As a financial consultant, I have my own office in Southfield. I meet with my clients monthly and go over their financial plans and long-term goals."

"I see."

"But the main thing is, I help people get out of debt and start living like they ought to live, which is debt free with the ability to have money left over to save and spend wisely."

"Sounds good." I sipped my water. "And the Internet business . . . ?"

"That, my friend, pretty much runs itself. I have my own virtual mall online, and since I became an independent business representative and began growing the business four years ago, I have acquired clients and other independent business reps of my own all over the country, in Michigan, Illinois, Florida, California-I even have clients in London."

"Impressive," I said, nodding.

"I don't have to do much of anything with that business, except collect monthly checks and make deposits into my checking account. Some executive level representatives may call on me occasionally to give a presentation about how I've succeeded in the business, but they even pay me to do that. The best part about it is, while I'm sleeping, I'm making money," he said with a large grin.

I had heard that e-commerce is a very lucrative business these days, and I could only imagine the amount of money that Pierre must be making. No wonder nearly every single woman in the church wanted to get with this brotha. So the rumors about his income were really true; he was pretty paid. I admired how he didn't wear his worth on his back in the form of zoot suits and seven-hundred dollar gators.

"It sounds like you have 'sincere passion' for what you do as well."

This man put the "p" in passion.

"Oh definitely. It's what I've been put on this earth to do."

"And what's that?" I asked.

"Become financially independent so I can help fund the spreading of the gospel."

Hold up. Did this man just say, "help fund the spreading of the gospel?" I was growing more and more interested in Pierre every minute. Saved, extremely handsome, goal-oriented, outspoken, and now a big giver concerned about spreading the good news? I believe I hit a gold mine with this man.

"Praise God," I said and gave Pierre a high-five across the table. The waitress returned with our food and placed it in front of us.

I was about to pray over my food quietly to myself when Pierre grabbed my hand, bowed his head and said, "Dear Lord, I thank you for the food we are about to receive for the nourishment of our bodies; may it be sanctified by the Word of God and prayer, and I thank you, Lord, for this opportunity to fellowship with this beautiful sister and your daughter, Michelle, that we may enjoy getting to know one another. In Jesus' Name, Amen."

"Amen." I said. I'm glad I decided to get over any anxieties and just come meet this man for dinner tonight. What a sweetheart!

"So, where do you serve at church?" Pierre continued.

"Where do I serve?" I asked as I cut a chicken finger with my fork and dipped it in honey mustard sauce. "I'm a Bible study leader and an altar call counselor."

"Oh yes, I do remember seeing you go down the aisle to help counsel those that responded to the altar call. Very faithful," Pierre observed.

"I try, I guess," I replied. "God has been so faithful to me, I can only try and do what He tells me to do as far as serving in the church, so that I can be faithful to Him."

I could tell Pierre liked that answer by the intense look on his face.

"And where do you serve?" I knew good and well that all the single ladies at Hype knew where this brotha served. Most of the single ladies with small kids couldn't wait until their kids turned six they could take their little rascals to children's church and have Pierre look after them.

"I currently serve in children's church with six-to-nine-year olds"

"Really?" I tried to sound surprised. "A suave and debonair brotha like you serving with the kids? I can't believe it." We laughed.

"I do have a soft side, now," Pierre admitted. "One Sunday they even made me wear a clown suit. Now that was funny."

"I bet it *was* funny. You, in a clown suit? You probably made a good clown."

"I don't know, now, not all the kids were laughing. Some of the younger ones even cried."

I was about to laugh so hard that I almost gagged as I took a sip of water. "Cried?" I asked in disbelief. "What kind of clown were you?"

"I was a good clown!" Pierre retorted with a laugh. "Those kids just weren't used to seeing me dressed like that. They didn't know who I was, so they were scared."

"Okay," I replied as I cut my eyes at him with a playful smirk.

"Michelle," Pierre said in a tone that was suddenly serious. "You have beautiful dark brown eyes. I love it when you look at me that way."

"What way?" I was starting to get the idea that Pierre

liked catching me off guard with compliments.

The remainder of the night went well. I discovered a lot about Pierre. He was the middle child of two brothers, and had no sisters. His parents recently divorced after being married sixteen years. He was originally from Virginia, but moved to Detroit to live near his older brother.

The only thing I wasn't sure of was Pierre's main reason for asking me out. Was it a date? It was very obvious that we enjoyed each other's company. I just secretly wished Pierre would go into detail about why we were here and where we were going from this point on.

Once the bill showed up, I started digging in my purse for money. Since I wasn't sure if this was a real date or not, I didn't want Pierre to think I expected him to pay for my meal.

"What are you doing?" asked Pierre.

"Oh, I'm just grabbing how much I owe for the meal."

"Michelle, get your hand out of your purse. I got it, baby."

Baby? Maybe we are going somewhere with this. Then again, a lot of men over thirty, even in the church, call women "baby."

"Why don't you let me be a blessing to you tonight," he added.

"I know Pierre, but I didn't want to be rude. I mean, I didn't want you to feel obligated to pay for my meal."

"Obligated? I'm not *obligated* to do anything. I wasn't *obligated* to ask you out tonight. And you weren't *obligated* to say yes. Or at least I would *hope* you didn't feel obligated. I'm offering to pay for your meal because I *want* to pay for your meal. I want to be a blessing, and I want you to know that I appreciate your agreeing to dine with me tonight."

Well, since he put it that way . . .

"I guess I didn't mean it when I said 'obligated.' And no, I definitely did not feel obligated to say yes to you tonight when you asked me out. But can I ask you something, Pierre?"

I mustered up enough courage to ask what really has

been on my mind during our interaction tonight. A lady has got to know these things.

"Sure, what is it?" Pierre responded. He set the bill aside after he placed his gold card inside the black dish. All of his attention was on me.

I took a deep breath, paused, and then finally asked, "Why am I here? Why did you ask me out, really? I mean, I know you're attracted to me and all, but are you looking to *date* someone right now? I don't mean to be all blunt, but I kinda need to know." I hesitated. "I just want us to be on the same page."

"I'm not sure about what you're saying, Michelle. You're wondering why I asked you out?"

"Yeah, why did you ask me out?"

"Because I feel that you are the kind of woman that I could eventually like, or be with." Pierre stated.

"Do you mean be with, for now, or be with, forever?" I hoped I wasn't too forward.

"Michelle, where are you going with this? It's our first date and you're talking about forever."

Aha! So it is a date! He admitted it. Okay, I can get with this now. Then again, I just remembered that I hardly ever saw Pierre at any of the Hype's Singles Meetings. They're held once a month in the sanctuary, and the main purpose is to show, through the Word of God, how unmarried Christians can have successful single lives.

The meetings also talk about how dating should be done for the purpose of getting to know someone for the ultimate goal of finding out, through the leading of the Holy Spirit and by spending time with another individual, whether or not the person you are with could be the one for you as a lifelong mate. Pierre hadn't attended any of the singles meetings, so he may not view *dating* the same way that I do.

Besides, I'm twenty-four now. I don't just casually date anymore. Been there, done that. I'm through with playing those games. My dates have to have purpose.

"Do you know what I mean, Pierre?" I asked.

"No, I'm sorry, I'm not sure I know what you mean."
Pierre looked confused as he wiped his mouth with his
napkin.

"I mean, are you just here with me tonight because you
think I'm attractive and you wanted some company while
you ate, or do you think that maybe, just maybe, we could
have a future together?"

"I don't know, sweetheart." He placed his hands on the
table and leaned forward.   "I don't know. I know right now
the Lord is doing some things with me that I don't feel I'm
ready to be *dating* someone in that way. But I also know
that I know a good thing when I see it, and you're definitely
it. So, Michelle, I can honestly say that I am attracted to you,
I want to know more about you, and I'll let the Lord handle
the rest." He then grabbed my hand and said, "Let's just
cherish the moment, okay, sweetheart?"

I wasn't quite sure where Pierre was going with that
'cop-out' response. And what's with all this "baby" and
"sweetheart" stuff? It was beginning to get on my nerves.
Even though I felt a bit awkward and unsure of myself after
Pierre's response, I still didn't feel like ruining an enjoyable
evening with any type of emotional fit. I decided to wait
and possibly bring up the subject again later, if there was
even going to be any later.

In the car on my way home from our date, or our
fellowship, or whatever it was, my mood changed and I
thought about the way I had acted in the restaurant.

Why was I so stupid, Lord? He probably thinks I'm some
over-zealous, over-emotional, super-spiritual, "needing-
a- man" feign! I couldn't get over how I acted, questioning
him like he was a common criminal. All he wanted to do
was dine together, and here I am sounding like I'm ready to
marry the man. Hopefully, I didn't scare him away. I guess
I'll find out by whether or not he decides to use the cell
number I gave him at the end of the night when he escorted
me to my car.

That night, in the privacy of my bedroom, I sat on my bed and prayed about this new man God has allowed me to get to know a little better. I prayed in tongues for fifteen minutes, and then I sat still to listen to what God had to say.

And a soft, gentle voice said to my spirit, "Yes, he is My child, no doubt, but I want you to wait on Me. Move when I say move. Go when I say go. Be not afraid; only believe. Believe you are all I've called you to be. You are My precious jewel, My loving princess, and I will always love you. Trust in My love and wait on Me."

Chapter 5

Freedom

"SANDY, IT'S 7:00 BABY, TIME TO GET UP!" sang a cheery older woman. It was Madear, yelling from the kitchen. Madear was such a morning person. Every morning she woke up at 5 a.m. to fix breakfast for herself and her granddaughter. Since Sandy was on the go a lot, Madear looked forward to their breakfasts together.

Sandy, on the other hand, didn't understand why her grandmother woke up so early since Madear was retired and only worked three days a week at Daisy's Gift Shop. However, Sandy didn't complain about receiving a home-cooked meal every morning.

"Sandy, did you hear me? It's 7:01, rise and shine!" Sandy grabbed her pillow and slammed it on top of her face. She was so tired from the night before, she didn't even know how she ended up in her own bed instead of still being on the floor near the couch, the same position she was in after she prayed to God about her situation with Mark.

"Okay, Madear. I'm up. Thanks," Sandy finally groaned. Really she was still lying in bed, unable to believe that it was morning already. The scent of fresh bacon cooking helped her wake up. She eventually crawled out of bed and headed to the bathroom.

Once Sandy was dressed in a pink and silver wraparound skirt and a light pink fitted top, she finally met her grandmother in the kitchen so that they could eat breakfast together.

"Morning, Madear," chimed a more alert Sandra Moore.

"Morning, sweetheart," sang Madear with a smile as she placed something from the skillet on a plate for Sandy.

"Mmm, what we got, bacon and eggs?"

"This time we have bacon, toast, and omelets," responded Madear.

"Praise the Lord! My favorite! Ham omelet with green pepper, mushrooms, and bacon bits!"

"You know it." Madear smiled.

Sandy felt like she was on "Leave it to Beaver."

"You're the best, Madear," Sandy chimed as she kissed Madear on her brown cheek and took a seat in front of a delicious breakfast prepared just for her.

"Lord," prayed Madear as she grabbed Sandy's hand and stroked the top of it with her thumb, "thank You for yet another day. Thank You for keeping us in our right mind. Thank You for our health and strength, and most of all, thank You for family. In Jesus' Name, Amen."

Madear has always loved God. Sandy believed it was Madear who prayed her into salvation. When Sandy used to come home late at night from messing around with "those little nappy head boys," as Madear called them, Sandy would sneak to her bedroom, afraid that she would wake Madear, but instead would hear Madear in her bedroom praying out loud in a boisterous, authoritative voice.

"Lord, protect that child!" Madear would pray, "Knock some sense into her head! And Satan, take your nasty hands off her! She ain't yours! She mine, you hear me? She mine! You may have thought you don' took my baby girl and her husband out, but you ain't gettin' this one. She mine!"

Sandy's parents were both killed in a car accident by a drunk driver when Sandy was six. After hearing the devastating news from her uncle one day after school seventeen years ago, Sandy raced to her bedroom, leaped on her canopy bed, grabbed her pink teddy bear, and cried inside her pillow for a full hour. As she cried, Madear entered her room and placed her massive body on top of Sandy to calm her. Sandy sometimes still remembered how Madear hummed the tune of "Precious Lord" in her ear that day, until little Sandy cried herself to sleep.

"Amen," repeated Sandy at the breakfast table.

"How you like your omelet, baby?" asked Madear.

"It's fine, Madear. You always know how to make 'em just how I like it."

"I wanted to make you a big breakfast to give you enough energy in the morning to keep you awake at work, since you were up so late last night," Madear said while still eating and staring into her plate. Sandy knew Madear was fishing for some answers about what went on last night.

"Thanks Madear, I really appreciate it," Sandy replied. She really didn't want to talk about what had happened with Mark, especially not at the breakfast table. Sandy was ready to just put the past behind her by not saying another word about it.

"And you know what else?" Madear continued, "When I got home last night, I come in and sees you all sprawled out in front of the couch. Know anything 'bout dat?"

"I know, Madear. I know about it."

"You know, Sandy, the day your mom and dad made their transition, I made a vow between me and God to never leave you alone and to always look after you. So if anything is ever worrying you in yo' life, I want you to know that you can come to Madear."

"Thanks, Madear." Sandy responded with a sheepish grin. She rose from the table and kissed her grandmother's warm cheek. "Gotta go to work now."

"Okay, baby, you have a lovely day. And don't forget to say your prayers this morning."

"Oh, shoot. I didn't wake up in enough time to say my morning prayer." Sandy thought, "Oh well. I guess I'll have to say it in the car; I'm almost late for work."

Sandy made a mad dash to her silver Neon, turned the ignition key, jolted out of the driveway, and began to recite her morning confession.

"Dear Lord, thank You for this great day!" she shouted in the car in order to boost her spirit. "Thank You that today I and my family walk in Divine Health, and that the Favor of God will follow me everywhere I go. I thank You that You are with me on the job today, and that I will never forget that I am never alone with You. Thank You that today You make me to prosper in everything I do, and I promise to give You and You alone all the praise, honor, and glory!"

As she shouted in her car with her window down, she noticed the person in the car next to her look at her like she was crazy. Sandy figured they probably thought she was screaming to herself, so she just glanced over and smiled.

Then, as if a light bulb came on in her head while she was driving, Sandy yelled, "And thank You, Lord, that I'm free! I'm free! I'm free! I'm free! No more Mark, no more pain! I'm finally free! Thank you, Lord, for restoring me, that I can now be alive again, without that punk Mark-I mean, your child, Mark! I'm free, woo hoo!"

Chapter 6

Home Sweet Home

AFTER A REWARDING BUT LONG MONDAY
with her favorite second graders, Liz was more than ready to
go home. She was ready for a soothing, hot bath while she
cuddled with a good book.

Monday nights were normally relaxing for Liz. She could
do what she desired to pamper herself, rather than spend all
her energy on the little ones at the academy. Liz was more
than looking forward to her Monday evening with just her
and the Lord. Her mom normally stayed out all night, so
Liz didn't anticipate her being there.

For some strange reason, tonight was different. As Liz

turned the key in her front door, she heard water running. In the bathroom, she saw the bathtub almost filled to overflowing with steamy hot water. She also saw red rose petals covering the top of the tub and all over the floor. Lit candles stood on each of the four corners of the bathtub.

"What the heck is going on here?" Liz thought to herself. She had hoped her mother hadn't gone crazy and started getting into voodoo meditation or something.

As soon as Liz turned the water off to keep it from overflowing, she heard laughter coming from her mother's bedroom. She figured her mother was probably home tonight, but what she was laughing about, Liz wasn't sure. As Liz tiptoed from the bathroom and eased closer to her mother's closed•bedroom door, Liz heard the bass voice of some strange man. It sounded like he was the author of whatever joke Ms. Coleman was laughing at. Liz's mom giggled like a high schooler, like it was the best joke she had ever heard in her entire life. Right then, Liz knew her own plans for a peaceful evening alone were now diminished.

Liz always knew her mother was loose, but she didn't usually air her dirty laundry by bringing these men home with her. She would normally go to their houses, or fly away with them on cruises or get-a-ways. Liz thought something really weird was going on tonight.

Liz headed for the front room, trying to put the pieces of the mystery houseguest together. She saw the man's clothes on the hardwood floor in front of the couch. Sprawled on the leopard skin throw rug was an extra-large, multi-colored sweater, some black pants, and a huge cowboy-looking brown belt.

He was so quick to take off his clothes that his wallet, some change, and a shiny gold object had fallen out of his pocket. Liz looked closer and then picked up the shiny gold object on the floor; it was a wedding band.

"This man is married!" Liz screamed. What in the world? She knew her mother did some dumb things to get back at men, but this is going a little too far. Married? What about his wife? What about his marriage?

As Liz began to fume, she heard the creak of her mother's bedroom door and saw her mother's brown body, scantily clad in a bright red bra and panties, slip away from her bedroom and head toward the bathroom.

"Liz!" Her mother jumped in shock as she noticed her daughter shooting darts at her with her eyes. "You're home." She tried to cover her half-nakedness with her hands. Apparently, it wasn't working.

"Yes, I'm home, and you're naked."

Liz's mother grinned sheepishly and replied, "Um, Liz, why don't you find something to do tonight." She shooed Liz away with her hand. "I have company over, and um, you know what I mean."

"No I *don't* know what you mean. Mom, do you know this man is married?" Liz proclaimed as she showed her mother the wedding band.

"Married?" Ms. Coleman pretended to be surprised. "Um, no, I didn't know he was married. How did you find that out?" She snatched the wedding band out of Liz's hand and placed it inside the pocket of the large pair of pants on the floor.

"C'mon, Mom. You knew he was married and you're in there sleeping with him-a married man!"

"What does his being married have to do with me?"

"C'mon, Mom!" Liz screamed. At this point Liz didn't care if the whole neighborhood heard her, let alone some sex-crazed adulterer in her mother's bedroom. "The man is married! Do you know what that means? He belongs to somebody else. He's not *yours*. He's using you, Mom! And you're just being so stupid, acting like you don't know what's going on."

"Oh, I know what's going on." Ms. Coleman darted her eyes at her daughter. She put on her black satin robe from off the chair in front of her. "What's going on is you better take you and your religious butt outta my house! Calling me stupid. If I'm so stupid, then you must be stupid, too, 'cuz I gave birth to yo' black butt!"

"Mom, that's not what I meant. I didn't say you were stupid, I just said you were *acting* stupid. Your behavior lately has been uncalled for. You are much better than that, and you don't have to stoop so low as having sex with a married man," Liz pleaded.

"Look, I appreciate your concern and I know you mean well, but I got something I got to take care of right now in the bedroom. So I would appreciate it if you would just find somewhere else to go tonight so I can enjoy myself in my own house. Comprendé?"

At that moment, a mountain of a man came walking out of Ms. Coleman's bedroom. He was so tall, his head touched the top of the bedroom doorway, and so big that he had to turn sideways to get through it. He came out with just brown satin shorts on, with his potbelly stomach hanging over his shorts. The man was bald with gray hair on the sides and looked like he was sixty.

He grabbed Ms. Coleman from the back and said in a gruff voice, "Is everything okay out here?"

Liz was so astonished by what stood before her eyes that she almost had to force herself to close her mouth and put her eyes back in their sockets. He wasn't attractive at all. He was light-skinned with acne and had a dented head. He looked like somebody's ex-bodyguard, not somebody's "boy-toy" for the night.

"Everything's just fine," sang Ms. Coleman as "Zeus, Jr." kissed her tiny neck and engulfed her entire frame with his ashy bare hands.

"This is my daughter Liz," she told him, "and she was just leaving."

On cue, Liz grabbed her black purse and ran out the door, slamming it so hard that the neighbors down the street probably heard it. She didn't care. She was just so upset that her mother was prostituting herself.

"Oh dear God," Liz said as she left the house, "please watch over my mother. I'm afraid if she doesn't change her behavior soon, she's going to end up ruining her life."

Chapter 7

In His Arms

I SNAPPED BACK INTO THE REALITY OF morning prayer service once I heard the minister lead the congregation in a shout of victory after everyone finished praying. The minister shouted, "We know that when we pray according to the will of God, He hears our prayers, and we also know that we have the petitions we desire of Him! Hallelujah!"

"Hallelujah!" the congregation shouted and praised God.

I had to remember where I was for a minute, so I lifted my hands to shout and praise God along with everyone else. I lost sight of the bright orange shirt in the crowd. I had hoped I could sneak out the sanctuary and head to my car without Pierre even noticing me. Unfortunately, he appeared in my sight on the other side of the sanctuary and was staring right at me. I made a mad dash towards the Exit sign but was stopped in my tracks.

"Michelle Williamson!" chimed Pierre.

I turned around slowly, put on a fake smile, and sang, "Pierre Dupree!"

"It's me," he said, "in the flesh."

"How have you been?" I asked. Like I really cared. I was just trying to be polite. I hoped his answer would be short and sweet so I can eventually head to my car.

"I've been doing well. I can't complain. I've been away on business for the last three weeks in Atlanta."

Whoopdeedoo.

"Atlanta? Niiiiiice. I'm sure you enjoyed it there."

"I *did* enjoy it there, besides the work, that is," he chuckled. There he goes again with that sneaky grin, the one that I thought was cute when I first met him eight months ago.

"Work? I know you're not talking about work. I thought you just loved your work?"

"I know, I know. You got me there. You're right. It's not really work to me. But when I'm done doing what I have to do, then sometimes I wanna have a little fun. If ya know what I mean?"

No, I don't know what you mean, Mr. Pierre. Enough of this pointless chatter.

"Pierre, I hate to cut you off, but I don't want to be late for work. You know how it is." I explained. I looked around to make sure no male prospects were eyeing our lengthy conversation.

"I understand, Michelle. Please, allow me to walk you to your car."

"No thanks, I'm okay," I said with a forced smile. I really didn't want to have anything to do with him after what he did to me last summer.

"You have a blessed day, okay?" I walked toward the parking lot, leaving Pierre standing in the sanctuary with a solemn expression on his face.

Once inside my car I felt relieved. Had he come to morning prayer just to harass me afterwards? The minute we stopped dating, or going out, or whatever it was, that brotha stopped coming to morning prayer, period.

And what was his little hint in his little small talk all about? *If* you know what I mean. If, Pierre, what you *mean* is compromising the Word of God in order to fulfill your little fantasies, then no, I *don't* know what you mean.

I was fuming inside. I know I'm supposed to forgive and walk in love and everything, but that man really made me mad! I better just pray in tongues quietly in my car so I can calm down.

In my cubicle at work, I looked at all of the paperwork in front of me and decided to work on my orientation program for new hires, which is supposed to be completed by this Monday. My company, Lazek, had recently adopted new policies and procedures, and I have to update the current training program to incorporate the changes. It shouldn't be too difficult, since most of it can be completed at my desk on my computer. I also have to present a PowerPoint presentation to my superiors. Fun.

One thing I do appreciate about this job is the autonomy. Like today, I don't have to worry about co-workers finding out that I allowed myself to get shaken up over some man. For them, I have to stay the calm, cool, and refreshing woman of God that I am. Every one in the office knows I'm saved, so I can't walk around the office with my head hanging down. I have to keep a smile on my face and let them continue to come to me with all their problems.

I turned on my computer and stared at it for a moment. *I'm a strong woman. I refuse to let some man get my emotions all bent out of shape and affect my performance on the job. Sure, my little heart was broken, but I have to know that God has something better for me, right?*

I started fumbling through the pages of the updated policy manual, and then my mind began to wander to the good times Pierre and I once shared.

I slammed the policy manual shut and put my hand on my forehead.

How could I be so stupid? Why didn't I listen to God's initial warning when He told me to take it slow? How did I allow this man to get to me, steal my heart, and capture my soul? What is wrong with you, Michelle Williamson?

I've never felt this way about anyone; why is this man so different? I started chewing the end of my ballpoint pen.

Maybe it's because Pierre was the first saved man I ever went out with. Maybe it's because I actually thought our relationship was going somewhere and that Pierre could possibly be "The One." Maybe it's because I actually believed him when he talked and walked like he was this sincere saint that would never do or say anything on purpose that would hurt God's heart. Maybe I was just in over my head.

"Where you are taking me?" I asked on an unusually warm night last May as Pierre and I were seated in his black Escalade headed on yet another date. Then again, no weather is unusual in Michigan; one never knew what to expect. We decided to take advantage of the warm weather tonight and go out. I felt cute and confident in my turquoise top with the back out, and long turquoise and white floral skirt. Pierre looked pretty sharp as well with his khaki shorts, showing off his hairy legs, and fitted black shirt.

After our initial encounter at dinner, Pierre had called me that very next night, and every night thereafter, and we had been going out together every weekend since for two

months. We'd gone to the movies, bowling, laser tag, and
several upscale restaurants downtown. Pierre spoiled me
by calling me sporadically at work just to say "Hi," or he
would call me after morning prayer on my cell just to say
"good morning, sweetheart." I got used to hearing his sexy
baritone voice every morning.

On this particular night last May, Pierre refused to tell me
where he was taking me. I really wanted to know, but then
again I am fond of surprises. Let's see, we're heading west
on Grand River, going towards Farmington Hills; we must
be going Go-Kart Racing and Putt-putt golfing! I figured it
out, but only after he turned left into the parking lot of my
favorite place to do those activities. I remembered telling
Pierre, during one of our late night phone conversations,
that I used to have so much fun going Go-Kart racing with
my dad when I was ten. I couldn't believe that Pierre took
heed to our phone conversation, and now here I am at the
very location where I used to have so much fun! I felt like a
kid again.

"I haven't been here since I was a little girl!" I shouted as
Pierre found a good parking space right in front. "Thanks,
Pierre," I sang and attempted to give him a huge hug as he
placed his ride in park.

"Whoa sweetheart, not while I'm driving," Pierre joked.
I just sat back with all smiles like an anxious four-year-old
waiting to get out of the car.

Once parked, I was ready to jump out and head for my
favorite yellow Go-Kart, but then I remembered how Pierre
is such a gentleman, he always likes to get out first and open
the door for me. Of course, I didn't want to rob him of that
privilege. He opened the door for me and I reached my
hand out toward him like a queen. I loved all of the royal
treatment from Pierre.

Once out of his ride, he whispered in my ear, "Now can I
have my hug?"

"Thank you Pierre," I repeated as I squeezed his body
tight. This was no church hug; this was a genuine thank-

you-from-the-bottom-of-my-heart kinda hug. I loved the feel of his broad shoulders and muscles hugging all over me, along with the smell of his spicy cologne. I eventually had to catch myself so I didn't kiss him, even though I really wanted to. I finally drew back, to Pierre's apparent dismay, and grabbed Pierre's hand and led him to the entrance gate.

"C'mon!" I sang like a child at an amusement park. "I got number 4!" I yelled and hopped inside the yellow Go-Kart, and Pierre hopped in the green one. As we raced, Pierre tried three times to run me off the road. He let me pass him twice, and I was even convinced that I was beating him in my own strength, not because he let me. However, because Pierre wasn't about to let a girl cross the finish line, he sped up, passed me, and won the race.

Next we walked hand-in-hand over to the putt-putt golfing area. Pierre likes to golf regularly, but I'm not much of a golf fan myself. I figured since he accompanied me on my favorite thing to do, which is Go-Kart racing, then it was my turn to accompany him on his favorite thing to do. Besides, as long as I had Pierre right beside me, I didn't mind. I can play like the "damsel in distress" who doesn't know a thing about golfing, and allow Pierre to show me how to hold that golf club and have him wrap his big arms around me once more.

The course was laid out with the little green hills and miniature pools for the golf balls to land in. There were about ten other people there that night. I noticed a few older couples looking at Pierre and me like we were the perfect young couple. Some of them even smiled at us.

Before we started at our first hole, Pierre struck up a conversation with a young white couple and, to my surprise, ended up talking to them about the Lord.

"Excuse me," Pierre asked the young boy, "if you were to die today, do you know where you would spend eternity?" The young couple looked like high schoolers; they shrugged their shoulders. The couple listened to Pierre, and he eventually led them in the sinners' prayer as I bowed my head and repeated the prayer with them for support. Right there, on the putt-putt golf course, the young couple received Jesus Christ as their personal Lord and Savior! I congratulated them, hugged the girl, and gave them one of our church cards since they both said they didn't have a church home.

I adoringly eyed my man of God. I always dreamed of marrying someone who loves people just like I do, and someone who obeys God's commands and preaches the gospel to every creature. As Pierre showed me how to hold the golf club at our first hole, I felt extremely safe in his arms.

During our ride home, I felt totally comfortable talking to this man. It was as if he brought out a side of me that very few rarely got to see. Pierre somehow brought out the excitement in me! He apparently noticed my giddiness and just nodded and smiled after every other phrase I said. He was a good listener and even looked as if he actually cared about what I had to say.

As Pierre pulled up into my driveway, instead of letting me out immediately and walking me to the door, he turned off the car's engine and lights and just looked at me with a flirtatious grin. I peeked at him.

God, this man is fine! His smooth caramel-brown skin shone under the moonlight, and his eyes looked at me like they had their own agenda. I stared at him and admired his beauty. He couldn't take his eyes off of me, either.

"You know, you are a very beautiful woman, Michelle," Pierre finally said with his deep voice. His voice sounded so good. I've had many men tell me before that I was beautiful, but none of them could compare to the way Pierre said it.

"Thank you, for the hundredth time," I said with a hint of nervousness. I was hoping he couldn't tell how much he turned me on.

"I really had a nice time tonight," Pierre added.

"You know I had a nice time. I couldn't stop talking.

Excuse me for talking your ear off; I was just a little excited, I guess."

"Oh no, that's fine. That's okay with me. I love to see you get excited. It means I'm doing my job, which is to make you happy and help you feel more comfortable around me. You do feel comfortable around me, don't you, Michelle?" Pierre asked with a concerned look.

"Very comfortable. So comfortable sometimes, it's scary. It's like, when I talk to you sometimes, even on the phone, it's like you're the brother I never had."

"Whoa now, lady," Pierre said with a slight chuckle. I loved it when he called me "lady." I just loved the way the word rolled off his tongue.

"I don't want you to get *that* comfortable. You my lady now, and I don't want you thinking I'm your brother." He grabbed my hand. "I'm your brother in Christ and all, but as it pertains to our relationship, I don't want us to be like brother and sister."

Butterflies formed in my stomach. We both knew that our "relationship" went far beyond that of a brother and sister, but I was satisfied in knowing that Pierre even acknowledged the fact that we even had a relationship. I'm his lady now? That was pretty deep. So I'm not just some woman he wants to spend time with outside of church; I'm his *lady*.

As he continued to talk, I discovered that not only was Pierre this smooth talker full of fun and romance, but he was also an overall nice guy. I felt like I could tell him anything and trust that he wouldn't go blabbing my secrets to the world.

We talked in the car for over an hour before Pierre looked at the clock and saw that it was 1:15 a.m.

"Well lady, I better get you inside." I was enjoying our conversation so much that I hadn't even noticed the time. I just remembered I had to serve at the altar call tomorrow during service, which meant I have to report to the church by 6:30 a.m.

"Oh shoot," I gasped as I glanced at the clock, "I didn't realize it was that late."

"I know; I have to go to first service at 8 a.m. myself. I didn't realize it was this late either. But I don't mind because it was time well spent with a very special woman," Pierre said with a sexy grin.

I was really getting turned on; I stared at his lips and noticed that they looked all wet and kissable.

The mood was set, the night was just right, the stars shone beautifully in the car, and the temptation almost became too much for me to bear. I wanted to leap on Pierre and just kiss all over him 'til the cops came knocking, but deep down on the inside I knew that wouldn't be right, and it would only make our relationship even more complicated.

I knew it was time for me to go inside.

Pierre then changed his tone to that of an old school rapper and said, "Now since I did come all the way over here to pick you up, and since I do have to go all the way to the other side of town to go home, you could just let me stay here so I can just go to sleep and get up for church in the morning." He grinned while waiting for my response.

He must be joking. I patted his hand and responded with an overly exaggerated motherly tone. "No, no, no Pierre. You must go home now to your own bed so you can get up bright and early for church in the morning. We don't want to give the appearance of evil now by having you stay over at my place. Run along now, Mr. Pierre." I joked while shooing him away with my hand. "I must get my beauty rest."

"We don't have to sleep in the same bed," Pierre whined like a ten-year old. "I can sleep on the couch," he insisted.

I was beginning to think he was actually serious.

I know this brotha didn't think I was about to let him spend the night, even if we don't sleep in the same bed. What, am I supposed to walk around in my nightie, see him with no shirt on, and then just be like, "Goodnight, you fine chunk of a man?" No, he'd probably follow me right into my bedroom and that would be the end of my twenty-four years of savin' it until my wedding night.

I continued to play along with Pierre's little game. "Now, now, young Pierre, run along." I laughed as Pierre pouted while sticking out his bottom lip. He looked so cute with a pouted lip, a pouted, wet, kissable-looking lip. *Stop, Michelle, stop. I must go, now.*

Pierre finally gave up and said, "Okay" and got out and headed to the passenger side.

As he helped me out of his ride, he yanked me close toward him and wouldn't let go. I rested my head on his chest, closed my eyes, and experienced what a piece of heaven might be like.

At that very moment, underneath the dark blue sky, I felt as if I was a young child and that Pierre was the nurturing father holding me in the safety of his arms. I felt like the world could not harm me in Pierre's arms; I felt like he was my protection and my refuge. After five minutes of simply holding one other, I let up from his grasp, looked intensely at Pierre with bedroom eyes, and whispered, "I gotta go."

I really had to leave. This man had me feeling all warm inside.

Pierre just looked at me with his hazel eyes that glowed and whispered back with his juicy lips, "I don't want you to go."

Now why did he have to say that? He was making it even harder for me to leave. This man must really want me. I wanted him, too.

"But I gotta go," I insisted, yet I rested my head again on his chest and allowed him to hold me once more.

"But I don't want you to go," Pierre responded while rubbing my back in a slow, circular motion. Just then it sounded as if I heard Pierre make a long moaning sound.

Now I really know I have to get out of this man's arms, quick, fast and in a hurry.

As he rubbed my back and moaned in my ear, I started to

feel sensations in my virgin body that I had never felt before. I started to get more overcome by what my body wanted; and my body wanted Pierre, and it wanted him bad.

"But I really gotta go." I said slightly louder a second time, while clutching him even tighter and beginning to tug on his shirt. It was as if I couldn't resist.

"But do you want to go?" Pierre asked. He knew what my response would be.

"No." He squeezed my body even tighter.

"Do you have to go?" Pierre asked in a low tone.

"No." I gave in. My body grew warmer and I knew I had to leave so I could stay holy. But I just loved the way his body felt holding mine.

"Then why go, Michelle?" Pierre asked as he continued to hold me tight and rub my back. His hands then began to move down from rubbing my back to caressing my thighs, then they went up and finally rested on my small behind.

Alright now, enough is enough. But, then again, I wasn't sure, maybe enough was not enough. I wanted Pierre tonight, and I wanted him now!

I finally answered his question of "then why go" with "because I have to."

"Won't you stay in my arms forever?" Pierre whispered softly in my ear and began to caress it with soft and tender kisses. "If not forever, just for tonight?" he said and began nibbling my ear.

I loved the feel of Pierre's breath on my ear with each whisper, and I also loved the sound of Pierre's sexy voice in the night begging me to stay. I couldn't resist his cry, and even though my spirit knew that our holding each other like this and stirring up all types of sexual energy inside wasn't right, my flesh was truly weak. This man was just so fine to me, from the inside out.

So I tried once again, while still resting my head on his rock-hard chest and having my arms clutched desperately around his waist. "But I gotta go . . . "

Pierre ignored my final plea. I didn't help the situation

either by pretending to be paralyzed in his arms. I held on tight.

"Michelle, how is that new orientation program coming along?" My boss snapped me back into the reality of the present day.

I popped up from holding my forehead in my hand and said, "Oh fine, fine; it's coming along great." I hoped she wouldn't ask me to elaborate on that.

"Good. We look forward to your presentation on Monday," Susan responded and then left my cubicle.

With this job, there is autonomy, and then there is Susan. She really caught me off guard that time.

The rest of the day went a lot smoother. I made a conscious decision to complete at least the introductory portion of the training program on my computer, while praying quietly in the Spirit.

During my lunch break, I pulled out my Bible and recited my scripture for the day: "There is therefore now no condemnation to them which are in Christ Jesus, who walk not after the flesh, but after the Spirit," which is found in Romans 8:1. Today's scripture reminds me that though I may have made mistakes as a Christian and may have gotten out of the perfect will of God at times, God does not condemn me, but yet He chastens me with His Word and covers me with His Grace. Thank God for His Grace, because if it weren't for His Grace, where in the world would I be?

Chapter 8

The One

SANDY SPENT MOST OF HER MORNING
working as a cashier at Donovan's Department Store. Sandy
took the job as a management-trainee a month after earning
a degree in history. She accepted the position mainly
because, out of four interviews with other companies, they
were the only ones that made her an offer. Besides, Sandy
figured that by working in an elite department store in
downtown Birmingham, a ritzy suburb outside of Detroit,
she could get a lot of good discounts. Almost nothing in the
store was less than a hundred dollars, and Sandy enjoyed
working in the elegant environment of classical music and
the smell of fresh potpourri.

   As a manager in training, Sandy's responsibilities on the

job rotated. Because she was fairly new, she had to perform the function of a cashier for at least a month, which Sandy didn't mind too much. The store was rarely crowded, and Sandy loved interacting with her customers when they did purchase something.

Today it was fairly quiet, as usual, with not that much traffic in or out of the store. Their customers were mainly older white women who liked to get out of the house once in a while to buy something nice for themselves, their daughters, or their granddaughters.

From 12 p.m. to 1 p.m., it could get a tad busier than usual, only because most people stop in the store during their lunch hour. By 1:30, it was so dead again that Sandy normally restocked the shelves and returned clothes to their proper places on the racks.

However, on this particular Monday, Sandy was at her register at 12:30 when she noticed a black man enter the store. *A man at Donovan's?* She noticed that this young man with no wife trailing behind him was particularly handsome, even fine, to say the least.

He was about 6'5", and had dark, smooth, milk-chocolatey skin, and a stocky, football-player build. His mustache and goatee were neatly trimmed to perfection.

"My Lord, this brotha look just like Morris Chestnut!" Sandy yelped on the inside.

Sandy glanced at his left hand; there was no wedding band.

Sandy's heart did jumping jacks as she watched him examine the jewelry on the display table. She was so anxious to speak to him that she slid away from the cash register and eased her way over to where he was standing. As he stood there wearing a burgundy sweater and black fitted dress pants, he rested his hand underneath his chin and pondered a possible purchase.

"Is there something I can help you with?" Sandy asked sweetly.

He looked at her as if his staring at the jewelry suddenly

became less important than her standing there. He looked her up and down and replied, "No, I'm just looking. Just looking."

Sandy was glad that she had just gotten a touch-up perm on her short hair. She was also glad she had decided to wear the outfit Michelle bought her for her birthday last month. Sandy knew she looked good, and didn't mind playing the flirting game with this brotha.

"Let me know if you need any help," Sandy replied with a smile as she rested her tiny cream-colored arm on the jewelry's display table. She was hoping she wasn't coming across too forward, but heck, she was having fun enjoying her womanhood.

"Actually, I may need your opinion on something. I'm buying a gift for my mother and . . ."

Glory to God Hallelujah! The man is getting a gift for his momma and not his boo!

". . . she's celebrating another birthday, and I want to get her a nice piece of jewelry. What do you suggest uh, I'm sorry, I didn't get your name."

Sandy had forgotten that she had taken her name tag off in the back room because the pin wouldn't work.

"I'm sorry; my name is Sandra A. Moore." Sandy was captivated by his big brown eyes, and those teeth! The man had perfectly white teeth! Sandy just loved a brotha with no cavities and pretty white teeth. Gleaming white teeth on a chocolate man go together like peanut butter and jelly to Sandy.

"What about a nice tennis bracelet for your mom's birthday?" Sandy suggested.

She hoped he could afford the bracelet. But then again, he was shopping in Donovan's; he *must* have the loot to go along with it.

"A tennis bracelet? That's a good idea. Could you show me where those are?"

"Sure, they're right over here." Sandy purposely walked with a little switch in her behind as she headed to one of the display cabinets.

"These are our tennis bracelets," she said while spreading her arms wide in order to present all of the tennis bracelets to Mr. Fine as Wine. He bent his football-player body over to view the bracelets and his big, bright eyes got even brighter.

"See anything you like?" Sandy asked with a smile.

"I do," he said as he eyeballed Sandy from her waist to her face. "And she's standing right in front of me."

Sandy's yellow skin turned pink. He threw her off guard with that one, but she wanted to remain cool, like the confident black woman who knows she looks good. He was the finest thing she had seen in a long time, and she prayed he didn't notice the tiny pimple on the side of her nose. She had tried to put mascara on it to make it look like a sexy mole, but it just ended up making it look more like a wart. So she just left it alone and hoped the redness wouldn't show.

"I meant the bracelets," Sandy said with a flirtatious chuckle. "Do you see a bracelet you like?"

"Oh, well in that case, I like this one." He pointed to a glittering 2-karat diamond tennis bracelet.

Wow, this brotha must have a lot of loot. Sandy pulled the tennis bracelet out of the case and replied, "Nice. Are you sure this is your mother's fit for a bracelet? This particular kind comes rather small. We could add additional links if necessary."

"Actually, even though I'm a big man and all, my mom is kinda small, like you. Her arm is so tiny," he said as he made a small circle with his fingers, "about as small as your arm. As a matter of fact, I can figure out if the size is right by using your arm. May I?" he asked politely as he reached for the tennis bracelet.

Brotha, you can use any part of me you want.

"Keep it holy Sandy, keep it holy," she whispered to herself. It's hard to stay holy when a fine brotha that looks this good comes walking into your place of business. Sandy composed herself as he grabbed her arm and slipped the bracelet around her wrist.

For ten seconds, Sandy imagined that this man was her knight in shining armor putting a beautiful bracelet on her bare arm. She imagined that he was her man of God that would love her from now until eternity. She was so caught up in her daydream that she didn't notice her boss, the manager of the store, peering at them from the cash register.

"Sandra, can you keep an eye on this?" ordered her boss, Geneva, pointing at the cash register. She said it loud enough so that Sandra and the other customers in the store could hear. Sandy shook herself back into reality and replied, "Sure Geneva, I'll keep an eye on the register."

That Geneva is always trying to check somebody. Ain't nobody hardly even in this store.

Besides the fine brotha Sandy was helping, there was only one other customer in the entire store, and that was an eighty-something-year-old woman looking through girdles, slips, and underwear. She just playa hatin', Sandy concluded.

"This is a perfect fit," Mr. Fine stated, ignoring Geneva's interruption. "I'll take it. But only if it's available."

"Oh, it's available." Sandy commented. *It's all yours.*

"Speaking of being available," Mr. Fine hinted as Sandy placed the demonstration bracelet back into its case and they made their way to the register with his soon-to-be-purchase, "are *you* available?"

Sandy began her response by leaning over the register and looking deeply into his eyes. "I never got *your* name, sir?"

"Sir? Excuse me for not introducing myself." He stood up straight and held out his right hand. "My name is Carter Maxwell."

"Nice to meet you, Carter Maxwell," Sandy replied and shook his hand briskly.

Carter continued, "I'm twenty-eight years old, drive a black Benz, and am a partner at Maxwell, Wright, and

Associates Law Firm downtown."

Sandy was impressed as the brotha recited his résumé.

"I own my own home in the city, and I'm a little disturbed that a lot of the women here are beautiful, yet lack intelligence and class. You, on the other hand, Miss Sandra A. Moore, immediately sparked my attention as one who could possibly be someone I would like to get to know better."

Sandy concluded that Carter was not only fine, sexy, and to-the-point, he also appeared to be rather intelligent and confident. Carter's words were like music to her ears. She hit the jackpot with this one.

Mr. Maxwell continued, "You're beautiful, and from my interaction with you so far, I perceive that you are an intelligent black woman, and by the way that you carry yourself, I can also tell that you have class. For these reasons, I, Carter Maxwell, would love to get to know you better, and would be honored and delighted if you would grace me with your phone number so I can call you in order to hear your beautiful voice and possibly set up a day and time when I can see your gorgeous face again."

Whoa! Sandy was taken aback. She was about ready to give him her home number, her cell number, and her work number, which Geneva definitely wouldn't condone.

Just then, as if an angel tapped her on the shoulder, Sandy remembered her horrific experience with Mark and wanted to make sure of one thing.

"So, Mr. Maxwell, are you saved?"

Please say yes, please say yes, please say yes!

Sandy prayed to God that he would say that he was saved, because if he said he wasn't, then she would go home again sour and then God would have a lot of explaining to do.

Mr. Maxwell's countenance remained unchanged. "Miss Moore, I'm glad you asked me that question." Carter paused. "I do believe in God. I am a member of Mt. Charity Methodist Church, and I also attend their weekly

Bible study when I can."

Sandy let out a sigh of relief.

"But right now," he added and leaned in closer, "I want to get to know *you*."

Sandy smiled from ear to ear. Before Mr. Maxwell left the store with his purchase, Sandy scribbled her cell number on his receipt. Carter pulled out a business card, kissed it, gave it to her, and then seemed to disappear in thin air as he left the store.

Sandy stood in a daze. *What just happened here? The finest thing in the whole world just waltzed in here and gave me his phone number. This man is fine, has mucho dinero, is a lawyer, drives a Benz, and is a saved. He got to be the one!*

Meeting and talking to Carter Maxwell was a definite ego-booster for Sandy. Lately she had felt like no guy wanted to talk to her since no man at the church had approached her in the four months that she had been saved.

At her new church home, Hype for Jesus, the guys there would barely even speak to her. They would just stare at her like she was the most beautiful goddess on earth, but they wouldn't open their mouths to say anything, like she would bite their heads off or something. She was starting to think that maybe she wasn't "super spiritual" enough for them or something. She knew it wasn't because of her looks.

"Maybe God didn't let any other guys approach me because He was leading me to Carter all along," Sandy thought. "The Bible does say the steps of a good man are ordered, I think. And shoot, God know what He doing. God sent Carter to me so we can go out and so that *I* can be his good thing. Thank you Lord for sending me a brotha so intelligent, so rich, and so fine! Praise the Lord!"

Chapter 9

Three's A Crowd

BACK AT HER APARTMENT, MICHELLE FIXED a homemade cheeseburger and fries for dinner. As she stood over the frying pan, she felt guilty as she thought about her older sister, Marqueeta, who lives in Atlanta with her husband and two sons. Marqueeta rarely kept in touch with Michelle or their parents. She may call on Christmas just to let grandma hear her two grandsons' voices, who were three and five.

Michelle didn't mind that she rarely heard from her only sister. She would prefer not to, because whenever she does, it only reminded her of an instance when she neglected to obey the Holy Spirit's unction and caused her sister to experience severe pain.

Last year on Memorial Day, Michelle had an extreme unction in her spirit to call and check on Marqueeta in Atlanta. She figured it was God since she rarely thinks to call her sister out of the blue on her own. But instead of obeying the check in her spirit, Michelle ignored it and kept watching an old movie.

Later that night, the Williamson household received a call that Marqueeta was in a serious car accident. Some woman ran a red light as Marqueeta was on the way to pick up her two boys from day care. Marqueeta's gold Sebring went ricocheting toward a telephone pole and finally hit the side of a large tree. She experienced whiplash and had to undergo physical therapy for her neck and her back. Michelle found out the accident occurred just ten minutes after she had the urge to call her sister. Michelle figured that if she had obeyed God and called her sister, Marqueeta would have been at home on the phone when that woman raced through the red light. Michelle still hadn't forgiven herself for that one.

After dinner, Michelle plopped on her long brown couch in the front room and grabbed the book she was reading off of the glass coffee table. She was reading Michelle McKinney Hammond's *What To Do Until Love Finds You* and had been reading it for a half hour when she heard a buzz from her intercom.

"Who is it?" Michelle shouted.

"It's Liz."

Michelle let her inside the complex and then opened her apartment door. It was unusual for Liz to visit during the week, since they both worked and normally only met on the weekends.

"Liz, what's wrong?"

Liz sat on the couch. Ignoring Michelle's question, she asked, "May I have some tea?"

"Sure," Michelle replied.

She and Liz often enjoyed having tea together. They
jokingly said it reminded them of rich older white ladies in
old black and white movies who had a butler bring out their
tea as they enjoyed tea and laughter in their landscaped
backyards.

Only tonight, Michelle concluded, was no laughing
matter.

Michelle brought out two cups of tea, each with a drop of
milk as they both liked it, and asked, "Is it your mom?"

"When is it *not* my mom." Liz shook her head and took a
sip of tea.

Michelle knew that Liz's mom hadn't given her life
completely to the Lord and that she was a little wild and
promiscuous, but Liz had never told her many details.
"What did she do now?"

"My mom is just still being my mom," Liz stated.

"Did you two have a fight?"

"A fight? No, not really I guess."

"Well then, what happened? Is she okay?"

"She's fine, or so she thinks."

"Liz, would you just tell me what happened?"

Liz took another sip of her tea, let out a long sigh, looked
Michelle straight in the eye, and said, "Right now, my
mother is in bed with a married man."

"No!" Michelle gasped and almost spilled her tea. She
didn't think Ms. Coleman would stoop that low.

"And she kicked me out tonight so she can be with him."

"You've got to be kidding me! How do you know he's
married?"

"Because I found his wedding band on the floor with his
pants."

"Does your mom know this?"

"She knows."

"What did she say?"

"She basically said, 'his being married is not my issue'."
Liz imitated her mother.

"No!"

"Yeah."

"She can't mean that?"

"Oh, she meant it all right." Liz took another sip of tea. "Got any cookies to go with this?"

Michelle wondered how Liz could remain so calm. But then again, it didn't surprise her. Liz could be pretty complicated at times. Michelle brought three large sugar cookies to Liz and asked, "So what are you going to do?"

"What am *I* going to do? I don't know. Pray, I guess. Like I been doing. That's about all I can do at this point." Liz nibbled on a cookie. "Is this fat-free?"

"No," Michelle said.

"Oh." Liz took another bite.

Like a light bulb turned on in her head, Michelle popped up from the couch and proclaimed, "You know what Liz, you're absolutely right! You *can* pray! We can pray, right now, for your mother. Because you and I both know that the prayers of the righteous availeth much, and that Satan can no longer have his hands on your mother!"

Michelle set her teacup on the glass coffee table, stood up, and reached her hands out toward Liz. Liz lazily set her tea and cookies on the table as well and stood up, joining hands with Michelle who began to fervently pray on behalf of Ms. Coleman.

"Father, God, in the Name of Jesus we come giving You Praise, Honor, and Glory. Satan, I bind you in the Name of Jesus, that you would loose your grasp on Ms. Coleman. I thank You, Lord, that Your Word says that it is the goodness of God that draws man to repentance, and because of Your goodness toward Ms. Coleman, in that You have spared her life and You keep and protect her every day, she will come to know that You sent Your Son Jesus to die for us so that we may no longer have to live according to the desires of the flesh, but to the desires of the Spirit."

Liz prayed quietly in tongues as Michelle continued in English.

"I pray for my sister, Liz, right now in the Name of Jesus,

that You would strengthen her with might according to Your Glorious Power. I pray that the words she speaks to her mother are Spirit and Life, and that Liz realizes that the battle is not hers, but the Lord's. I speak restoration to Liz and her mother, and I call Ms. Coleman saved, sanctified, and filled with the Holy Ghost! In Jesus' Name, Amen! Hallelujah!"

Michelle began to shout up a storm, and Liz shouted along with her. They praised God for fifteen minutes, so much so that Liz's voice began to grow hoarse. They shouted the victory because they knew that what they prayed had already come to pass.

Just then, the telephone rang. At first Michelle wasn't going to answer it, but then she thought it might be her parents calling from out of town. She saw the number on the caller ID and recognized immediately who it was. It wasn't her parents.

"Hey, Mickey!" screeched a loud voice before Michelle even had a chance to say "hello."

"Hey, Sandy girl," Michelle said while hunched over, attempting to catch her breath.

Michelle hoped Sandy's call was important this time. Sandy often called every day just to talk about nothing.

"You wouldn't believe what just happened to me today!" Sandy began as she lay sprawled out on her white canopy bed with pink satin sheets. She was holding on to her pink teddy bear as she talked on the phone.

"What?" Michelle responded, still out of breath.

"This fine, I mean fiiiine brotha asked for my number today! And get this, not only is he fine, but he's a lawyer, *and* he saved! Praise the Lord! I done found my mate!"

Michelle rolled her eyes, took a seat on the couch and said, "Hold on now, Sandy. Where did you meet this guy?"

"At work. He was buying a *phat* tennis bracelet for his momma. Bling bling! That thing cost almost three grand!"

"For his momma, huh? What church does he go to?"

Sandy hesitated. "I think he said he goes to Mt. Chastity

Episcopal Church, or something like that. He even said he goes to their Bible study every week!"

"Bible study every week, huh? Hmmmmm."

"Yeah, and guess what else?"

"What?"

"He look just like Morris Chestnut! You know, from all those movies you watch. And you know how I just love my chocolate men."

"Well, I'm happy for you, Sandy. I'm happy that you met someone today who is nice looking and saved. My only caution is that you don't go running off to get your wedding gown just yet. Be patient. Pray about it. Have you prayed about it yet?"

"Well, not really, but this guy did appear in my life at a time I didn't think anybody else was interested. And I been praying for God to send me my mate. Then this brotha showed up, and man, did he show up!"

"Well, Sandy-" Michelle began, then paused, watching Liz as she sat on the brown love seat and wiped the sweat from her forehead. Liz hadn't shouted like that in a long time. She picked up another sugar cookie and settled down to listen to Michelle's phone conversation.

Michelle continued, "All I'm saying is, pray about it. Pray about him, specifically, to see if you should be going out with him. You don't want to be wasting your time going out with somebody who ain't the one."

"You right about that. Ain't no time for that. I don't want to start having no kids at age thirty-five because I kept going out with the wrong ones and wasting my time." If it were up to Sandy, she would be married and about to have kids right now at twenty-three.

"What's this guy's name, anyway?" Michelle inquired.

"Carter Maxwell," Sandy responded with a syrupy sweet smile as she sat up on her bed, "and his teeth, girl, his teeth are so white! And his shoulders girl, his shoulders are so big! And his eyes girl, his eyes are so bright!" Sandy sighed and gave her pink teddy bear a big squeeze.

"Well, just slow down, okay? Don't go making any wedding plans just yet and you barely even know the guy. Besides, have you completely gotten over Mark?"

"Mark who?" Sandy exclaimed and threw the teddy bear on her pillow. "Mark ain't nobody. This brotha has class. He got it goin' on! Forget Mark! Carter probably makes more money in one day than Mark does in an entire year!" Sandy got up from her bed, stood in front of her mirror on her dresser and started playing with her hair.

"Shoot, I'm beginning to like this 'being saved' stuff." Sandy smiled at herself in the mirror. "At first I thought it was kinda boring, but now I'm starting to realize that it's actually kinda fun."

"Alright Sandy, we'll definitely have to finish this conversation later. I'm about to let you go. Liz is over, and we just got through praying and praising God."

"Oh, Liz is over there? Tell her I said 'hey'."

"I will."

"Okay, Michelle. I'll talk to you later."

"Bye." Michelle hung up and looked at Liz. "That girl."

"Well, what was Miss Sandra Moore ranting and raving about this time? Some man?"

Liz sometimes missed the good ole days when it was just her and Michelle; she was used to having Michelle all to herself. Liz was almost convinced of the truth in the phrase, "two is company, but three's a crowd," especially when the third person was Miss Sandra A. Moore.

"Oh yeah. Sandy just going on about some *fine* guy she met at work today."

"Oh. I shoulda known. Is he saved?"

"Well, he says he is, but you know how some of these guys are now-a-days. They'll say anything just so they can get yo' goodies."

"I don't understand why that girl gets so riled up over some man. If she was as excited about God as she was about men, then she would be more happy about herself."

"I know what you mean."

"So what did she say?"

"Basically, she think he's the one."

"Oh, God."

"I told her we'll talk more about it later."

"Please do. The girl just got saved yesterday and here she is trying to get a man."

"I know. She say he's a lawyer."

"Oh. A honey with money?" Liz said and the two of them laughed. "But is he a *holy* honey with money?"

"I know that's right, girl," Michelle responded.

Chapter 10

Goodbye, Past

THAT NIGHT MICHELLE GRABBED A YELLOW blanket and pillow from the closet and handed it to Liz. Liz made herself comfortable on the couch. The two of them were in bed by 10 p.m. because Liz had agreed to go to morning prayer with Michelle, though she usually preferred to pray at home.

Liz's alarm on her cell phone woke her up at 5 a.m. She wanted to wake up before Michelle so she could hurry and take her shower to leave the bathroom free for her friend when she finally got up.

Liz didn't bring any clothes from home with her, since

she left her mom's house so abruptly. Before she went to Michelle's place, she did stop at Value K to pick up some essentials: deodorant, a toothbrush, a package of white panties, and a jumper-dress to wear to work the next day. There used to be a time when Liz could have borrowed a suit from Michelle to wear to work, but Liz had gained so much weight that she couldn't wear any of Michelle's size 8 clothes anymore.

By the time Michelle woke up and hopped in the shower, Liz was already dressed and in the kitchen fixing tea and toast. She was seated at the table eating when Michelle walked into the kitchen clad in a white robe and plastic shower cap.

"Michelle," Liz asked as Michelle peeked in the frig to see what she could make for lunch.

"Yes?" She was looking for the salad dressing to spread on her ham and cheese sandwich.

"Can I borrow a pair of your shoes to wear with this outfit? I rushed out of mom's house so fast that I didn't pack anything or bring anything with me from home. I actually bought this outfit from Value K."

Michelle looked up from the frig to see what Liz was wearing. "You bought *that* from Value K?"

"It was close-by and every thing else was closed," Liz defended herself.

"I was actually going to tell you I thought it was cute," Michelle said with a smile.

The outfit was a long, light blue jean jumpsuit with a white shirt underneath. It definitely looked like something Liz would wear.

"Yeah, you can borrow a pair of my shoes Liz," Michelle assured her. She went to the hall closet and found a pair of blue loafers a shade darker than Liz's jumpsuit.

"Thanks," Liz responded and slipped the shoes on her flawless feet. Liz's feet always seemed so perfect, partly because she hardly ever wore high-heeled shoes. As a teacher, she was on her feet practically all day, and she chose comfort over being cute.

Michelle and Liz took separate cars and met at the morning prayer service by 7:05 a.m. Liz was a little disturbed because she didn't like to arrive late to anything, including morning prayer.

Once inside the sanctuary, Michelle went to her usual corner to pray and Liz sat on one of the pews. As the minister led the prayer, Liz remained seated while the majority of the one hundred people stood. By 7:30, the minister no longer led the prayer and the congregation was given the opportunity to pray about their own needs or the needs of others.

Liz prayed for her mother, and then remembered that she hadn't called her mother last night or this morning. As Liz prayed, she could hear the Spirit of the Lord say to her spirit, "Be careful for nothing, but in everything by prayer and supplication with thanksgiving, let your requests be made known unto God." As soon as she heard this scripture from Philippians 4:6, she immediately wrote it in her prayer journal. Liz sighed a sigh of relief. She didn't get much sleep last night because she kept waking up thinking about her mother.

In her corner facing the wall, Michelle also prayed for Ms. Coleman. Michelle was mainly mad at the devil for causing her friend be so worried about the whole situation, which led to Liz overeating and not being as happy or joyous as she used to be.

Though Liz had always been the most reserved one in the bunch, she still had a joy factor within that was evident at most times. Michelle knew that this trial in Liz's life was Satan's way of distracting Liz from what God had planned for her life, which included walking in her evangelistic calling.

At 8 a.m., the minister dismissed everyone and Michelle greeted those she recognized with a huge smile and a, "Have a blessed day!" After hugging one person, she turned around and saw someone she hadn't seen in a while, her friend, David Parker.

"Hey, Michelle!" shouted an animated David.

"David!" Michelle shouted with the same amount of enthusiasm as they gave each other a nice, big, church hug.

"Where have you been, man?" Michelle asked with a light-hearted punch to David's shoulder.

"Oh, I been here and there." David's signature Kool-Aid grin showed off all of his bright white teeth. "I was out of town for two weeks visiting my dad and his side of the family in Boston."

David, a dark-skinned, short, slim brotha whom everyone at Hype just adored for his talented singing ability and his charm, currently lived at home with his momma. Michelle remembered he had told her once that he was saving to buy a house. Even though he was 26 and still living at home, he definitely took good care of his mom. He was his mom's own personal chauffeur and accompanied her at almost every church event.

"Boston, huh? What in the world did your momma do while you were away?" Michelle teased.

"Oh, mom was a'ight. She managed somehow." The two of them laughed. David was an only child and Michelle knew that his momma was just crazy about her baby boy with the baby face.

Michelle always thought David looked young for his age. He was also an inch shorter than she was, and Michelle was 5'6". He and Michelle had known each other for over two years now, and neither of them expressed any interest in the other, beyond a cool friendship. Besides, David wasn't her type. She liked a nice tall man, one that she can look up to and rest her head on his chest.

Liz joined Michelle and David while they were talking.

"Hi David," Liz said with slight enthusiasm and a forced smile.

"Hey, Liz!" David sang as he gave her a hug like the one that he gave Michelle.

"I haven't seen you in a while," Liz stated.

"Boy," David joked, "you guys really missed me! I didn't realize I was so loved around here!" They all chuckled.

"Like I was telling Miss Michelle here, I had been in Boston for two weeks visiting my dad."

"Oh. How is your dad doing?" Liz remembered that the last time David mentioned anything about his dad, he said that he wanted her to pray for him because he was battling a drinking problem.

"Oh, he's doing real good. When I went down there, I was able to minister to him and he rededicated his life to Christ!"

"Praise God!" both Michelle and Liz proclaimed.

"I told him how liquor is Satan's counterfeit high, while believers, on the other hand, have the Holy Ghost as a spiritual high." David added, "And once you get drunk in Christ, ain't no turning back, 'cause there ain't no high like the Most High!"

All three of them laughed.

"I showed him the verse where it says, 'Wine is a mocker and strong drink is raging.' I think it's like Proverbs 20 or something."

Michelle and Liz nodded their heads. "Preach preacha'!" Michelle sang.

"Next thing you know, my dad was emptying all his liquor bottles in his kitchen cabinets and pouring out all the liquor in the toilet and tossing all of the empty bottles in the trash! He even grabbed the vodka bottle from the secret stash in his room and threw that out. Man, I tell ya, God is Good!"

"All the time," Michelle and Liz sang together.

As Liz and David continued to talk about David's father, Michelle felt as if she was being watched. She looked across the sanctuary and sure enough there were a set of almond-shaped, hazel eyes staring at her.

As soon as Pierre saw Michelle return his glare, he shot up from the pew and headed toward the three of them.

Hoping to avoid him, Michelle interrupted David and

Liz. "Well, you guys, I hate to cut you off, but I have to go in to work early today to get a few things done."

"Oh yeah, you have that project you're working on," Liz said. "That's fine; I'm leaving, too. I have to make sure my study lesson is in order for my students today."

As the two ladies left David behind and swiftly walked to the door, Pierre caught up with them.

"Ladies, ladies, allow me," he chimed and opened the door for Michelle and Liz as they exited the sanctuary.

"Thank you," Liz said sheepishly.

"Pierre Dupree," Liz thought to herself, "now there's a face I hadn't seen in a while. I wonder why he's trying to be so nice now, after all he put Michelle through."

As the three of them walked down the porch stairs to the parking lot, Pierre asked, "You mind if I walk you ladies to your cars?"

"Oh, Pierre," Michelle said, "I'm really in a rush to get to work. You can walk Liz to her car if you like, but I have to go. Thanks, though." Michelle thought she accomplished "giving him the cold shoulder in a nice way" rather smoothly. Liz, however, thought otherwise.

"Oh, I understand, a busy, corporate woman like you is always on the go," Pierre responded sarcastically.

"You know what, Pierre, I'm kinda in a rush, too." Liz piggy-backed off of Michelle's tactic. "I have to review my lesson for the students, and while we were in there chatting after prayer, I didn't realize it was almost 8:30. I really have to go."

"Okay, Okay, I get it. No one wants to allow Pierre Dupree to be the gentleman that God has called him to be. Well, that's okay, I guess. Maybe some other time." He headed in the opposite direction toward his ride with a "your loss, not mine" attitude.

"Or maybe some other planet," Michelle thought.

As Michelle drove toward the freeway on her way to work listening to her favorite gospel rap artists, Cross Movement, her cell phone rang. Liz's name appeared on the caller ID

"Hey, girl," answered Michelle.

"What was that all about?" Liz asked, referring to their encounter with Mr. Dupree.

"Girl, I don't know."

"I thought the two of you were through with each other, period."

"I thought so, too. I know *I'm* trying to get over it. But lately he's been coming to morning prayer again. He hadn't been to morning prayer since he first started talking to me almost a year ago. Then once we started going out, or whatever we were doing, Mr. Holier-than-thou stopped coming to morning prayer. Maybe he's trying to reconcile things with God or something."

"Or maybe he's just trying to see you," Liz speculated.

"I don't know. I mean, I'm trying to forget all the former things and move on to the new. I'm trying to prepare myself right now for the man of God that God has for me. And I ain't tryin' to let Pierre, or anybody for that matter, keep me from receiving my Boaz."

"I know that's right, girl. Well you keep on confessing that thing and surely it will come to pass."

"Thanks, Liz."

Liz closed her cell phone.

As Liz drove to work, she thought about her mom. She wondered if that man was still there from last night and if her mom decided to go to Golidecko this morning, where she worked full-time as an insurance sales agent.

Liz mustered her courage, took a deep breath, and dialed the number.

The phone rang three times; just as Liz was about to hang up, a gruff male voice said, "Hello." Liz hung up.

Chapter 11

Boss Issues

TUESDAY AT DONOVAN'S, SANDY WORKED THE
sales floor and checked inventory to make sure selected
items were marked on sale. She could barely concentrate;
her mind was filled with thoughts of Carter. She marked the
last blouse on sale for 50 percent off; then she realized all of
the items on the rack were supposed to have been marked
off only 20 percent.

She wondered why he didn't call her last night. She gave
him her correct number yesterday when they met, which she
rarely does with most men. She hoped he didn't lose her
number on his way home; maybe the receipt she wrote it on

fell out of his pocket.

Her day moved slowly, as usual. Not even ten customers had visited the store, and it was almost lunchtime. Sandy hadn't had a single bona fide purchase by anyone yet. She felt hopeful when an older man walked in and asked her to show him their diamond rings. He was looking for a ring for his wife of fifty years as of tomorrow. Eventually, after spending about forty-five minutes showing him what seemed like 100 rings, he decided he wanted to get her something else for their anniversary. Frustrated, Sandy put all of the rings back in their cases and in the showcase.

"That's what happens when you wait until the last minute to buy an anniversary gift for your wife," Sandy thought.

After the older man left and Sandy returned to her register, Geneva came out from the backroom and asked, "So how'd it go with that last customer?"

"It went okay, I guess," Sandy said.

"Did he buy anything?"

"Well, no."

"No? After all of that time you spent with him? What were you showing him?"

"I was showing him our rings. He was looking for a gift for his wife for their anniversary. After showing him practically all the rings in our store, he decided he wanted to buy her something else."

"You mean you spent *all that time* with him and he didn't buy *anything*?" Geneva asked again, as if she didn't just hear the whole story.

Kellie, the girl working next to Sandy who had just started working two weeks ago, looked up to listen more intently to their conversation.

"No, he didn't buy anything," Sandy repeated with an attitude.

"Sandra Moore, we're going to have to work on that," Geneva stated.

"What do you mean, Geneva?" Sandy kept an attitude

while avoiding Geneva's eyes.

"You can't spend that much time with customers who don't buy anything. Were you asking him personal questions about himself, building rapport, and were you being polite?"

"Yes," Sandy responded.

"Were you telling him the advantages of buying jewelry from our store, about how all of our products here are 100-percent guaranteed and come with a two-year warranty?"

"Yes."

"In other words, Sandy, were you pushing the product?" Geneva probed.

"Yes, I was *pushing the product*," Sandy said, gritting her teeth.

In the middle of Geneva's lecture, Sandy noticed someone enter the store with a huge crystal vase filled with two dozen long-stem red roses. Sandy's eyes widened as she watched the deliveryman make his way to the counter.

"Is there a Miss Sandra A. Moore here?" he asked with a country accent.

"I'm Sandra A. Moore." She raised her hand like she was in kindergarten.

"These are for you." He placed the vase on the counter.

"For me?" Sandy asked, almost bewildered.

"Uh yeah," he answered, "Miss Sandra A. Moore." He looked at the name again.

Sandy signed for the delivery and opened the card attached that read, "Beautiful Flowers for a Beautiful Lady, Love, Carter Maxwell."

Sandy was ecstatic. The roses were extremely beautiful; most of them were already in full bloom. The vase was gorgeous. Sandy's heart raced as she stood in awe of the surprise blessing. Kellie acted like she was working, but she smiled secretly at Sandy as if to say, "You go, girl."

"Um, can you get that vase off the glass counter before you spill water all over it? And can you take that to the back?" Geneva demanded.

Instead of saying, "This is not a 'that'; this is two dozen red roses in an expensive crystal vase which you obviously know nothing about because you've probably never received flowers from anybody," which is what Sandy really wanted to say, she replied sweetly, with a hint of sarcasm, "Why certainly, Geneva, I'll take *my* flowers, which were bought for me from the man I just met yesterday, back to the back room. If it is okay with you, I'll set them in the back by the *window* so they can get some light."

Sandy's thoughts went back to Carter. He hadn't forgotten her after all. She was so elated that she wanted to do the Holy Ghost dance right in the back room. She set the roses by a window, smelled them one last time, and felt their smooth, velvety red petals.

She continued to gaze at them in awe while she envisioned Carter's fine self until she heard a familiar cackly cry of, "Sandra, you have a customer!" Of course it was Geneva spoiling the moment for her yet again. Sandy couldn't get over how her boss had been hatin' on her lately.

As Geneva entered the back room and Sandy exited it at the same time to go up front, Geneva muttered, "Maybe you can get a sale this time."

Sandy shot an evil look at Geneva. She couldn't understand why her boss was treating her like this. Sandy wished she'd had a tape recorder to record all that Geneva has said to her, because no one would believe it otherwise. But instead of retaliating and reacting negatively, like her flesh really wanted to, Sandy ignored Geneva's comment, forced a smile, and went up front.

"She better not touch my flowers," Sandy said underneath her breath.

Chapter 12

Love, or Infatuation?

AT WORK I DECIDED TO REALLY BUCKLE down and work toward completion of the orientation project before Susan asks me about it again. I have to remember that when I work, it is unto the Lord, or as if I were working directly for Him. With this in mind, even though the boss-lady can get to me sometimes, I can respect her and be grateful for the job that God has given me, which allows me to help others. Besides, I want this project to be the best ever of its kind; I want to represent myself, Michelle Williamson, but most of all, I want to represent God.

I finished my caramel latte, munched on a powdered doughnut from a box of doughnuts that a co-worker brought in, and then zeroed in on the task at hand. I was eager to complete this project with sheer excellence. Besides, Lazek had just acquired another automotive supply company, so I anticipated a lot of their employees eventually joining the team within the next month or so, which meant completion of this project was top priority.

I must stay focused.

Just before lunchtime, I completed my PowerPoint presentation uninterrupted when the telephone at my desk rang.

Argh! Who could this be? I was on a roll.

"Hello," I answered while trying to sound professional and not agitated.

"Hey, lady, how are you?" asked a familiar voice.

I know this is not Pierre calling me at work. What is his problem?

I was ready to hang up on him.

"Fine," I said dryly.

I didn't want him to think I was excited about hearing his deep voice. I hate when I get interrupted while I'm working, especially when it's over some foolishness like this.

"Who's calling?" I asked. Maybe he'd get the hint that I no longer remembered his voice and no longer wanted to.

"It's me, Pierre. What, you forgot my voice already?"

"Maybe."

"Oh, it's like that, now?"

He knew I hadn't forgotten his voice. It was the same voice I had heard consistently every day for the six months we went together. It was the same voice that I, at one point in my life, loved to hear call my name under a deep blue moonlit sky. It was the same voice that used to bring butterflies to my stomach, especially when we used to talk for several hours at night. His voice would grow deeper and deeper and even sexier and sexier on the telephone.

I used to love to hear Pierre Dupree's voice, but not anymore. Especially since he made the conscious decision to humiliate me and ruin my emotions. If only I hadn't fallen for the smoothness of his voice when he gave me the slightest impression that he may have been sincere, then maybe I wouldn't have gotten hurt so badly.

Pierre and I had been going out with each other consistently for six months. I'd never dated a guy more than four months without having to break up with him because he wanted to have sex and I wouldn't, so I was really excited about this one. Since Pierre was the first saved man I ever dated, I knew that this just wasn't some weekend hangin' buddy. Going out with the same person consistently every weekend was pretty serious to me, especially since I was believing God to be married soon.

As we spent more and more time together, and countless hours on the phone each night, I developed a peace inside my spirit which began to show me that Pierre may be the one God has ordained me to be with for the rest of my life. Now don't get me wrong, I've never been one to jump ahead of myself and just "run with the vision," like I witness so many saved women do when it comes to men and marriage.

 I wasn't like some saved women who, when they are approached by a somewhat decent looking man in the church with a job that just says "hello" after service, start picturing themselves in a wedding gown going down the aisle with him.

I wasn't like some saved women, who, "by faith," are getting married this particular year, at this particular time, and at this particular place, and then start telling everybody and spending money on flower arrangements, knowing they don't have a single prospect in sight.

No, I wasn't like some saved women who prefer not to use the common sense that God gave them.

But I do know a good thing when I see it, and from the looks of everything, Pierre was a good thing. Pierre was my dream come true, my knight in shining armor, and I thanked God for him.

On this particular hot summer day in August, Pierre took me out on a surprise date. We were in the car headed west on I-96 as I kept trying to figure out where we were going. I loved how Pierre always kept our relationship fresh and exciting. It kept everything fun; I never knew what to expect.

"So, where are we going this afternoon?" I asked. I knew he wouldn't tell me; I just liked bugging him with questions.

"You'll see," Pierre responded.

As we drove on the freeway, I noticed that everything looked so perfect. The sky was beautiful, a picture-perfect blue with an orange sun slightly hidden under a big white cloud. There was not a dark cloud in sight, and no one could have asked for a better day.

As I enjoyed the view during the ride, I still tried to figure out where we were going. Maybe we're going swimming. Nah, because I didn't bring my swim suit. Unless . . . maybe he bought me one, but how would he know my size? I just couldn't quite figure it out. I hated being stumped.

After crossing a dirt road, I noticed that somehow we ended up going in circles in what looked like a park. It finally dawned on me that he was taking me to one of the largest parks in Michigan.

How sweet, a trip to the park. I should have known Pierre would conjure something romantic for our date.

Once we found a nice parking spot near the lake, Pierre parked and opened the door to let me out.

"Madam," he said as he reached for my hand. I gave Pierre a playful royal nod as he ever so gently led me out of his ride.

I just knew I looked good in my yellow sundress and matching straw hat. I carefully stepped out of his ride so that the heel of my yellow sandal wouldn't get caught anywhere and cause me to fall flat on my face and lose all of my cool points.

Pierre lifted the back of his ride, and my eyes popped open as I saw a huge wicker picnic basket and two small baby blue blankets. "A picnic, Pierre? You're taking me on a picnic? How sweet!" I gasped. No other man had ever been so thoughtful and so creative.

Since Pierre was taking me on a surprise picnic this weekend, I couldn't wait to see what he had in store for my twenty-fifth birthday, which would be exactly a week from today. I figured I could spend Friday night with my man, my actual birthday with family and my man, and Sunday night with my girls.

"Nothing's too sweet for my lady." Pierre responded while giving me that same boyish grin that I simply adored. He looked extremely handsome that day with his beige polo shirt and brown shorts. I loved the way the sun shone on his big, hairy legs.

Once we discovered a nice spot under a shade tree, Pierre laid out one of the blankets and sat down. I sat across from him, and he began to unpack his big basket of goodies.

"What are we having for lunch?" I was nosy and peeked inside.

I had gotten hungry during our long journey to the park. My mouth watered as Pierre pulled out two huge submarine sandwiches with the works, two bags of plain potato chips, two cans of pop, grapes and strawberries in a plastic container, and a canister of pineapples, all my favorite fruits.

After everything was laid out, Pierre grabbed my hands, bowed his head and prayed, "Dear Father God in Heaven, I thank You for the food we are about to receive for the nourishment of our bodies. May it be well received and may it be sanctified by the Word and prayer so that if there is any deadly or toxic thing within it that it would not cause sickness to come upon us. Father, I bless this occasion and fellowship, as we celebrate six months of our being together. May You bless Michelle and keep her in Your Peace. I thank You for bringing her into my life, and I praise You in advance for all that You will do in our relationship. In Jesus' Name, Amen."

I couldn't believe he remembered our sixth-month

anniversary! Most men don't remember things like that!
What a mighty man of God! I just wanted to give him
a huge hug on the blanket for praying such an awesome
and sincere prayer, but I figured that would probably
be inappropriate, so I just topped out his prayer with a
resounding, "Amen!"

As I took a huge bite into my long-awaited submarine
sandwich, Pierre motioned me closer to where he was
seated on the blanket. I scooted over and rested my head
on his shoulder as I ate. When I grabbed a bunch of purple
grapes, Pierre put his head back and opened his mouth wide
so that I could feed him some. I dangled the grapes above
his mouth, allowing them to fall, and he acted like he was
going to bite my hand off.

We laughed and then Pierre reached up and grabbed my
hand and ate the grapes; then he pulled my hand to his lips
and lightly kissed every single one of my fingers. He looked
at me longingly, and I stared at him with an adoring smile.

After lunch, Pierre picked me up and whisked me toward
the water. Once we reached our destination, Pierre let
me down, and I took off my shoes to show off my french-
manicured toes. Pierre held my shoes in one hand and
grabbed my hand with the other as we walked along the
lake.

We watched several speedboats as they passed by, and we
spoke to the children and other couples that walked past.
I couldn't have asked for a better afternoon until Pierre
spotted a dock with canoes and decided that we should go
on a canoe ride.

A short Latino man with a thick mustache greeted us as
he explained how he would be the one giving us our ride.
At least that meant I didn't have to worry about rowing any
boat, praise God.

Pierre escorted me inside a rather large canoe and then
he sat in the back and I plopped directly in front of him as
he wrapped his arms around me. I loved feeling Pierre's
arms and body wrapped around me and feeling the breeze

that flowed through my hair.

The little man rowed the canoe and I could almost hear him humming. I took a sniff of the fresh air and exhaled.

Pierre started caressing my neck with his fingers and stroking my hair while staring at me.

Finally, I broke the silence. "Pierre, why are you staring at me?"

"Because you're beautiful."

"Well, then, why are you so good to me?" I had to ask.

"Because you deserve it. You're beautiful, you're intelligent, you're saved, sanctified, and filled with the Holy Ghost," Pierre added while playfully poking me in the side.

"Oh yeah," I thought. For a minute there I almost forgot that I *was* saved, sanctified, and filled with the Holy Ghost. For a minute there I thought I was just a girl who was falling in love with a guy. I closed my eyes, smiled, and captured the moment.

At that moment I felt something I never felt before.

I felt loved.

I felt loved by a man who chose to love me for who I am, and not just for what I have to offer, and it felt good.

"Pierre," I said still with my eyes closed, "why do you treat me the way you do?"

I had hoped he wasn't getting tired of my questioning him, but sometimes a sistah's gotta know, even if it means being told over, and over, and over again.

"Because I respect you. I respect you more than anyone in the world right now. I respect who you are and the fact that you are my beautiful sister in Christ," he said while stroking my hair from top to bottom.

"I respect that," he repeated and kissed the top of my head.

With each word he spoke, I found myself growing to love him yet more and more. I'd never been in love before, and I hoped I wasn't confusing it with some type of infatuation, but this man sparked feelings in me that had never been sparked by any other man.

I knew that not a single day went by without my thinking of him or longing to talk to him or be with him. If I could be with him every waking hour of the day, I would; I just hoped he felt the same way.

Instead of asking Pierre if he loved me, I laid my head back on his broad shoulder, closed my eyes, and smiled like he was the man God ordained me to be with for the rest of my life.

As if the two of us were the only two people in the world, Pierre ignored the man rowing the boat, moved my hair from my neck, and kissed it. He kissed it ever so lightly once, twice, and by the third time I helped him by leaning my head forward. I turned around to face him and he did exactly what I wanted him to do-exactly what I had been wanting him to do for the last six months-but I knew that he was just waiting for the right time to do it.

He kissed me. He gave me the longest and most passionate kiss I had ever had in my entire life. As he kissed me passionately with his tongue, I tilted my head back and rubbed his ear with my hand.

As we kissed even more, I heard a tiny little voice inside me tell me to stop; however, the voice of my hungry flesh overrode that small still voice as Pierre held me even tighter.

That afternoon I figured, even if this man isn't "The One," I'll just pretend for the moment that he is mine, all mine, forever.

When we returned to my apartment complex, I didn't want Pierre to leave. It was as if he had some sort of magical spell put on me, or some soul-tie. I couldn't imagine being without him, even for one second.

I still couldn't figure out how this man managed to make me feel this way. I've always been such an independent, industrious, virtuous woman of God who never needed anyone but God. But right now, as he stood in front of me in the parking lot of my complex, at the end of the most romantic date I've ever been on, I felt like I needed him.

"Thank you again for taking me out on a wonderful

date," I said.

It was the only thing I could think to say, besides, "I love you, you man of God! Take me now and forever!"

"You say that like you're trying to get rid of me," Pierre stated.

"You know I'm not trying to get rid of you," I said and flirtatiously poked him in his broad chest.

"Oh, you're just trying to feel my hard chest, that's all," Pierre said with a smile. He was starting to give me goose bumps. Did he know what he was doing to me?

"You really don't want me to leave tonight, now, do you, Michelle?" He kissed my hand.

"No," I admitted, "I don't necessarily want you to go this instant."

"Good." Pierre stated. "Then I'll stay. So what you got in there to eat?" He acted like he was about to enter the apartment complex with no key.

"Pierre, stop playin'. You know I can't let you in."

"Why not?" he whined.

"Because . . . you know."

"What? You know I won't try and do anything. I'm just hungry, that's all." Pierre looked innocent.

"Hungry? You just ate!"

"I know, but that was hours ago, and that was a little bitty submarine sandwich. I'm ready for some real food now," Pierre proclaimed with a sneaky look in his eye.

"Well, I don't know what you think we have to eat at my place because all I have are leftovers and T.V. dinners."

"That's fine."

"Oh, okay." I gave in and went to open the door to the complex with my keys.

This brotha betta not try anything.

Once in my apartment, I headed toward the kitchen while Pierre sat on the couch in the front room, turned on the big-screen T.V., and made himself right at home.

"Hey, Michelle," Pierre yelled from the living room, "why don't we just order pizza and watch a movie?"

Actually, his idea sounded a lot better than my trying to scrounge around in my skimpy frig searching for a meal. I could stand to watch a good DVD. Besides, watching a movie together is pretty harmless, as long as we both watch the movie and not each other.

"That's a great idea!" I yelled from the kitchen.

I headed toward the living room and Pierre asked, "Got any good movies?"

"We have my all time favorite movie in the world, 'Love Jones'!"

"Oh Lord, I should have known you would pick some sappy love story," Pierre teased.

"And what's wrong with that?" I retorted.

Then again, maybe Pierre was right. Maybe I should have chosen a comedy like "Friday" or something, a movie that wouldn't have any love scenes in it which could give us some ideas.

"Oh, alright, then, 'Love Jones' it is." Pierre gave in.

"Well, maybe we can watch an old western movie." I picked up the DVD from beside the T.V.

"Oh Lord no, put in 'Love Jones', please!" he pleaded.

We laughed.

Pierre used his cell phone and ordered the pizza as I popped in 'Love Jones' and sat on the opposite end of the couch.

Pierre let me sit far away from him for about fifteen minutes into the movie; then he finally whispered loudly to me, "Michelle!"

I looked at him to see what he wanted. He motioned for me to come over to him.

I vigorously shook my head.

"I'm cold," Pierre whined.

Did he think that wimpy excuse was going to work?

I shook my head again.

"I'm lonely," Pierre tried again, this time sounding like a helpless child.

I mouthed the word, "no" this time.

"Why not? I won't bite." He looked angelic.

I shook my head a final time and then attempted to ignore him by focusing on the movie with my arms folded.

Then Pierre said out loud to himself, "The kingdom of God suffereth violence," then he got up and crawled toward me and quoted the rest of the passage of scripture, "and the violent take it by force!"

With that he grabbed me playfully toward him like a maniac, and I just burst out laughing in his face.

"Now sit here." he said, still acting like a wild man as he forcefully sat me close to him.

"Have we completely lost our minds here?" I asked while still trying to hold in laughter. Pierre never ceased to amaze me.

"No," Pierre said abruptly. "Now I can enjoy the movie, with my woman by my side!"

"Oh, so that's all it was. All you had to do was ask; I would've sat next to you." I fibbed jokingly, " I thought you were asking me something else."

"What else did you think I was asking you?" He looked me straight in my eyes.

"I don't know." I nestled my head against his shoulder. "I didn't know what you wanted; you didn't open your mouth."

After another twenty minutes of watching the movie, the intercom buzzed and I let the pizza deliveryman inside the complex. Pierre opened the door, grabbed the pizza, and tipped the deliveryman with a five dollar bill. He then returned to the couch where I was sitting upright and ready to eat.

I ate about three slices with orange pop and was full while Pierre ate about six slices in all.

Now we both were not only full but also tired from all of that food. I put the pizza away in the kitchen, snuck a mint in my mouth, and came back in the living room to sit up under my man.

"Thanks for the pizza," I said.

Pierre looked at me with his seductive, hypnotizing hazel eyes and said, "You're welcome."

Then he said loudly, out of the blue, "Now can I get on with watching the movie, huh?"

I propped up and said playfully, "Oh, so we want to be rude now, is that it?"

"C'mon now, Michelle," Pierre said, feeding into my routine.

"The movie is more important than my showing my appreciation, is that what this is?" I stood up above him with my hand on my hip.

"Girl, sit down," Pierre jokingly said.

"No, I will not sit down. I have a right to do whatever I want to do in my own apartment!" I yelled.

I was in a mood to playfully get on his nerves, since he tried to playfully get on mine earlier.

"Then I'll make you sit down!" Pierre said as he shot up and threw me down on the couch.

I picked up one of my two brown pillows and started swinging at him.

"Take that, you punk!" I yelled.

Pierre then grabbed the pillow I was hitting him with and threw it clear across the room. He then threw his whole body on top of me in an attempt to calm my little self down.

"Now you're going to be a nice little girl today, okay?" Pierre gnarled as he had me pinned to the couch.

I nodded my head vigorously like the little girl again.

"You're not going to do any more crazy things, like disturb me while I'm watching this movie again are you?" Pierre asked.

I shook my head wildly.

"You're not going to tick me off are you?" Pierre asked with gritted teeth.

I shook my head violently again.

Then I couldn't stand it anymore and just burst out laughing.

I laughed so hard that I may have even spit in his face. Pierre looked at me as if to say, "What's so funny?" and then finally started laughing himself.

He picked me up and propped me on his lap and said, "Girl, you know you are a trip."

I kept giggling inside. I loved messing with Pierre; he was so fun.

"You are a trip," he repeated and with the last part he spanked me on my butt.

"I'm a trip for you," I added in my normal speaking voice. Pierre softly said, "I'm a trip for you, too" and then kissed me sweetly on my forehead, then on my right eyelid, then my nose, then my cheek, until his lips rested on my mouth and we kissed long and passionately again for the second time in the same day.

Before I knew it, Pierre somehow managed to lay me on the couch and we started kissing more heavily. My body didn't want him to stop, even though deep down I knew I was treading upon forbidden territory.

His body was pressed hard against mine and his hands rose higher and higher underneath my dress.

"Pierre," I said, trying to stop him before it was too late. Pierre ignored me.

"Pierre," I said, more firmly.

"What, Michelle?" He was kissing my neck. "Don't worry baby, I won't do anything. I just want to make you feel good." With that, he attempted to slide my panties down.

"Pierre, no!" I screamed and struggled to sit up.

"What, Michelle? We're not doing anything!" Pierre shouted in defense.

"We're not doing anything?" I sat up straight and fixed my clothes. Pierre sat up as well. He was sweating like a dog in heat.

"What do you mean, 'we're not doing anything'? Your hand was underneath my dress!"

"So, what's wrong with that? My God, Michelle, we weren't about to have sex or anything."

"We weren't?" I asked.

"No, Michelle, I care about you too much for that. Besides, if we did have sex, then I would be obligated to marry you."

What? Was this man fo'real?

"Oh really," I said with a suspicious look. "Well, then, what in the heck were you just doing?"

"Dangit, Michelle!" Pierre shouted in frustration. " I was just trying to make you feel good, that's all! Don't you know that by now? I want to make you *feel good*. I want to make you happy!"

"Well, you don't have to make me happy by trying to-"

"Look, you know as well as I do that I wasn't about to have sex with you. We are two grown adults, and I know when to stop!"

"But Pierre, you didn't think what we were just doing was . . . wrong?" I asked. I was in desperate need of an honest response.

"No," Pierre said firmly. "There is nothing wrong with two consenting adults wanting to make each other feel good. Especially when the person you're doing it with is the person you may want to-oh, never mind."

"No what, what were you going to say, Pierre?" I insisted.

"Well, I don't want you to take this the wrong way, Michelle, but I don't see nothing wrong in doing what we were just doing if you're doing it with the person you may want to marry in the future."

"In the future? Of course we may one day hopefully get married *in the future*. I don't go out with just anybody unless I think we may have a future together. But what about what we were doing just now? You're not convicted at all about the fact that we're two single Christians that were just acting like the world by slobbering all over each other and feeling all on each other's bodies? You didn't feel like you shouldn't have been doing what you were just doing?" I asked again.

I had hoped that this conversation was merely part of

some nightmare that I would eventually wake up from.

"No, I didn't. I mean, I ask God for forgiveness every day," Pierre stated.

I couldn't believe it. So Pierre was just another one of those saved, sanctified, tongue-talking, Word-having brothas that just wanted to have their cake and eat it, too? I had no idea Pierre would be one to use God's grace as a credit card; sin now, repent later. I thought Pierre was better than that.

I was fuming inside; I wanted to cry right in front of him. But I refused to let this man see one single tear trickle from this woman's eye.

"Besides Pierre, you told me before that you weren't even ready to date anybody seriously now. So what's all this talk about getting married?" I asked with a cracking voice.

Nope, he won't see me shed a single tear.

"Nothing," Pierre said, "forget I ever said anything. Forget I ever came." Pierre got up from the couch and headed toward the front door.

"Wait, Pierre, wait! We have to talk this out!" I screamed with tears now streaming down my face. "I'm still trying to understand what you are saying, and what you mean!" He couldn't just be like all the rest. He couldn't just leave. Not like this.

"You'll never understand what I'm saying, and you'll never know what I mean," Pierre declared as he stopped at the front door and looked at me with a cold glare.

"I knew I shouldn't have messed with a young girl like you. I need a real woman, one who doesn't like to play games."

With that, Pierre opened the door and said, "I'm outta here," then slammed the door and left, exactly one week before my twenty-fifth birthday.

And after that night I didn't hear from Pierre ever again. No phone calls, no morning prayer "hellos," no nothing. I spent my birthday the following week at a seafood restaurant downtown. I pretended like I was having a good time, and even laughed while listening to Sandy talk my ear off, but deep down inside, I was hurting.

▼

"Yeah, it's like that. What do you want Pierre?" I asked him, still upset that he had the audacity to interrupt me at work. This man hadn't called me since he stormed out of my apartment that day eight months ago.

"Oh, I see how it is, Michelle. You all smiles at church, but when you step outside the sanctuary, you turn into something nasty."

Can I hang up the phone now, Lord, please?

"Pierre, I'm really busy here at work. May I ask why you're calling me?" I chewed on my already battered pen.

"My, my, aren't we a little touchy? I see you still have that little fire in your voice."

"Pierre-"

"Okay, okay. I know you're busy and all. I was just wondering if maybe, after you get off work today, we can meet somewhere and talk . . . "

"Talk? What do you mean talk? There is nothing to talk about. At least that's what you told me when you stormed out of my place eight months ago."

I wondered if he had forgotten. I, personally, remembered that day quite vividly. He dumped me, broke my heart, and didn't even bother to say why. And now he was trying to stir up old flames?

"Okay, I get it. I'm terribly sorry for what happened that day. I had a whole lot of things on my mind back then, that's all."

"That's all?" I said. He talked as if breaking up with me went right along with deciding not to take the trash out one week or something.

"Michelle, I know you're a busy woman and that you have a lot of things going on, but I was just wondering if tonight the two of us can meet at *Starbucks*, just to talk. I have some important things on my mind that I have to talk to you about."

Important things, huh? What did he have to spring on me this time? I didn't know what to think of his "out-of-the-blue" request for conversation, a whole eight months after he disappeared from my life. And why would he call and try to set something up with me the same day? Does he think I don't have a life now, since he's been out of the picture?

Then again, it was this same sense of spontaneity that I liked about him in the first place. Maybe that was why I fell for him so hard. Now that I think about it, maybe this would be the perfect opportunity to bring some closure to the whole thing. It would definitely make me feel better once I knew that it was finally over and that I have total and complete peace about it. Maybe it wouldn't be such a bad idea to meet with him after all.

"Okay Pierre," I finally said. "I'll take you up on that offer. What time do you want to meet?"

"Can we meet there at 8:00 tonight?"

"8:00 is fine."

"Okay, Michelle, I'll see you then."

"Bye."

Chapter 13

Dream Man

"THANK YOU FOR THE ROSES; THEY'RE BEAUTIFUL," chimed Sandy as she spoke to Carter on the telephone in the back room during her lunch break.

"Did you read the card?" asked Carter.

"Yes, I did," Sandy sang, blushing.

"I'm glad you liked the flowers. Sandra Moore, when can I see you again? Are you doing anything tonight?"

"Well, no, it's Tuesday, and I really don't have anything planned. Why, did you want to get together?" Sandy asked.

"As a matter of fact, I do. A friend of mine has four tickets to see Kirk Franklin tonight in concert. My friend is going with his girlfriend and I was wondering if you would join us."

A Kirk Franklin concert? Carter must be really saved!

"Sure, why not?" Sandy didn't hesitate. The fact that they would be going with another couple made Sandy feel comfortable. It proved he was willing to take things slow by going out as a group first instead of one-on-one dating. Michelle had told Sandy that was the best thing to do when going out with someone new.

"Cool," the voice on the other line said. "I'll pick you up at work."

"Wait a minute. I have to go home and change. I can't just wear what I have on now." Sandy looked at her pastel blue suit with a pink rose pinned on the lapel and pink heels.

"I'm sure what you have on now is fine and that you still look good."

"Thanks for the compliment, but I want to look my best for you," Sandy said with a sexy voice.

"Then I'll pick you up at your place at seven? The concert starts at eight."

"Seven is fine," Sandy reassured him.

"Okay then, it's a date. Don't be looking too good tonight, now. I don't want to be distracted from the concert," Carter stated with a chuckle.

"I'll try not to." But really, after work, Sandy planned to make herself look the best she had ever looked in a long time. She wanted this man to know that she was definitely fine and that he made the right choice in asking her to go out with him and not some other woman. Sandy didn't mind being his trophy for the night and was more than prepared to look the part.

After doing eighty on the freeway headed home, Sandy rushed into her house and ran for the bathroom. She flew by Madear, barely saying "hello."

"Baby, you alright?" Madear asked. By this time the shower was already running in the bathroom so Sandy couldn't hear her grandmother's inquiry.

After much thought, Sandy had decided to wear her hot pink sleeveless dress and hot pink heels. The dress wasn't too tight, but it did fit snug around her round behind.

Sandy looked at herself in her full-length mirror and attempted to pump up her nearly nonexistent breasts. Sandy then put on her pink lipstick, brown eyeliner, and a hint of pink blush to make her cheeks look extra rosy.

She was fumbling around with her short hair, trying to do something a little different with it, when Madear entered her room with her arms folded.

"Going somewhere tonight?"

"Yes, Madear; I'm going to a gospel concert."

"A gospel concert? You lookin' kinda spiffied up there to be going to any gospel concert." Madear looked her grandbaby up and down.

"Yes, Madear. I want to look nice." She wished Madear would leave her alone and not pry so much into her life.

"Nice is hardly the word," Madear commented. Sandy rolled her eyes.

"You going with a man or something?" Madear probed.

"Yes, Madear, I'm going with a man," Sandy hissed.

"Who?"

"A man I met on the job."

"Oh, you must have *just* met him, 'cuz I don't 'member no men calling for you 'round here."

Sandy continued to play with her hair while ignoring the woman who practically raised her.

"Is he saved?" Madear asked.

"Yes, Madear, he's saved."

"That's good."

Sandy stared at her grandmother. Madear finally got the hint and walked out of Sandy's room.

Sandy decided to just leave her jet-black hair the way it is as she sprayed it with oil sheen and called it a night. Ten minutes later the doorbell rang.

"I'll get it," Sandy sang as she raced downstairs toward the front door, all dolled-up and ready to go. She didn't want Carter to have to sit through twenty questions with Madear.

When Sandy opened the door, she couldn't believe it, but Carter looked even finer than he had yesterday.   He had on a black silk shirt with black slacks, and his hair was freshly cut with waves swimming toward his widow's peak. His smooth chocolate skin almost shone and was freshly shaven with a perfectly trimmed mustache and goatee. Sandy's heart raced when she saw his gleaming white teeth smiling at her.

Sandy was so elated by his appearance that she didn't notice that he had something in his hand for her. He held a heart-shaped box of chocolates and a white teddy bear, and it wasn't even Valentine's Day.

"Thank you, Carter!" Sandy beamed as she grabbed her gifts and invited him in.

"You look gorgeous." Carter eyed her from head to toe; his tongue was nearly hanging out of his mouth.

"Thank you," Sandy said with a sly grin.

"No, I mean it. You look really good. Now I told you I didn't want you to distract me now, but hey, that is okay. Girl, you look fine."

"Thank you," Sandy said again shyly this time.

"Well, can I get a hug?" Carter asked.

"Sure, why not?"

Sandy set her chocolates and teddy bear on her grandmother's plastic-covered couch, opened her arms wide, and Carter fell into her arms and squeezed tight. Sandy felt like she was in heaven as she held on to his bulging arms and whiffed the scent of his cologne.

He picked her up and started swinging her around in the living room until they heard Madear clear her throat. Carter stopped swinging Sandy and placed her back on solid ground.

"Oh, Madear, this is Carter." Sandy regained her composure and pulled down her dress.

"Oh, uh, hello Madear," Carter said, embarrassed. He extended his hand.

Madear just looked at it. "Hello, Carter," she said, looking him straight in the eyes. "Do you know the Lord, Carter?"

After a slight pause, Carter responded, "Yes, ma'am. I do."

"Do you *really* know the Lord, Carter," Madear asked again, arching an eyebrow.

"Sorry, Madear, we really have to go because the concert is about to start," interrupted Sandy. Sandy grabbed Carter's hand and led him out with a final good-bye.

"What was that all about?" asked Carter once they were outside.

"Oh, that was just my grandmother who raised me since I was six-years-old. Sometimes I feel like she thinks she's still raising me."

"Oh," Carter said.

"She treats all my guy friends like that, don't pay her no mind."

"Oh, *all* your guy friends?"

"I didn't mean it like that," Sandy exclaimed quickly in order to regain her cool points while protecting Carter's ego. "I don't have a lot of guy friends, at least not anymore." She gave Carter a flirtatious glance. He smiled.

"Wow, look at your ride." Sandy screeched as she eyed Carter's black Benz, "This is a baaaaad car you got here!"

"Thanks," Carter proclaimed proudly and waltzed over to the passenger side to open the door for Sandy.

"For you, madam," he said as he led her inside with his right hand.

As the two of them headed downtown, Sandy was so excited about going on a date with a guy that she really liked that she almost couldn't contain herself.

Carter sure was different from Mark, who never took Sandy anywhere except to the dollar show and, even then, he would make her buy her own popcorn. He never bought her anything, even last year when he was out of town on Valentine's Day, Sandy mailed him two cards, but what did he buy her? Nothing. Not a thing. If Mark had made Sandy a card with a poem written in crayon, she would have cherished it just the same as if he bought her diamond earrings. She was glad to be rid of that loser.

During the ride, Sandy suddenly realized that she didn't call and tell Michelle that she was going on a real date with the man of her dreams.

"She probably would say I shouldn't make myself so available by going out with him the same day that he asked me," Sandy thought. "But, shoot, I just met the man yesterday and his friend probably just told him today that he got tickets for the concert. Besides, maybe he had initially had someone else in mind he wanted to take, like a friend or something, but then when he met me, hey, gotta go gotta go, praise the Lord." Sandy chuckled out loud at that thought.

"What's so funny?" Carter asked.

"Nothing," Sandy stated, "I was just thinking about something, that's all."

"Oh," Carter replied.

"So how did your friend get tickets to the concert?" Sandy asked.

"My friend knows the producer of the opening act of the show, so he was able to grab four tickets from him the other day."

"Oh," Sandy replied in relief. So it was a last minute, grab-the-opportunity-while-it's-there type-a-thing. Sandy felt better. Michelle couldn't complain about that.

Suddenly, sounds of R. Kelly's song, "12 Play," blasted throughout the car. Carter sang along with the chorus, and Sandy looked at him with a weird expression. Pretty soon, Sandy began swaying to one of her old jams.

"You remember this here?" Carter asked with a southern drawl.

"Yes, I do." Sandy stated. "Are you from here?" she asked suspiciously.

"Well, no. I'm originally from Atlanta."

Sandy sighed with relief. So that explained the slight southern accent.

"You from Atlanta? I love Atlanta! I visited there about three years ago with some of my girlfriends. The weather there was just beautiful, and the people were so friendly. When did you move here?"

"I only been here for a year and a half. One of my partners in the law firm is from here and I and another brotha from St. Louis moved here to start it."

"So, you mean to tell me you've been here a year and a half and you haven't been able to meet a decent, intelligent woman?"

"Is that so hard to believe?"

"Oh!" Sandy exclaimed. "So now you cracking on the sistahs in the D?"

Carter chuckled. "I'm just kidding. Besides, I met you didn't I?" he said as he grabbed her left hand, "and it didn't take me too long to find you, now did it?"

Chapter 14

Who Cares?

TUESDAY, AFTER ANOTHER DAY OF TEACHING
and encouraging her students, Liz left the school parking
lot wondering if she should even try to go home.   She was
afraid that her mom and that married man would still be
there, but she didn't want to be a burden to Michelle by
staying at her place two nights in a row.

"Besides," Liz thought, "Michelle and I just prayed about
the situation, so I'm supposed to expect change, right?"
Liz didn't want to admit that she was secretly afraid that
nothing had changed.

As Liz pulled into her driveway, she noticed no cars were
there. "Maybe that man did like most cheaters do and took
Mom to a motel or something. Or maybe she got some
sense put in her brain and decided to go to work today."

123

Inside, everything was pretty much intact. She headed for the kitchen and warmed up a pot of leftover beef stew. Liz was glad that she didn't have to take anything out to thaw and cook; she was "starvin' like Marvin" and wanted something to fix and eat fast.

She turned on the television to find a channel that showed news instead of the countless talk shows, court shows, or soap operas that are on around three o'clock. Then the telephone rang.

"Who that could be?" Liz wondered. The caller ID read, "Private." She didn't think it was Michelle. Maybe it was her mother calling from work to apologize for her childish behavior last night. Liz picked up the cordless phone. "Hello."

Click.

"That was weird," Liz thought after the person hung up. "Maybe they had the wrong number."

As Liz went to stir her stew on the stove, the phone rang again.

"Hello," Liz answered the "Private" caller again.

This time there was a brief pause. *Click.*

Who could be calling just to hang up on her? Liz filled her bowl with beef stew, grabbed a slice of bread, and poured a glass of water, eyeing the phone suspiciously. Fifteen minutes passed, so Liz hoped the anonymous caller was finished with his or her harassment for one day, but as she carried her dinner to the living room, the phone rang again.

The caller ID read "Private," and this time Liz decided she would just let it ring. The phone rang eight times before it got on her nerves. On the tenth ring, Liz picked up the phone and shouted, "Hello!"

"Tramp!" a female screamed on the other end and hung up.

Liz was dumbfounded. The caller must be "lover boy's" wife, trying to harass Ms. Coleman. "What in the world has my mom gotten herself into?" Liz thought. "This woman could be crazy or something."

Just then Liz heard keys rattling in the door and in walked Ms. Coleman.

"You're home," Ms. Coleman stated as soon as she saw her daughter seated on the black leather couch with a bowl of beef stew on her lap.

"Yes, I'm home," Liz said with confidence, knowing that her mom wouldn't have the guts to kick her out permanently, especially since Liz contributed $600 a month toward the mortgage.

"You're home, too. You didn't go to work?"

"Don't start with me, Liz. I don't feel like hearing another lecture from my own child," Ms. Coleman proclaimed as she hung up her navy blue windbreaker in the closet.

Since her mother was wearing a casual two-piece purple outfit, Liz knew she hadn't gone to work.

The telephone rang again.

"It's for you," Liz stated.

When Ms. Coleman picked up the phone, Liz could hear screaming from the other end and then another *click*.

"What was that?" Ms. Coleman asked in disbelief. From the look on her face, Liz knew the caller must have called her mom something more severe than "tramp."

"That, my dear mother, was what I've been experiencing ever since I got home today. Apparently that man of yours now has an angry wife who knows where you live." Liz took a sip of water.

"Shut up, Liz, just shut up!" Ms. Coleman stormed toward her bedroom and slammed the door. Liz's college graduation picture on the mantle crashed to the floor.

Liz wondered what else was going on in this drama circle. Ms. Coleman had tears in her eyes, which was definitely unusual. Liz finished her stew and then sat pondering whether she should check on her mom.

Eventually, Liz got up and lightly tapped on her mother's bedroom door before Liz slowly opened it. There sat Ms. Coleman, the most strong-minded one in the family, clutching her black comforter and rocking herself on the side of the bed with rivers of tears streaming down her brown face.

Liz looked at her mom as if the lady who sat before her was not the same woman who raised her. It was not the same woman who would drop a man at the drop of a hat the minute he stopped giving gifts in exchange for some good sex.

"Mom," Liz asked quietly, "are you okay?"

Ms. Coleman said nothing.

"Mom- "

"No, Elizabeth, I'm not okay," Ms. Coleman hissed. "Is that what you want to hear?"

"Is there anything I can do to help?"

"Yeah," Ms. Coleman began, staring intently at her only child. "You can make that man love me!"

Liz entered the room completely and sat next to her mother at the foot of the bed.

"Who?"

"Richard!" Ms. Coleman screamed, as if Liz was somehow supposed to know his name.

"He doesn't love you, Mom?" Liz couldn't think of anything else to say.

"No! He don't love me! He never did, even though he said he did! I'm sure you'd be glad to know that you won't be seeing or hearing from Richard anymore."

"Why?"

"You were right," Ms. Coleman admitted. "It's no fun messing around with a married man, because after a while they leave you and go back to they wife and kids."

Kids? That made matters even worse. Liz wondered what kind of hold this man had on her mother; she had never seen her cry over a man in her entire life.

"So, he left you?" Liz asked, depending on the Lord to give her the right words to say.

"Yeah," Ms. Coleman confessed. "He did it this afternoon. We had sex in his cabin up north, then we came back and had lunch downtown. And right there at the restaurant, he tells me he's going back home to his wife . . . for good."

"Good for him," Liz thought. But of course she couldn't tell her mother that. "Just like that?" she asked.

"Just like that."

"You must have really loved him, Mom," Liz said with her head down staring at her hands in her lap.

"I did love him. The rat."

Liz grabbed a box of tissue from the dresser and gave some to her mother. "So how long have you been, um, seeing him?"

"We been screwing each other off and on for about two years now."

"Two years!" Liz shouted and grabbed her mouth. Ms. Coleman glared at her. Liz couldn't believe her mother's eyes were so blinded for two full years. At that point it was very hard for Liz to remain sympathetic. "So what are you going to do, Mom?"

"What am *I* going to do? Nothing, I guess. I guess I just have to move on, and hope that crazy wife of his don't come and try to burn this house down."

"Don't say that."

"It's true. Richard told me how crazy she was."

"I bet he also told you that eventually he was going to leave her for you, right?"

"Don't go there, Liz. I don't need that right now."

"It's true, Mom. What other lies of his did you believe?"

"Look, all I know is I loved him and I thought that one day, when the time was right, he would be able to make his transition and leave his wife so he could be with me. Obviously, the woman found out about us and is now calling this house. She probably checked his cell phone and found the number or something. Crazy heffa."

"Mom, why do you keep calling the woman crazy? She has every right to know if her husband is cheating on her. And you had no right to invade their home and cause all of this confusion. Especially if he has kids, too."

"Oh boy, here we go again. I repent, I repent!" Ms. Coleman proclaimed with dried eyes and one hand waved in the sky.

"It's not even about that, Mom. It's not even about the fact that you sinned against God. It's about the fact that you don't realize how much God loves you in that He has spared you this long and kept you from going crazy or even catching a sexually transmitted disease with the way you've been acting lately."

Ms. Coleman looked at her daughter with sheer disgust.

"Mom," Liz said more quietly, " I just want you to realize that God does love you, no matter what."

Ms. Coleman's face appeared to be in deep thought, and with a sigh she said, through clenched teeth, "God don't love me."

Liz looked shocked. "What did you just say?"

"God . . . does not . . . love . . . me!" Ms. Coleman proclaimed louder as tears filled her eyes again.

"That's not true, Mom."

"It's not true? Then why is my life the way it is now? My momma died a year after I had you, my daddy's I don't know where, and the one man I did love, your father, left me at the altar while I was pregnant with you. So, if you ask me, nobody care about me!"

"Mom, that's not true." Liz insisted. "I care about you!"

"You don't care about me!" Ms. Coleman shot up from her bed and faced Liz. "For the past twenty-seven years, all I been trying to do is be your mother, and maybe even your friend, but ever since you got all high and mighty with all this religion, all you ever tried to do was be my judge!"

Liz grew silent as her mother's words stung her ears. She didn't know what to say as her own mother looked at her like she was the enemy. Liz rose from the bed and quietly walked out of her mother's bedroom. She closed the door behind her, backed against the door, wrapped her arms around herself, and held back tears.

Chapter 15

Praying in Tears

THE CONCERT HALL WAS PACKED. PEOPLE
from all walks of life came to see the show. Sandy and
Carter waited in the lobby for Carter's friends, Nick and
Tracey. They were supposed to meet them at 7:50, and it
was now 8:15; the opening act was already performing.
Feeling restless in the hot, crowded lobby, Sandy excused
herself to go to the restroom to check her hair and make-up.

Sandy thought she could get away from the crowd by
going to the spacious restroom downstairs, but she was
obviously wrong. There was a long line as Sandy squeezed
through to the mirror. She noticed all of the different outfits
some of the ladies had on. Some wore skirts that were so
tight and short that she could almost see their underwear.

Others wore tops that showed nothing but cleavage.

From the looks of things, Sandy almost forgot she was even at a gospel concert. Then she remembered how she used to dress like that, except she didn't have any cleavage to show off. She used to try and show off her skinny legs, big booty, and pouch-less belly. The day after she got saved, one of the first things she did was throw away her favorite pink and silver belly ring. It reminded her too much of her past. Sandy just shook her head as she finally made her way to the mirror in front of the sink.

One look in the mirror proved Sandy's suspicion to be true. Her face was shiny with sweat, and her curls had almost all fallen out. Sandy sighed and pulled out a comb from her purse.

As Sandy fixed her hair she heard a heavy-set woman next to her say to another lady, "Girl, did you see Darnell walk up in here with Laqueeta? The nerve of that brotha. Wait 'til I tell Chantelle."

"Yeah, girl, I saw him," the other lady said. She was fixing her makeup in the mirror and combing her super long, curly black weave.

"I think you should tell her. Chantelle was just telling me he was about to propose to her, and now here he is at a gospel concert with another woman."

"Ain't that something?" chimed in the first woman who pulled out some hand lotion from her fake designer purse. "Girl, I tell you, men."

"Yeah, men."

Listening to their conversation made Sandy boil inside. She wanted to scream, "What about men? Yeah, they can be mean at times, and some of them can be outright dogs, but there still are some good ones out there!" Sandy was fed up with women down-talking her men. For all those two women knew, that brotha Darnell could've been taking his cousin Sally Sue to the concert.

Sandy reapplied her lipstick and went back into the lobby where Carter was conversing with another couple. The lady was cute, short, and bubbly with a short bob hairstyle, light brown skin, and a thick frame. She had braces but continued to smile with every word. The man she held on her arm was light-skinned, about six feet tall, extremely skinny and handsome. He was real friendly acting, too.

Sandy threw on a fake smile as she eased her way next to Carter.

Carter proclaimed, "Sandy, there you are! I want you to meet my good friends, Nick and Tracey."

Sandy kept smiling and shook their hands. "Nice to meet you both." She failed to mention how she was upset that they were late and she was ready to head inside.

Finally, they all headed to their seats in the second row of the first balcony. Sandy hated when people came in after a concert had started, and now here she was the late one having to say, "Excuse me" to everyone in the row. By the time they all sat down, the opening act was finished and another act was about to perform.

The next act was a set of overweight brothers called "The Light." Sandy was impressed by how they moved ferociously across the stage while singing and praising God with such vigor.

Sandy wanted to stand up but decided not to because the three people with her stayed seated and just clapped their hands to the beat. But after a while, she did stand up, and Tracey and Nick soon followed. All three were really into an upbeat song entitled "Lord, I Thank You." Sandy envisioned all of the good things in her life that she has to be thankful for.

Sandy was thankful that, for the past twenty-three years, God had kept her in perfect peace. Even though her parents were killed in a car accident, God saw that she was still taken care of by her loving, yet sometimes over-protective grandmother.

Sandy was also thankful that God saved her four months ago and surrounded her with good Christian friends like Michelle and Liz. Sandy clapped her hands and praised

God right along with the act that was ministering to her in song.

Sandy wondered why Carter didn't stand up like everyone else. He just sat in his seat, calmly clapping his hands and staring at the stage.

"Maybe he had a long day at work," Sandy thought. "Maybe he's not the type to show outwardly how he feels."

After The Light's performance, a local radio personality returned to the stage and prepared the crowd for the next performer.

"Alright ya'll!" the vibrant, older woman wearing a silver gown and a white wig screamed into the microphone. "Get ready now. I want ya'll to stand up on yo' feet and give a warm Detroit welcome to the one, the only, Mr. Kirk Franklin!"

The audience grew extremely loud as everyone stood up and cheered as the main attraction entered the stage. The blaring music revitalized the whole crowd; even Carter stood on his feet and clapped his hands to the beat.

After several songs, and several tears of joy shed by Sandy, she was having the time of her life and was glad that she had the opportunity to spend it with Carter.

Once the concert was over, the four of them decided to wait a few minutes before diving into the crowd heading for the exit.

"Did you enjoy the show?" Carter asked Sandy as they sat waiting.

"I sure did," Sandy said as she looked at Carter with a huge grin. Deep down inside Sandy wanted to show how much she enjoyed it by planting a kiss on Carter's juicy lips, but she decided against doing that. It wouldn't seem appropriate at a gospel concert, and besides, Michelle has always told Sandy that the male is supposed to lead in the relationship, so she didn't want to seem like the aggressor.

"I'm glad," Carter said as he returned Sandy's smile. Sandy just loved the way his bright white teeth shone in the dim light.

"Well, it's looking a little more cleared up now. Plus, I have to get up and go to work in the morning. Are we ready to head for the door?" Nick insisted.

"Yeah," everyone agreed. Sandy held on to Carter's bulging arm as he led her through the crowd.

Once in the lobby, Sandy thought her eyes deceived her as she spotted a familiar face. Among several people, Sandy saw a short, caramel-complexioned brotha walking toward the exit and holding hands with a tall, light-skinned woman with long, wavy hair, and slanted eyes that made her look Chinese. The woman was gorgeous in her white mini-dress. After a second look, Sandy was sure the man was no other than her ex, Mark.

"That two-timing low-life!" Sandy immediately thought to herself. Then she remembered that they were no longer a couple, even though it was only two days ago that Mark was just at her house trying to sleep with her. Sandy was sure that Mark didn't *just* start talking to the girl he was with now.

"That punk!" Sandy thought. Jealousy and disappointment boiled up inside her. "I didn't know tall women were his type. What's he trying to prove, anyway?"

Carter noticed her changed expression and asked, "Is everything okay, Sandy?"

"Oh, everything's fine," Sandy snapped. "Just fine."

"Well, you look a little disturbed." Carter looked in the direction Sandy was looking to see what caused her disgruntled look.

"No, I'm okay." Sandy said. "Can we walk a little faster? I'm really tired, and I have to get up and go to work in the morning, too."

"Sure," Carter said, looking at Sandy strangely.

During the ride home, Sandy barely said a word to her date. She stared straight ahead and remained expressionless.

Carter broke the silence at a red light. "Sandy, are you okay?"

"I'm fine, Carter," Sandy said. She finally turned to him.

"I really had a good time, Carter. Thanks again for inviting me."

"No problem. You know I had to invite *you*. I just wanted to show a beautiful lady a good time."

Sandy cracked a smile. "Thanks."

As they pulled up into her driveway, Carter hopped out of the car and opened Sandy's door.

"Carter is really a sweet guy," Sandy thought as he walked her to the door.

"Thank you, Carter. I really had a nice time," Sandy repeated while they faced each other.

"The pleasure was all mine," Carter said with a sexy look into Sandy's dark brown eyes. He grabbed her right hand and kissed it.

Sandy smiled sweetly and stared at him in return. She wondered if he was going to try and kiss her; she hoped he would.

Ten seconds later, the porch light came on.

"I gotta go; my grandmother's giving me 'the hint,' Sandy said with a motion to go inside.

"I understand," Carter said. Sandy respected Carter because he didn't make a move on their first date.

"May I call you tomorrow?" Carter asked.

"Sure." Sandy stepped inside and watched him drive off from her front door peephole.

Once Carter disappeared from her sight, Sandy turned around, leaned her back against the front door, closed her eyes, and let out a huge sigh.

"How was your date?" Madear was wearing rollers and a dingy white robe.

Sandy opened her eyes wide and said, "Fine," and then rushed upstairs to her room.

Sandy plopped on her canopy bed, grabbed her pink teddy bear, smashed it into her face and screamed. She couldn't stand the thought of seeing Mark with another woman, especially after he just tried to get back with her.

"He never took me to any concert," Sandy complained

to Teddy. "He never took me anywhere!" Sandy yelled and sent Teddy flying across the room.

Sandy wished she had never given it up to Mark, but now, she couldn't even stand the thought of his being in bed with someone else. She wished she had saved herself for marriage, like Michelle and Liz were doing. She felt like she never could measure up to them, no matter how hard she tried.

Sandy lay down on her bed and cried softly in her pillow. More than anything, she was mad at herself for even caring. All types of emotions were built up inside her as she thought about her life and what happened tonight. She was starting to get a headache.

Sandy rolled over on her back and cried out to the ceiling, "God, what is wrong with me!"

No response.

Sandy thought about calling Michelle, but then decided against it because it was almost midnight. Instead, she knelt by her bed and began to pray in the midst of her tears.

"God, I need Your help. I don't know what to do, Lord. I try to stand on my own two feet, but it seems like every time I try, I get knocked down again."

She concluded that living the saved life is not as easy as she thought it would be. Sandy didn't feel so saved as she thought about grabbing some scissors and cutting all of that other woman's long, pretty hair off. Sandy figured if she were really saved, she wouldn't be harboring such vengeance in her heart. She thought if she were really saved, she wouldn't feel all jealous and betrayed. She also thought if she were really saved, she wouldn't be having the sexual thoughts about making sweet love to Carter and allowing him to hold and caress her to make all of the pain go away.

With nothing else left to do, Sandy wondered what Michelle might do or say if she were here. Sandy reached for her Bible on her nightstand and opened it to the book of Ephesians. The first scripture she saw and read out loud was Ephesians 2:8-9, "For by grace are you saved through faith; and that not of yourselves: it is the gift of God: Not of works, lest any man should boast."

Sandy was amazed that God led her to the very scripture she needed. It was the same verse that the altar call counselor had her highlight on the day she got saved at Hype. The counselor told Sandy, "No matter what you feel like, or no matter what you do, you are now saved by the grace of God. There is nothing you can do to get into heaven; God sent Jesus so that you could go to heaven, so even when there are times when you might not feel saved, you are saved because of the grace of God."

Comforted by God's Word, Sandy climbed into bed and fell asleep.

Chapter 16

A Cup of Latte

I WAS RELIEVED ONCE I MADE IT INSIDE
Starbucks. I shook the water from my drenched umbrella
and looked around for Pierre. Since he hadn't made it yet,
I ordered my usual, a nice warm cup of latte with a shot of
caramel and whipped cream.

I sat at a small table for two, removed my rain coat, and
revealed my corporate brown suit. I was taking tiny sips of
my latte when Pierre walked in around 8:10.

"I'm sorry I'm late," he said. He shook his long, black
umbrella and wiped his black dress shoes on the mat at the
doorway.

Even half wet, Pierre looked extremely sexy. I hoped he
would just get to the point so that I wouldn't be mesmerized
once again by certain looks from his hypnotizing hazel eyes.

"That's okay. It's wet out; I figured traffic was probably bad," I said.

"It was, especially I-696 on the way getting here from my last meeting with a client."

"Oh, how'd it go?"

"It went extremely well," Pierre responded with utter confidence. "I believe this client will definitely be utilizing my services. At least that is the impression he gave me."

"Good," I chirped while sipping my latte.

Okay, enough of the small talk, let's get down to the nitty gritty. I waited for him to place his coat on the back of the chair and have a seat; then I asked, "Are you going to order something, Pierre?"

"Yeah," he said and then popped up from his seat. "Did you want anything else?"

"No, but thanks for asking." I couldn't help smiling. He was still trying to be Mr. Considerate, always thinking of others before himself, which was another distinct quality that I used to admire.

Pierre returned to the tiny table with a regular coffee, black. Pierre always did like to drink straight black coffee. Sometimes he would even drink three cups a day. He always told me it helped his nerves. Maybe that was his problem, too much coffee.

"So how ya been, girl?" Pierre asked in a lively tone.

"I've been doing real good," I said calmly. "And how you been?"

"I've been doing wonderful, just wonderful," Pierre responded. "How's your job going?"

"Oh, it's going. Let's just say I'm pretty content in my present position." I was ready to cut right to the chase, and I think he sensed it by the serious look on my face.

"Well, as I mentioned to you on the telephone, Michelle, I really have something I want to talk to you about." Pierre switched his tone from upbeat to extremely serious.

"What?" I tried to sound unconcerned, as if I hadn't been wondering ever since he called what in the world was so pressing that he had to re-appear in my life and tell me here on this cold and rainy night.

"Again, I want to apologize for the way I treated you when I last saw you at your place."

Okay . . . an apology almost a year later. . .

"And I want you to know that I've grown a lot spiritually and mentally since then."

Time to break out the violin so he can 'cry me a river'.

"And since then, I've been spending a lot of time alone just thinking about life, and . . . "

What, he figured out that breaking up with me was absolutely the dumbest thing he could ever do and now he wants me back? Well, too late, buddy. You should've thought of that before you walked out on me.

". . . and about some choices I've made in the past . . ."

I just wanted to rub his hand and say, "It's okay, baby, I understand," like Madear would say.

"And lately I've been seeing someone and . . . "

Hold up. Seeing someone? Who, a psychiatrist?

"And instead of making the same mistake twice I decided to really settle down this time."

Settle down?

I took another casual sip of my latte and asked politely, "What are you saying, Pierre?"

"I'm saying," began Pierre with a slight pause, "this weekend, on Saturday, May 4th, I'm going to ask the woman I love to marry me."

I almost choked on my latte.

No, this man didn't drag me out in the rain on a bad hair day to tell me he was about to propose to some other chick. He could have told me this crap over the phone.

What was the big deal anyway? What did he expect me to say?

"Married?" I asked, clearing my throat. Boy, it didn't take him long to kick me to the curb and then move on to someone else.

"Yes, married," Pierre repeated. "I'm going to ask the

woman I love to marry me."

Oh, what is he trying to rub it in now by repeating it? What next, is he going to pull out the box and show me the ring he bought her?

Who is this woman, anyway? Does she go to Hype, or did he just drag her from off the street? Maybe, when I chose to say no to his cocky, arrogant advances, she said yes.

"Well, Pierre," I said, "What can I say? I'm really . . . happy . . . for you."

And the Academy Award goes to...

"You're happy for me?" Pierre asked in disbelief.

"Sure, why wouldn't I be?" I kept my composure by taking another sip of my latte, which was almost gone now. I wanted to appear as calm, cool, and collected as possible, even though deep down I felt like asking the man behind the counter to add a shot of vodka to my latte.

"Oh." Pierre stated.

"Why, should I not be?" I asked. "Aren't *you* happy?"

"Me? Oh, I'm *very* happy." Pierre proclaimed.

"Well, good. Now is that all you had to tell me?" I asked with a smile.

"Uh, yeah, yeah. That's all." Pierre gulped his black coffee.

"Well, thanks for sharing that piece of information with me."

"And what about you, Michelle?"

"What about me?"

"Are *you* seeing anybody?"

No, he didn't just go there. First, he tells me he's about to propose to somebody just so he'd see how I would react, and now he's trying to get all up in my business. I will never be able to figure this man out. I felt like really telling this brotha off; if it weren't for the Holy Ghost constraining me I would've thrown the rest of my latte right in his "fine" face.

"Yes, I *am* seeing somebody."

I hope he doesn't ask me who it is, because then I would have to tell him it's Jesus. He's the only man I'm seeing right now, and at least He won't go out with me just for sex and leave me crying at the door.

"Oh," Pierre said solemnly. "Are *you* happy?"

"Oh, I'm very happy."

"That's good. Well, I'm happy for you, then."

"Well, Pierre, if you've nothing else to say, I think I'll be going." I gathered my beige rain coat. "I should try to head home before it starts raining again."

"You know, I think you're right." Pierre gathered his black trench coat as well. "Mind if I walk you to your car?" Pierre asked as we headed for the door.

No, thank you. But, then again, maybe I shouldn't let on that I'm fuming inside.

"Sure, why not?" I forced a smile as we walked to the parking lot.

Pierre opened the car door like the normal gentleman that he always has been, and then waved goodbye as I drove off.

In a strange way, I guess I did finally receive the closure that I thought I needed; however, I never thought it would come in the form of an engagement announcement.

Chapter 17

The Playground

"OKAY KIDS, IT'S 11:30; TIME TO LINE UP for recess." Liz herded her second graders toward the classroom door. Today was Liz's day to monitor the children on the playground during lunch period. "Now I want to see a straight, single file line or else we won't be going out," Liz announced as she watched the tiny second graders scurry like frightened mice. They grew loud with excitement.

"Okay now, quiet down, kids. Don't make me have to count to three."

The noise and laughter continued.

"One . . . "

It got a little quieter but playful Jason was still hopping

143

around screaming.

"Two . . . "

At this point, even Jason stopped screaming and found his proper place in line behind Renita.

"Three!" Liz proclaimed. Everyone was now silent.

Liz prided herself on the fact that her students were always the quietest ones to leave the building for recess. Her second graders were also the best behaved during practice fire drills, and Liz would reward them with extra free-play time at the end of class.

Liz hadn't been outside sitting on a bench fifteen minutes trying to enjoy her own lunch when suddenly she saw a huge crowd of kids, big and small, rush toward the far east corner of the playground.

Children began to yell loudly, and she heard one little boy scream, "Fight! Fight!" as he rushed to the scene.

"A fight? At the academy?" Liz jumped up and ran to the crowd. She squeezed herself through the herd of at least fifty kids trying to get in on the action.

Inside the circle, she saw a tall fourth grader who was at least forty pounds overweight fighting with one of her second graders, little Matthew Long.

The fourth grader had Matthew pinned against the fence with both his hands wrapped around Matthew's neck when Liz shouted, "Stop! You're hurting him!"

Liz pushed forward to stop the fight herself when Mr. Fletcher, a black male teacher in his late thirties, rushed in between the two boys. Mr. Fletcher yanked the big kid off of Matthew and held him as Matthew coughed and rubbed his neck.

A few more lunch monitors entered the scene. Mrs. Clooney and Liz ran to Matthew's aid. The big kid yelled at Matthew, "You little punk! You coward! You snake!" Mr. Fletcher and Mr. Hobson escorted him back to the school building.

Matthew, one of the smallest pupils in Liz's class, looked pretty bruised and beat-up; blood rushed from the side of his swollen little mouth as he rested on the fence with his eyes half closed. His pants were torn in the knees, and grass and pebbles were all caught in his head full of curly brown hair.

"Matthew, are you okay?" Liz asked. Mrs. Clooney gave her a wet towel to wipe his face. "Matthew, can you hear me?" Liz asked in a state of panic. She felt like her own child had gotten hurt.

"Uh huh," Matthew managed to mutter with his busted lip.

"C'mon Matthew, we gotta get you inside."

Mrs. Clooney and two other lunch monitors disseminated the crowd and asked the students to return to regular play.

Inside, Liz escorted Matthew to the nurse's office so he could get cleaned up. The nurse wiped Matthew's open wounds with peroxide, and Matthew cringed because of the stings. Liz held Matthew's hand; he squeezed her hand every time he felt pain. Once bandaged up, Matthew appeared to be a little calmer, but he still remained silent.

"Matthew, are you all right now?" Liz finally asked him. She was ready to get to the bottom of all this.

"Yes, Miss Coleman," Matthew muttered. He looked down at the blue band-aid that the nurse put on his right knee.

"Can you tell me what just happened out there on the playground?" Liz asked.

Matthew just continued to look down.

"You know you're going to have to tell the principal what happened."

Matthew nodded.

"And you know we're going to have to tell your father."

Tears began to run from Matthew's eyes. Matthew suddenly lifted his head in desperation.

"No!" He knew that once his father found out, that would mean his hide. Mr. Long was already having difficulty raising Matthew alone.

"It wasn't my fault!" Matthew pleaded.

"Can you tell me what happened then?" Liz asked again.

Matthew looked down and twiddled his thumbs.

"Okay, since you don't want to tell me what happened, you're going to have to explain it to the principal, and your father will be notified."

Liz knew his father would have been notified whether or not Matthew told her what happened, but she just wanted to stress the consequences of what took place.

"Do you understand, Matthew?"

Liz hated disciplining her students, especially Matthew who was normally the best-behaved student in her class, but she could find no other way to teach him to respect her and to answer her when she asked a question.

Matthew maintained a sad, glassy-eyed look on his ruddy face.

Liz didn't budge from her initial request. "I'm going to have the principal's office call your dad at work." She escorted him to the principal's office.

By 2:00, Matthew returned to Liz's class and took his normal seat in the back. Liz was notified by the principal's office that Mr. Long, Matthew's father, was unable to leave work early and would pick up his son at 3:30. Liz dismissed her class and little Matthew remained seated at his desk waiting for his father. He grabbed a piece of paper and some crayons and began to draw.

At 3:45, Matthew was still drawing while Liz reviewed her lesson for tomorrow.

At 3:50, an extremely handsome, thirty-something, tall, light-skinned male with curly brown hair and a thin mustache walked into Liz's classroom. Liz noticed his light brown eyes twinkle as he entered the room. He was wearing a blue and gold polo shirt with matching navy blue pants and navy blue shoes. His choice of clothing definitely complimented his medium build. He looked around as if he wasn't sure he had the right room.

Liz slowly rose from her chair, purposely not showing

any excitement, as Matthew looked up at his father and Mr. Long gave him a disappointed glance. Liz noticed that Matthew looked exactly like Mr. Long, except for his height and the mustache.

"Mr. Long, I'm Liz Coleman." She offered an aggressive handshake.

"Nice to meet you, Mrs. Coleman."

Liz wanted to correct Mr. Long by proclaiming, "No, no, it's not Mrs. Coleman, it's Miss, Miss!" but she didn't want to sound desperate. "Besides," Liz thought, "if he really cared, he would have noticed the absence of a wedding ring on my left hand."

"Please, call me Liz," she said with a professional smile.

Liz decided to take control of the conversation by saying, in her prosecutor tone of voice, "As you know, little Matthew here got into a fight today during lunchtime."

"Oh yes, I heard about that. Matt Jr. and I will be having a long talk once we get home, if we talk at all." Little Matthew just continued to draw. A tear fell from his eye to his paper.

"Well, I hope he tells you what happened. He didn't give me much to work with, but I'm sure there's a logical explanation behind all of this," Liz said sternly.

Just then Liz noticed that Mr. Long was staring at her, like he was not paying attention to a word she just said, but was lost looking deep into her eyes.

Liz had no idea Mr. Long would look so appealing to her in person. If Liz had known, she would have worn something besides her same ole navy blue jumpsuit and white tennis shoes. She would have spent a little more time in the bathroom styling her braids, which were currently in a messy ponytail. She would have even possibly put on a little lipstick, instead of the strawberry lip-gloss she used everyday.

"But, then again," Liz rationed, "he might not even be saved. He's raising a child alone, and he probably never been married, or he probably got a divorce. He might be like those parents who just drop their kids off, expecting the school to raise them and teach them about God while they themselves sit at home not even thinking about God or living the Word of God in front of their children."

Liz was determined not to let this man's good looks and charm fool her into thinking about something that was not even there. Besides, Liz didn't have time for a man right now. She was solely focused on God and served Him by teaching His children at the academy and volunteering in the church nursery every other Sunday and Thursday night.

"Matthew, are you ready to go?" Liz asked sternly in an attempt to redirect Mr. Long's extensive glance. She walked to his desk and peeked at his drawing.

Matthew had drawn two stick figures. One was a small figure, and the other was a taller figure with a dress on and long, curly orange hair. It looked as if the two stick figures were holding hands.

"Who is that, Matthew?" Liz asked.

"This is a picture of me and my mommy," Matthew said without looking up. "Oh." Liz could tell that little Matthew loved his mother a lot. She wondered who she was and why he didn't stay with her.

"C'mon son," Mr. Long interrupted as little Matthew gathered his navy blue book bag and light blue jacket. "But before we go," Mr. Long said to Matthew as he turned his little body around to face his teacher, "I want you to apologize to your teacher for disrupting lunch hour today."

Matthew paused for a moment and then looked at Liz with glassy eyes. "I'm sorry, Miss Coleman." He choked up and allowed several tears to fall.

Liz was so touched by little Matthew's apology; she knew it was sincere. She knew he didn't mean to hurt any body today or cause any trouble.

Liz sensed that there was something else deeply hurting the little boy who stood before her, but she couldn't figure out what.

Chapter 18

The Perfect Date

WEDNESDAY MORNING, SANDY FELT MUCH better. She woke up early enough to pray for thirty minutes before she left the house.

During her drive to work, Sandy cranked on her Mary Mary CD, which was the first contemporary gospel CD that she had received as a gift from Michelle. She turned on the first track entitled "Thankful" and started singing right along with them.

Sandy felt one hundred percent better as she sang one of her favorite songs. Sandy just loved how music could take her from one emotional state to a completely different state of mind with a melodic rhythm and heartfelt lyrics.

At a red light, Sandy noticed a frail black man holding a

cardboard sign that read, "Lost Everything due to Burn Out." Sandy reached into her ashtray, pulled out all of the change she had accumulated in the past month, and held it out toward the man. The man walked up to the car, took the change, gave her a bright yellow smile, and said, "God bless you."

By the time she made it to work, Sandy felt ready to take on anything, even another day with her boss. "Well, it's good to see you here early," Geneva chimed with a hint of sarcasm as Sandy entered the store at 8:15 rather than 8:30. Geneva always arrived at 8 a.m. so she could get her morning smoke and drink her cup of coffee in the back room.

"And how are you today, Geneva?" Sandy sang.

"I'm here," Geneva grunted.

Just then Kellie entered the store with a bag of bagels.

"Praise the Lord! Kellie brought bagels!" Sandy shouted.

Geneva gave Sandy a look that said, "Oh Lord, here we go again with this 'praise the Lord' crap. Not this early in the morning."

Geneva's usual glances and unwanted stares normally made Sandy feel uneasy and uncomfortable, but not on this particular Wednesday. On this particular Wednesday, the birds were singing, the sun was shining, and Sandy was thankful!

She was mainly thankful for the new man in her life, Mr. Carter Maxwell.

"He definitely could be the one," Sandy thought as she situated herself at the cash register.

Today Sandy wore a fuchsia pink two-piece suit with a silver shell shirt, matching silver shoes, and small cubic zirconium earrings. She hummed to herself as she envisioned her pink and blue wedding with her bridesmaids wearing pastel pink, strapless dresses.

"They can't look prettier than me, though," Sandy thought as she cleared off the cashier's area from the night before.

Just then, the phone rang. Kellie was closer, so she answered it. After a moment, she motioned for Sandy to take the phone. "It's for you," she said with a grin.

Sandy had a feeling who it might be calling her this early in the morning. Who else could it have been but her new main squeeze.

"Hello, this is Sandra Moore." She used the most professional voice she could muster.

"Hello, beautiful," a familiar deep voice said, sounding even deeper than usual.

"Carter!" Sandy screeched, acting surprised. "I was just thinking about you."

"Don't lie to me, Sandy; I thought you were a church-going woman?" he joked.

Sandy laughed slightly. "And how are you on this beautiful Wednesday morning?"

"Fine, just fine."

"I didn't asked how you looked," Sandy chided. "I asked how you been."

Carter laughed out loud. "I thought I was supposed to be the one coming up with the one liners," he said.

"Well, you know me; you gotta come quick, or I'll beat you at your own game."

"O-kay," Carter responded. "Sandy, I was wondering if I can, I mean if you would allow me to take you out to lunch today?"

"Sure, where are we going?"

"Will you leave *something* up to me?" Carter asked.

"Sure, I'll leave it as a surprise then," Sandy pouted.

"Good," Carter snickered. "What time do you normally break for lunch?"

"Oh, around noon," Sandy said. "Hold on one second, Carter." Sandy placed her hand over the phone and asked Kellie in a loud whisper, "What time are you going to lunch today?"

"Anytime you go is fine," Kellie whispered. "Just whenever you go, let me know, and I'll work around it."

"Thanks, Kel," Sandy said and kissed the air. "Noon is fine," she assured Carter.

"Okay then, I'll see you around noon."

"Until then."

"Bye, gorgeous," Carter said in his smooth sexy voice.

"Bye."

"Yessss!" Sandy sang.   "Praise the Lord!"

Geneva then yelled from the back, "Sandra, since today is normally slow we're going to use this day to work on inventory to get ready for our summer line and get rid of a lot of this winter stuff. We're gonna mark these clearance items down even lower so we can get them out of here!"

Sandy sometimes wondered if she were the only employee in the entire store. It always seemed like Geneva had Sandy doing more work than Kellie. Kellie would work at the register with the customers who trickled in every now and then, while Sandy would often get stuck in the back.

"Is it just me, or does it seem like she just picking on me today?" Sandy asked her sidekick.

Kellie shrugged.

"Oh, and thanks for bringing the bagels; that was really sweet of you," Sandy said as she grabbed a cinnamon raisin bagel from the bag.

"You're welcome," Kellie replied with a smile. "Oh, and don't worry about today, Sandy," she mentioned in reference to Geneva's orders. "I got 'cha covered." Kellie winked at her co-worker.

"Thanks," Sandy whispered.

By 11:30, Sandy stopped marking down already ticketed winter merchandise and went into the restroom to get ready for Carter's visit. She was so nervous about seeing him again it almost seemed unreal. She normally knew how to be well-behaved, prim, and proper in the presence of a man, but she had never met a man quite like him. She hoped that he didn't remember how strange she acted last night after the concert.

"Today I'll make that all up to him," Sandy said as she

applied a fresh coat of lipstick. "He won't even remember yesterday." She smacked her lips and winked at herself in the mirror.

As she exited the restroom, she met Kellie. "Sandy, there is someone here to see you."

Sandy figured it must be Carter so she walked briskly to the front with a flirtatious and confident smile on her face. However, when Sandy made it to the front, she saw a white man with long blond hair and a white T-shirt and blue jeans standing at the register with a dozen pink roses in his hand.

"Are you Miss Sandra A. Moore?" He looked like a hippie from the 60's.

With a confused look, Sandy responded, "That's me."

"These are for you," he said and handed her the roses.

Sandy just stared at the flowers, not realizing that the deliveryman was still standing there waiting for a tip. Soon he figured he wasn't getting anything and just left.

Sandy smelled the roses as Kellie said, "Nice flowers."

"Yeah, really nice. They're my favorite color. But where is Carter?" She hoped that the flowers weren't his way of saying he couldn't make it. She was really looking forward to seeing him again. "We were supposed to meet for lunch."

Kellie shrugged her shoulders and grinned.

Sandy read the outside of the card: If you seek me, you will find me. I'm closer than you think.

The inside read: I'll be right there just before you even blink.

"What in the world does that mean?" Sandy asked out loud.

Kellie smiled and pointed toward the door.

Sandy saw a tall, dark-skinned man wearing a cream custom made suit, a cream shirt, and a tan tie; his shoes matched his tie perfectly.

Carter was standing at the door with one leg crossed over the other and one hand underneath his chin and was staring at Sandy intensely.

Sandy's heart raced. "There is a God," she thought.

She just wanted to run to him and hug him and allow him to take her to lunch, never to return to this place called work again.

As if in slow motion, Carter worked his way down the aisle and finally made it to Sandy's register. Carter leaned his whole body against the counter and said, with minty-fresh breath, "Hey, girl."

Sandy replied with a shy, "Hey."

"Is that all I get from you? Hey?"

"Well, what do you want, a kiss?" Sandy said. *Oh God, I didn't mean to say that.*

"Well, I would like a kiss," Carter said, "but I'll settle for a hug." He opened his arms wide.

After making sure no one had entered the store, Sandy gave Carter a hug. He could smell her perfume that she had just re-applied in the restroom.

"Mmm, you smell good," he purred. "You look good, too."

"Thanks," Sandy said, "You don't look too bad yourself. Oh, and I wonder who these are from?" Sandy picked up the roses and smelled them as she stared at Carter with an accusing grin.

"I wonder," Carter said as if he was trying to figure it out himself.

"You're a poet now?"

"And you know this, man!" Carter said while twisting his head wildly with a grin.

"How did you know my favorite color was pink?" Sandy asked.

"Let's just say, I know my women, or shall I say, my woman."

He's claiming me now. That's a good sign.

"Are you ready to grab a bite?" Carter asked.

I'd like to take a bite out of you. Bad thought, Sandy, bad. He just looked so good that she just wanted to run away to Vegas or somewhere far, far away to be with him forever.

"I can give this man a lot of babies," Sandy thought as

she pictured herself with a house on a hill, a white picket fence, and little kids running around in their backyard screaming, "Daddy! Daddy!"

"God is good," Sandy thought. "Yeah," she told Carter, "let me grab my purse so we can be on our way."

Carter opened Sandy's car door for her as she entered his spotless ride. She recognized the "like brand new" smell which was present the last time she was inside.

As he drove, Sandy was overtaken by sounds of Yolanda Adams' "I Open My Heart" blasting from his CD player. "Yolanda Adams!" Sandy yelped.

"Oh yes. Yolanda," Carter proclaimed.

"You like her?" Sandy asked.

"I do. I do." Carter responded.

"See, men can change their tune," Sandy said to herself as she sang right along with Yolanda.

"So, where are we going?" Sandy asked.

"Don't worry about it; just relax." Carter drove down Woodward Avenue toward downtown. He parked inside a parking garage, and got out of the car to open Sandy's door for her.

Sandy held on to Carter's arm as she walked down the streets of downtown Detroit and nodded to a gentleman who looked homeless.

"Got some change, man?" The older white man with a rugged beard and torn clothes asked Carter. To Sandy's surprise, Carter reached in his pocket and gave the man a five-dollar bill.

"A giver," Sandy thought as she clutched Carter's arm. "What an angel."

Carter finally opened the glass entrance door to one of Detroit's most elite restaurants.

"Praise the Lord," Sandy sang as Carter escorted her inside. The atmosphere was totally divine. Dim blue lights and a live band made the occasion even more special.

A cordial and attractive hostess seated Carter and Sandy in a snug booth in a corner. Sandy peeked out the window beside her and saw an exquisite view of the Detroit River. She was so excited that she almost couldn't contain herself.

"Are you two lovebirds ready to order or would you like a few more minutes?" the blonde waitress asked.

"No, I'm ready," Sandy chimed in anticipation. "I'll have the lobster and jumbo lump crab cakes, please."

"And for you, sir?" the waitress asked Carter.

"I'll have the filet mignon." He gave his and Sandy's menu to the waitress.

"I could get used to this," Sandy said while again looking around the restaurant at all the brown, yellow, and white faces in business suits.

Carter suddenly grabbed Sandy's glass of water and hid it behind his back.

Sandy couldn't see exactly what he was doing with the glass; however, when he brought it back to the table, he held it up to the light in the ceiling and said, "Are you sure you want to drink this; it looks like something is in it."

"What?" Sandy asked. "Is something floating in my water?"

"Well, it's not floating, it's just sort of . . . sitting there."

"What is it?"

"I don't know," Carter said as he handed her the glass.

Sandy looked and saw a distorted gold glimmer on the bottom of the glass.

"Maybe you should get it out with this." Carter handed her a spoon.

Looking suspiciously at Carter, Sandy scooped up the disfigured looking item from the water.

As it finally rose to the top, Sandy pulled it out and discovered that it was a tennis bracelet, just like the one Carter picked out Monday for his mother.

"A tennis bracelet!" Sandy screamed loud enough for three couples in the restaurant to turn their heads. "Is this *the* bracelet?"

"Yes, it is *the* bracelet. I bought one for my mom, and the next day while you were at lunch, I bought one for you."

"Carter, I, I don't know what to say-"

"You don't have to say a word," Carter said. "Just making you smile is enough for me."

"Carter, you're so sweet."

"I figured you'd be impressed."

"But why did you go to all this trouble just for me?" Sandy asked.

She wanted him to be totally honest with her; she didn't want just any blanket response. Sandy had never had any man make her feel as special as Carter did. She felt as if she was in some dream that she never wanted to wake up from.

"Why?" Carter repeated and grabbed Sandy's left hand. With his right hand he gently placed Sandy's bracelet on a nearby napkin.

"Why?" Carter repeated again and kissed her hand.

Carter sang the classic Joe Cocker song in his own crackling tenor voice, "Because you are so beautiful to me…"

A tear trickled from Sandy's right eye.

Carter then stood up, dropped down to one knee, and continued to sing. People seated at surrounding tables looked at the two of them and smiled.

Carter completed the entire chorus to one of Sandy's most favorite songs in the world. He held on to Sandy's hand, not caring who watched or heard him. He didn't sound like any Luther, but he did get an "A" for effort. Sandy laughed lightly as more tears fell from her eyes.

By the end of the chorus, Carter stood up, raised Sandy from her seat, pulled her close and rocked her from side to side in his arms.

"You are sooooo beautiful," Carter sang off key, "to me." And with that he kissed her on the lips, soft and slowly at first, and then fervently and passionately, as if no one else were in the restaurant.

Chapter 19

Stop the Wedding!

"NOOOO!!!!" I SCREAMED AS THE BUZZ OF the alarm clock woke me up Wednesday morning. I had just had the worst dream. I dreamed that Pierre was in a small wedding chapel about to get married and when he lifted the bride-to-be's veil, it was Sandy! In a fit of rage, I stormed to the center of the aisle and screamed, "No! Stop the wedding! Stop the wedding!" and waved my hands like I was some kind of a nutcase.

I woke up sweating after the nightmare. I had to look around at my own surroundings in my bedroom to convince myself that it wasn't real. I wasn't sure if I was so frightened by the dream because one of my close friends was about to marry my ex-man, or because Pierre was getting married, but not to me.

Why am I trippin'?

I wiped the sweat off my forehead and wondered what in the world was wrong with me. I'm supposed to be completely over this man, and for some strange reason, I'm not.

To calm my nerves, I hopped out of bed without a fight this time, took a quick shower, and got dressed in time for morning prayer service. I definitely needed to hear from the Lord and sense that corporate anointing from the prayers of other saints.

Afterwards, I decided I would just make a mad dash to the door and not stop to speak to anybody. People might think I'm rude, but oh well. For all they know, I could just be in a rush to get to work. Besides, I wasn't about to let Pierre keep me from doing what I normally do every morning, which is attend morning prayer service.

At morning prayer, I found my normal corner and sat down and started praying quietly to myself with a rocking motion. I sensed the wonderful Peace of God come upon me as I heard a small, still voice whisper to my spirit, "I will never leave you, nor forsake you."

I was definitely comforted in knowing that through all of what I was going through, God was still here by my side. The Spirit of God didn't say much else to me during my morning fellowship with Him; however, that one reassuring phrase was really all I needed to help me throughout the entire day.

The Lord led me to one of my favorite passages of scripture, found in Isaiah 26:3, which reads, "Thou will keep him in perfect peace, whose mind is stayed on thee: because he trusteth in thee." The scripture encouraged me to keep my mind focused on God, and trust Him with the outcome.

At the end of my time with the Lord in prayer, I rose from my seat and shouted the victory along with the other saints. I shouted in faith knowing that all the prayers I prayed this morning have been answered, and that I have the victory over everything in life. With God, nothing is impossible, and after giving God a nice, long, shout of praise, I truly believed I could do anything! I was ready to conquer the world as I shouted for joy at the top of my lungs.

Once the minister dismissed us, I was determined to head to the front door discreetly and uninterrupted. I didn't see Pierre this morning, which meant I didn't have to worry about dodging him. I turned around and reached for my raincoat and small Bible when my plans were thwarted as I heard someone belt out my name.

"Hey, Michelle!"

Erika Richardson stood right beside me. I had served with her two years ago in the youth department until she felt the call of God on her life to full-time ministry and left for Revelation Bible School in Houston, Texas. Erika is also the beautiful daughter of one of the most popular and well-loved ministers on staff at our church, and I was somewhat surprised to see her now since she was about to graduate from Revelation next month.

"Erika! Praise God, I'm so glad to see you!" I've always loved Erika because she has always been so beautiful and so sweet.

"I thought you were finishing up your second year at Revelation, or did you already graduate?" I asked.

"No, I graduate next month; however, my great-grandmother passed away last Saturday and the home-going service is today, so dad flew me in for it."

"Oh, I'm sorry to hear that," I said. Come to think of it, I do remember Pastor Wilkins announcing to the congregation that Minister Richardson's grandmother made her transition to be with the Lord last week.

"Oh, that's okay," Erika said, still as cheerful as ever. "She lived a long and prosperous life. She was one hundred and two, ya'know."

"Wow, Praise God," I said. Erika still looked good with her long brown hair, skin the color of the sun, and wide, beautiful red smile.

To tell the truth, I used to be so jealous of Erika. Well, maybe not jealous, because I didn't dislike her or anything. Let's just say I always thought she was one of the most beautiful young women I have ever known.

"So what you been up to, girl? You look good," I added.

"Girl, God is so good. I feel good, too. I'm loving Revelation; it is such a wonderful school."

"Well praise God."

"Oh, and also," Erika said with a slight pause, as if this is where the drum roll would come in. "I'm dating!"

"Praise the Lord!" I shouted.

I knew she would be telling me one day real soon that she's dating. By "dating," she meant that she is consistently going out with and learning about the person God may have intended for her to marry. And since she is a minister's daughter, I knew she meant business because they hold an even higher standard when it comes to dating. She was practically engaged.

"Go Jesus! Go Jesus!" I cheered.

"And girl, he is definitely the man of my dreams! You know how the Bible says in Ephesians 3:20 that God would do exceeding abundantly above all you could ask or think? Well, that's this man, and more!"

"Praise God, Erika; tell me about him." I had a little time to hear this.

"He's fine. He's saved and on fire for God, and he is even called to the ministry, like me!" Erika proclaimed like an excited kid in a candy store.

"So, did you meet him at Revelation?" I asked. A sistah's gotta know who's off the market.

"Actually, I didn't, which is the weird thing," Erika said. "You know how a lot of people go to Revelation Bible School, and then the next thing you know they find their mate and run off and get married somewhere?"

"Uh huh," I agreed.

"Well, this man I met right here. It's so weird because it's like he's been right under my nose the whole time, but I hadn't really noticed him before, until he approached me, of course." Erika smirked slyly.

"So he goes to Hype?"

"Yeah, he goes here. And actually, we've being seeing each other for the past nine months now. As a matter of fact, we celebrate our nine month anniversary this Saturday!" Erika beamed. "He's probably going to do something special for me this Saturday; he is always full of surprises."

I just gotta know who this is.

"Every month since we've been seeing each other he would always do something new in order to celebrate. One time he even took me on a picnic, and it was so romantic," Erika reminisced.

"Oh, well, praise God," I said half-heartedly.

Did she just say "picnic?"

"May I ask who it is, if you don't mind?"

I definitely had to clear my conscience of this one; it can't be who I think it is.

"Sure, it's Pierre. Pierre Dupree," Erika proclaimed, "and what a man of God!"

My heart dropped. Hearing Erika say Pierre's name stung my ears. Pierre is the man of God, the Ephesians 3:20 man of God that is the man of her dreams? *Say it ain't so, Lord.*

And what does she mean, they've been talking for the past nine months? Pierre broke it off with me just eight months ago, not nine. You mean to tell me that he dumped me a month after he was already going out with Erika Richardson?

That two-timing— I felt like swearing right in the sanctuary.

"You know Pierre, don't you? He's right over there talking to my dad." Erika pointed to the other side of the sanctuary to Pierre joking with Minister Richardson.

I thought he wasn't here this morning. I guess I was wrong.

Just look at him, sucking up to his future father-in-law.

"I gotta go," I said, grabbing my belongings. "Good seeing you, Erika," I said as I gave her a final hug. "Sorry to cut you off, but I don't want to be late for work."

I stormed out of morning prayer, maintaining a smile and holding back tears until I made it inside my car.

Chapter 20

Tired

LIZ THOUGHT ABOUT LITTLE MATTHEW AND
his dad during her drive home from school Wednesday
afternoon. She hoped everything was alright and that
little Matthew explained everything that happened on the
playground to his father. As she sat pondering at a red light,
a Muslim brotha in a brown suit tapped on her car window
and held up a "Final Call" newspaper and a bag of cherries.
Liz shook herself into reality and mouthed the words, "No
thank you."

Finally, at home in her driveway, she fumbled around in
her tan purse for her house keys. Liz noticed her mother's
red car in the driveway, which meant this was the third day

she had skipped work. Surely her mother was not allowing some man to keep her bedridden.

"Mom!" Liz yelled soon as she got in the house and grabbed the mail on the closet floor where it fell in from the chute. Liz didn't hear the answering machine beeping, which meant there were no messages waiting for her, but she still checked the caller ID for those people who call and just refuse to leave a message.

Liz was hoping that the 'Private' message wouldn't show up, indicating that the estranged wife of Ms. Coleman's ex-fling had been calling again. It wasn't there.

"Maybe he had a long talk with his wife," Liz thought.

As she scrolled through the caller ID, she saw that Dr. Logan had called, Ms. Coleman's personal doctor. Liz wondered why he would call their home, and if everything was all right.

"Mom!" Liz yelled again and didn't hear a response. Just then Liz heard the toilet flush and saw that the bathroom door was closed.

"Mom," Liz said quieter this time and walked over and tapped on the bathroom door, "are you okay in there?" Liz still didn't hear a response from her mother but what she did hear was the sound of someone regurgitating.

Liz slowly opened the bathroom door. Her mother was on her knees wearing a white bathrobe with her hair halfway in rollers. Liz rushed toward her, rubbed her back and asked, "Are you okay?" Ms. Coleman vigorously shook her head up and down.

The telephone rang, and Ms. Coleman motioned Liz to get the phone. The caller ID indicated that it was Dr. Logan's office calling again.

"Hello?" Liz answered.

"This is Dr. Logan calling; may I speak with Ms. Pauletta Coleman?"

"She's, uh, indisposed right now," Liz said, but then realized that Dr. Logan could possibly answer the question of what was wrong with her mother. "Actually, Dr. Logan, she's in the bathroom right now throwing-up. May I ask if you know what's wrong with my mother?"

Liz heard the toilet flush again and then water running; Ms. Coleman came stumbling out of the bathroom looking extremely worn out and disheveled as she reached for the phone.

"Hold on, Dr. Logan, here she is."

Ms. Coleman walked into her bedroom and closed her door shut leaving Liz in the front room wondering what was going on. Liz sat on the couch with her arms folded for ten minutes, and then decided to knock on her mother's bedroom door.

"Mom?" Maybe she was off the phone. Liz walked in the room and saw her mother curled on her queen-sized bed wrapped in black satin sheets, clutching her pillow tight, and staring at the wall.

Liz sat on her mother's bedside. "Mom? Is everything okay?" Liz really didn't know what to expect; her mother hasn't been sick like this for a long time, and Liz wondered why it was so serious that it involved Dr. Logan.

Ms. Coleman sat up slowly and rested her head against the headboard.

Liz grabbed her mother's pillow from Ms. Coleman's lap and placed it behind her mother's head.

"Liz," Ms. Coleman began with dimmed eyes, "I know that I haven't been a saint in front of you, and not even a saint for the sake of myself."

Liz wasn't quite sure what her mother was getting at.

"I've made a lot of mistakes in my life, and I regret a lot of them."

Liz grabbed her mother's hand.

"But the one thing in my whole life I don't regret, is having you as my daughter." Ms. Coleman caressed Liz's cheek and Liz smiled.

"Even though it had to take that no good man to be your father," Ms. Coleman said with a frown, "I thank God for bringing you in this world."

Liz could sympathize with her mother's approach, but she still couldn't figure out what she was trying to say.

"And if I had it to do over, I would, in a heartbeat," her mother said and pinched Liz's cheek. A single tear streamed from Ms. Coleman's eye.

"But right now, I'm tired." she continued. "I'm tired, and this body is old." Ms. Coleman sighed. "And I don't have any more energy in these old bones to raise any more kids."

"What are you talking about, Mom?" Liz asked.

After two minutes of silence, Ms. Coleman admitted, "I'm pregnant."

Liz's heart dropped.

"And I'm not . . . keeping it." Ms. Coleman's voice cracked.

Liz gasped and abruptly let go of her mother's hand. "What do you mean, you're not keeping it? You can't abort it!" Liz screamed.

"Oh yes I can . . . "

"You can't do that!" Liz shouted as tears welled up in her own eyes. She thought about the innocent child in her mother's womb that her own mother was considering murdering.

"Liz, I know how you feel, but I'm tired."

"Tired? Tired? You can't use that as an excuse to refuse to give birth to a child! That child didn't ask to be put in this world! That child is innocent! Before the foundation of the earth, God knew that child, and God called and predestined that child!"

"Liz, you're talking as if the baby is already here and I'm about to kill it or something."

"But you are! Don't you understand? You can't play God by taking the life of another human being. No matter how many weeks old that child is, not even if he's a day old, he is still a human being! It's still a baby!"

"I knew I should've never told you nothing." Ms. Coleman hissed. "I knew I should've just gone down to the clinic and-"

"Mom, no!" Liz screamed. "I can't believe you're talking like this!" Liz wiped her drenched face with her hands. "Why don't you just put the child up for adoption if you don't want it?" Liz pleaded.

"Because then I would have to carry it for nine months and have to go through giving birth for something that ain't mine. When I had you, it was nothing but pain. I went through almost twenty hours of labor for you. So, like I said, I'm tired, and this old body ain't up for it anymore," Ms. Coleman reasoned. "Besides, I don't want to give birth to a child knowing ten years down the line that somebody else raised it. I can't live with that."

"You can't live with that?" Liz shouted. "How selfish can you be? Instead of preserving the child's life, you kill it because you 'can't live with that?' How can you *live* with knowing you killed a baby? You should have thought about that before you laid in bed with some married man!"

Ms. Coleman reached over and slapped the mess out of her only child.

With an extremely painful sting in her right cheek, Liz glared at her mother with utter disgust in her teary eyes.

"Look," Ms. Coleman stated with her finger pointed directly in Liz's face, "you better be glad I didn't abort yo' butt when I had the chance." Shouting and cursing, she ordered Liz out of her room. "As a matter of fact, get outta my HOUSE!"

Liz stormed out of her mother's bedroom, rushed to her own room and stuffed a large brown suitcase with five outfits, underwear, three pairs of shoes, deodorant, toothbrush and toothpaste, and a curling iron.

She wasn't about to allow her mother to throw her out of the house with nothing this time; she wasn't about to waste money on stuff she already had. Besides, Liz needed to keep as much cash on hand as possible because this time she decided not to bug Michelle about spending the night. This time Liz was prepared to stay as many nights as necessary in a nearby motel, until she found an apartment.

On Liz's way out the door, the telephone rang.

Liz figured it was probably that man's wife calling again.

"Let her deal with her own drama," Liz muttered. "I don't think 'wifey' will be too thrilled to know that my mom is about to have a baby by her no-good husband." Liz checked her purse to make sure her flip cell phone was inside and then slammed the door behind her.

Minutes later Liz pulled up into a nearby motel, which was only a few miles from the church. Liz wasn't too fond of this particular motel, especially since the last time she visited she saw holes in the towels in the bathroom, but she figured for $45 a night with her auto insurance card discount, what else could she expect?

In the lobby, an older white couple was playing cards at a small table in the guest area. Near the vending machine stood an older black man wearing sunglasses and a black hat and smoking a cigarette.

"I didn't know smoking was allowed in this place," Liz thought as she watched the man puffing desperately from the cigarette.

Liz made her way to the counter and set her bag down beside her.

"May I help you?" a cheerful older white lady with white hair asked.

"Sure, I would like a room, please."

"Smoking or non?" the lady asked.

"Non, please."

Liz noticed the smoking stranger head her way.

"Lord, please don't let this man say anything to me. I don't feel like it tonight," Liz pleaded within.

Liz gave the woman her credit card and the lady gave her the key and said, "Down the hall and to your right,"

Liz was praising God that she didn't have to go upstairs with her overloaded suitcase on wheels. She reached for her suitcase handle when the stranger asked, "Need some help there, baby?"

"No, I'm fine, thank you," Liz said, really praying for

added strength so that she could make a mad dash to her room.

"You sure?" the man asked, looking like a sugar-daddy-wanna-be with his opened red shirt showing off his hairy chest, and black pinstriped pants.

"I'm fine, but thanks for offering," Liz said with a forced smile.

The persistent man followed her with a pimp stride as she headed toward the corridor. "Ay, ay, wait up! You new in town?"

"No, I'm not." Liz kept walking.

"You stayin' wit' somebody?"

Liz stopped suddenly. "Sir, I would rather not answer that. You have a nice night, okay?" She was almost hesitant to go to her room for fear of his knowing which room was hers.

"Oh, I see, you must be stayin' wit' yo' man, den. Mind if I call you sometime?"

"I'm flattered, but no."

"Oh, I'm sorry, I thought I would just ask to keep in touch, that's all, with a woman like you and all."

Liz was tempted to ask, "What woman like me?" but she decided not to go there tonight. Besides, she could have her ego stroked some other time by someone more worthy of her time rather than this chain smoking "playa playa" who just wouldn't go away.

"Is Charlie giving you a hard time?" the woman from the front desk chimed in. "Go home to your wife Charlie, and stop hittin' on the young, pretty ladies who come in our motel, okay?"

To Liz's surprise, Charlie obeyed and then got on the elevator.

"Don't mind Charlie," the lady said to Liz. "He hits on all the pretty ladies, and he needs to be home with his wife; she puts him out a lot, ya know."

"Figures," Liz thought as she headed down the hallway to her room.

Liz was tired of hearing about all of these trifling, unfaithful men. Men just like her father. It was getting harder and harder to trust any man these days, saved or unsaved.

Liz walked inside a small room with a single bed with a brown cover, a desk with a chair and lamp, and a small television set. She forgot to bring her small radio, which appeases her sometimes since she barely watches T.V. At least she remembered her favorite book, the Bible. After she set her bag near her bed, she pulled it out, got on her knees, and prayed.

"Dear God," Liz began and wiped a tear. "Forgive me for being so insensitive and so uncaring toward my mother. Help me to bridle my tongue and walk in love. It's just that, when I think of the possibility of her killing one of Your . . . " Liz choked up and finished praying, "As I read Your Word tonight, Lord, I pray for strength, for guidance, and for courage. Lord I need Your help. I need You to help me make it through."

Chapter 21

A Gem

SANDY RETURNED TO WORK FROM LUNCH thirty-five minutes late to six older ladies looking agitated and impatient while waiting in line. Kellie was working hard, trying to ring them all up with a smile, and was relieved when she spotted Sandy. Sandy rushed in the back room and was about to head toward the restroom.

"Sandra Moore, you are extremely late," Geneva announced.

"I'm sorry, Geneva; we got caught in traffic on the way back," Sandy lied. She decided right then to ask God for forgiveness later.

"Well, Christina called in sick, so it's just you two working today," Geneva said in reference to the other employee who was scheduled to come in at noon. "The line is backed up, so I need you up front now!"

"Sure, but can I go to the bathroom first?" Sandy asked.

Geneva rolled her eyes and continued marking down already ticketed items.

Sandy thought, "Why can't *her* lazy butt help Kellie up front, as if she's allergic to the cash register," as she stormed to the ladies' room.

Sandy finally made it up front after freshening up her lipstick and eyeliner; Kellie looked over at her with a slight grin. Sandy could tell that Kellie was anxious to know what happened on her date with Carter, but they would have to wait until the line went down.

"I can help you over here," Sandy chimed.

"You ladies need more help in this store," complained an older black woman. "I've been waiting in this line for twenty minutes."

"I'm sorry for the wait, ma'am; one of our employees called in sick and I just returned from lunch." Sandy said.

"Well, y'all gotta do betta than this," the lady said as Sandy rang up the woman's powder blue nightgown and blue fuzzy slippers.

"You have a great day," Sandy said with a smile as she accepted the woman's cash and gave her the receipt. After ten minutes, Kellie and Sandy had taken care of all customers in line.

"Kellie . . . " Sandy sang as she held up her left hand to show off the gleaming diamond tennis bracelet from Carter.

"You got it!" Kellie yelped.

"Yeah I got it, and I heard that your little butt was in on it!"

"Well, he came in the store yesterday, when you were gone to lunch, and he asked for it. He told me he was buying it for you, and guess what else?"

"What?"

"He told me to make sure you got the credit for it."

"What?" Sandy asked.

"He knew this was a partly commissioned job, so he

asked me to make sure you got the credit; I guess that's why he bought it from this store and not somewhere else," Kellie concluded.

"You know what, Kellie, I think you are absolutely right," Sandy proclaimed. "Guess what he did after he gave me the bracelet."

"What?"

"Girl, he got up and sang to me, girl, in front of everybody in the restaurant!"

"Whaaaat?"

"Yes, girl. He did. He didn't sound like no idol, but it was sooooo sweeeet."

"I bet it was."

"Girl, then he picked me up and held me in his arms." Kellie sighed.

"Then he gave me a long, passionate kiss in the restaurant. It was our first one ever, and it lasted forever."

"I wish something like that would happened to me," Kellie said with dreamy eyes.

"Don't worry; it will," Sandy said reassuringly with a smile.

"Sandy, I think you've found yourself a gem," Kellie concluded.

"I think you're right, girl." Sandy stared at her bling-blinging tennis bracelet, fit for a queen.

Chapter 22

Chosen

I TURNED IN MY PROJECT TO SUSAN BEFORE I went to lunch Wednesday; when I returned, I found it in my "in box" with about a thousand red marks on it. She had crossed out paragraphs and written suggestions for improvement in the margins.

I picked up the packet and thumbed through the pages that bled red all over. From the way she marked it all up, no one would ever guess that I had a bachelor's degree in human resources with a minor in journalism.

I let out a huge sigh and dejectedly flopped the packet on top of my desk. I sat down, took a sip of my caramel latte and placed my hand on my forehead.

Now what? Back to the drawing board, I guess.

As I picked it up again and reviewed Susan's notes, I concluded that maybe this wasn't my best work. Maybe I didn't really put my best foot forward. Maybe I had my mind on other things, or other people.

I don't know. I put the project back on the desk a second time and decided I'd start all over first thing in the morning. I'd even come in super early tomorrow and leave late if I had to. I had to give the company what they wanted, and as long as I'm receiving a paycheck from them every other week, they deserved the best that I could give them.

As I sipped my latte, my mind filled with thoughts of Pierre and his sorry self. All this time, I thought he broke up with me because of something I said, or something I did, or because I wasn't willing to let him "make me feel good." But even as he was trying to arouse me, he was already putting the moves on Miss Erika Richardson.

Who does this brotha think he is? He may be fine, but he is no Denzel. Even still, I wouldn't let *no man* cause me to compromise my Christianity and be used as some toy. Pierre ain't put no rings on these fingers. Heck, I'm glad our relationship wasn't that deep anyway. This way, I was able to find out who he really was without having to discover the mistake I made later, after saying, "I do."

I wondered if he tried to make Miss Erika do the nasty with him?

Probably not.

He's probably just marrying her for clout so he can end up on the church staff or something.

I rubbed my temple and then reached for my purse and grabbed two generic aspirin capsules. I washed them down with a swig of bottled water that was on my desk.

The worst part was that a little part of me really was a tad-bit jealous. I guess deep down inside, a part of me wished Pierre had chosen me instead of Erika. To be chosen by any man at this point in my life would be nice.

During my drive home from work, I left the radio off and just pondered about life. Let's see, I'm twenty-five, I have a degree, a nice job, my own place, and some money in the bank. I'm a beautiful woman with a good head on my shoulders, but it looks like I'm just lacking in one little area: I don't have a man.

I want to get married soon, and as a young girl I always figured I would be married with a child and maybe another one on the way by now. My sister, Marqueeta, who is only four years older than I am, is married with two little boys. She seems to be doing okay. I don't hear her complaining too much about her husband, Robert, except that he may forget a birthday or two, or an anniversary, but that's to be expected with some men.

I should at least be seriously dating someone right now, if not practically engaged. I've been believing God for a mate for the past two years, and the first saved man I went out with turned out to be a wolf in sheep's clothing posing as a mature saint.

Pierre really had me fooled. I really thought he truly cared about me with all his smooth talk and kind gestures, but they were just words in the air. And to think, I almost thought for one minute, or even for a second, that I loved him.

At a red light, I looked over and saw a man selling fake designer purses on one corner, and an older white man selling watermelons for six dollars across the street. The light turned green and I proceeded along with my thoughts.

Maybe I did really love him and just didn't know it, which is why I can't stop thinking about him. Or maybe I didn't love him at all but was just intrigued about being in love. Maybe I just wanted to love someone so badly, that just the idea of being in love somehow swept me off my feet. Maybe it wasn't Pierre's extremely good looks, wide smile, and dreamy eyes. Maybe it was the fact that he treated me like a queen, and actually paid attention to me. He made me believe he could love me for the rest of my life. Maybe I should have just listened to God's initial warning and taken it slow. Then my emotions wouldn't be so disturbed, and my mind wouldn't be so confused.

I stopped at another red light and this time pulled the car visor down and examined the chocolate woman in the mirror. I used my finger to wipe the excess lipstick off that wasn't quite perfectly lined with my thick, dark-red lips. I then wiped away the mascara that was smeared on the bottom of my right eye.

My hairstyle was tired. I've had this same wrap style for going on two years now. I've never been one to switch hairstyles, but maybe it's time for a change.

As I pondered about what I would do next with my hair, a black jeep behind me honked its horn and gave me a dirty look to tell me that the light turned green. Startled, I popped the mirror back up and continued to drive as the jeep whisked around me.

Who cares about Pierre, anyway?

I put on my gold-tinted sunglasses that were resting in the box in between the two front seats. Every time I wore them, I felt like a movie star.

Pierre isn't the only fine brotha out there; I can have my pick. There are many *fine* brothas out here, and at my church. I just hadn't put my *moves* on 'em yet.

Who was I kidding?

I knew that I wasn't about to be putting any *moves* on any man, especially not a man of God. If I did, he would think I was one of three types of women: loose, easy, or desperate, and no man of valor wants that.

The man would have to be the one initiating any romance with me. Besides, that's the way it was for me even before I was saved.

As a matter of fact, before I was saved, I never had to approach any man that I was interested in. If I was attracted to a man, all I had to do was catch a brotha's eye, bat my dark brown eyes, flash an inviting smile, and the brotha would be making his way over to me like I was his momma calling him home for dinner. I never had any trouble getting a man when I was in the world. I wondered why it was so hard to get a brotha to holla at me in the church?

Then again, before I was saved, a lot of the men I went out with, after about two dates, or sometimes even after just one, would take me back to their place or come back to mine and we would end up all over each other on the couch. I always made it a point not to have sex with any of them; I was determined to only sleep with the one that I really loved. But a lot of them liked to test me to see how far I was willing to go.

One brotha I made out with, after I told him I wouldn't have sex with him, had to raise up from the couch to take a long sip of his ice-cold water. I actually thought it was kinda funny as he tried to rationalize why it was "okay" for two casual friends to have sex.

I used to take a lot of risks with strange men, before I was saved. But thank God he saved me when he did, four years ago at Hype, because I used to make stupid choices with the men I went out with.

Because I made mistakes, I can empathize with Sandy. I know where she's coming from, and I've been where she's been. I want to make sure that where she goes is along the road of living a victorious, single life, not giving in to the pressures of this world.

At home at last, I threw my purse on the couch only to hear the answering machine beeping.

Who left me a message?

"Hi baby, it's your mother!" Mom yelled, sounding as chipper as ever. I should have known.

"And your dad!" chimed in Dad.

"We just wanted to call to see how you were doing, to make sure everything was okay!" Mom sang.

Yeah right. If they really wanted to call and see how I was doing, they would have just called me on my cell and talked to me right away. Knowing the two of them, they still might not know the number by heart yet, even though I had given it to them a thousand times.

"We're doing great down here in Florida! Your father goes to meetings all day and I go shopping!" Mom squealed. Mom loves shopping more than I do.

"At my expense!" Dad interjected.

"Honey . . . " Mom interrupted.

"Well, anyway, if you need anything, you know where to reach us, or you can always reach me directly on my cell," Dad continued. "Love you, sweetheart."

My parents love to travel so much that sometimes I wonder why they don't just give their house up and buy a condo in Florida.

I deleted the message and then grabbed the phone to check caller ID. As I scrolled through the phone numbers, I was surprised to see a phone call about twenty minutes ago from Pierre.

What did he want?

I must have just missed his call due to the annoying and unusual traffic on my way home from work. Thank goodness I never gave him my new cell number. Why is he calling me anyway if he's about to make his big announcement to Erika? I tell you, I will never understand that man.

I took the cordless phone into the kitchen and starting dialing Liz's house. After four rings, no one answered, so I hung up before the answering machine picked up.

That's weird. I thought Liz would be home by now. She didn't say she was going anywhere.

I grabbed the whole chicken that had thawed out on the black counter next to the sink, rinsed it, cut it up, floured and seasoned it, and left it sitting in a plate as I wiped off my floury white hands with a paper towel and again reached for the cordless phone.

Before I could dial Liz's cell number, my home phone rang again. Afraid that it might be Pierre calling again, I checked the caller ID. It was Sandy.

The phone rang a third time. I wondered if I should answer it.

I just didn't feel like being stuck on the phone all night ministering to my young sister in the Lord who likes to dramatize every little detail of her life. Right about now, I felt like I need to be ministered to, not the one ministering. I then remembered that God placed Sandy in my life so I could help her mature in the things of God. I picked up the phone after the fourth ring.

"Hello," I answered sheepishly.

"Mickey!" sang Sandy in her normal, cheerful tone.

"Hey, girl, what's up?" I put vegetable oil in the frying pan and cut the fire on low.

"Girl, I got so much to tell you!"

"What is it?" I responded, trying to sound interested. *What drama is it this time?*

"I went out to lunch with Carter today, and he gave me a 2-karat diamond tennis bracelet!"

"What?" I said in shock as I plopped the pieces of chicken into the pan, praying that none of the grease would pop on me.

"He gave me the same one he bought for his momma!"

"His momma?" I exclaimed. *What is this child talking about now?*

"Yeah," Sandy went on, as excited as ever. "He came into the store and bought the same tennis bracelet he bought for his mom while I was at lunch yesterday! Can you believe that?"

During the short time that I have been reunited with my outspoken friend and fellow classmate from Kingsley High School, I have learned that anything is possible with Miss

Sandra A. Moore.

"I'm not surprised," I stated. Then I began my miniature sermon. "Sandy, how long have you known this man?"

"Well, we met on Monday, but he's really nice."

"Monday? You mean you've only known this man for three days, and he bought you a tennis bracelet?"

"Yeah, God is good, ain't He?" Sandy sang.

Now I knew that it was my turn to tell Sandy something she might not necessarily want to hear. Here she was trying to bring God in the midst off all this foolishness. She barely even knew the man!

"Yes, Sandy, God *is* good," I told her. "However, just because someone gives you something doesn't mean you always have to take it," I attempted to explain in a loving yet simple way.

"What do you mean?" Sandy asked, confused. "The Bible says anything that is good comes from above, right?" Sandy said. I wondered if she was deliberately misinterpreting that passage of scripture.

"Yes, the scripture does say that, Sandy . . ."

"So this diamond tennis bracelet is a good thing, and I receive it in Jesus' Name, Hallelujah!"

I couldn't believe this girl's naivety. I hoped what I was about to say wouldn't break her little heart, but it needed to be said. I'd rather she be mad at me now then be mad at herself in the long run.

"Sandy," I began with a deep breath, "just because a man gives you an extremely expensive gift after only knowing you for a short time does not necessarily mean he is sent from God."

"What do you mean?" Sandy asked.

I could hear the disappointment in her voice. I paused for a moment and silently asked God for the right thing to say.

"Let me put it to you like this. You're a woman of God, right?"

"Right."

"And right now you're believing God for a husband, right?"

"Right."

"Well, God knows your desires, and He will fulfill those desires in due time; however, Satan knows your desires as well and can sometimes send you a counterfeit that may look good, smell good, say all the right things and may even buy you expensive gifts, but he may not be the right person for you."

There was complete silence on the other end.

"So what are you saying, Michelle?" Sandy finally asked. "You're saying Carter was sent to me by Satan?"

"All I'm saying is, proceed with caution. Just because a man buys you a really expensive gift doesn't mean that God necessarily did it; it could mean that the man may have other plans for you, or that he may want to take advantage of you later."

"Advantage?" Sandy screamed. "Advantage? Just because I pray to God for a man, meet somebody that is saved, got much bank, takes me out, and loves the very thought of being with me-how in the world does that mean he may want to take advantage of me?"

"Again, all I'm saying is, be careful," I stated. "Don't get too excited or all worked up about nothing."

"You just mad 'cuz you ain't got a man," Sandy remarked.

That did it.

Here I am, trying to help the girl out and look out for her best interest, and she insults me.

Just then Sandy's other line beeped.

"Hold on, okay," Sandy said in her cheerful tone again, like she didn't just offend me. It took the grace of God to keep me from just hanging up on her little behind.

I turned over my frying chicken and waited for what seemed like forever for Sandy to click back over. I wished that she would open her eyes and see that she's no "Cinderella" and that this man is not her fairytale prince. The girl not even sure about the name of the church he goes to. I wondered if he attended church at all, or was that just another line he was giving Sandy, trying to act like he was all "holy." I tapped the chicken with a fork, and Sandy finally clicked back over.

"Michelle, I'ma call you back, okay? It's Carter."

Figures.

"Okay, Sandy," I said, "Maybe we can talk more tomorrow night, after Thursday night service."

"Okay," Sandy rushed.

"You are coming to service tomorrow, aren't you?"

"Yeah, yeah. I'll be there," Sandy snapped and hung up the phone.

I actually thought that I handled the conversation rather well, considering that if she would have come at me the way she did six months ago, I probably would have hung up in her face and written her off of my friend list.

I set my fried chicken on a plate with a napkin, patting another napkin on top of it to squeeze out the excess grease, picked up the phone, and dialed Liz's cell phone number.

The phone rang three times before Liz finally answered.

"Hello."

"Hey, girl, what's up? I called your house and you weren't home. Where are you?"

"Oh, I'm at a room right now."

"A room? What kinda room?"

"Oh, a nice little room."

Liz can be so secretive at times; doesn't she know by now that her best friend can tell when she's hiding something?

"A nice little room? Girl, where are you at?" I asked impatiently.

"I'm at a motel." Liz finally gave in.

"A motel? What are you doing at a motel?"

"Oh, Ms. Coleman and I had another intense fellowship," Liz stated, using her phrase for a heated argument.

"What about this time?" I couldn't believe Ms. Coleman's audacity lately to continue to throw Liz out of the house.

"Do you remember that guy that she was sleeping with that was married?"

"Yeah."

"Well, he got her pregnant,"

"No!"

"Yup."

"You've got to be kidding me?"

"I wish I was, but the thing that really upset me is that she's considering killing the baby."

"An abortion?"

"Mm hmm," Liz stated.

"Not your mom! She can't have an abortion; that's murder!"

"Apparently she doesn't see it that way."

"I'm surprised your mom can still get pregnant. She's what, forty-five?"

"Mm hmm."

"How can she talk about gettin' an abortion?"

"She says she just doesn't want to go through with it," Liz said in a shaky tone.

"Liz, why don't you come over here. You don't have to be in any janky little motel. Come to my place so we can talk . . . and have cookies." I had hoped that would lure her over to my place.

"That's sweet of you Michelle, but I think this time I want to stay here. I really have to pray out some things and get some rest; I really have to figure this one out on my own."

"But Liz, you're not alone, and this is a *big* thing. I'm here for you Liz, and we can pray this out together," I pleaded.

"Thanks for your thoughtfulness, Michelle, but I really want to stay here and pray," Liz said quietly. "Now is the perfect time for me to seek the face of God alone. But thanks for the offer."

"Okay, since you insist."

"Bye, Michelle."

"Bye."

I hung up the phone and placed it back on the counter. An abortion?

I spread my arms wide and clutched the end of the counter and just stared into the endless hole in the kitchen sink. How in the world could Ms. Coleman even consider aborting a baby? Why doesn't she consider adoption? I've heard of people who were born as a result of rape, or so-called "unwanted children" who were born and turned out to be perfectly healthy and happy adults.

I knew that this was just tearing Liz apart. Liz loved children with her whole heart and soul, and could never imagine anyone killing an innocent child, let alone her own mother doing it. Liz would even be willing to birth the baby herself, if she could.

I remembered that Liz said her mother would have aborted her. Ms. Coleman was eighteen at the time, and Liz's father, Dominic, who was twenty-four, was very abusive and controlling. He had even burned Ms. Coleman on her arm while she was pregnant with Liz; the huge scar was still visible today.

Ms. Coleman did not want to give birth to Liz because she didn't want to be reminded of Dominic. Liz's grandmother insisted that her daughter and Dominic get married for the sake of the child. He did not show up for the wedding, which was two weeks before Liz was born, and he hasn't been seen since.

On the delivery table, Liz's grandmother prophesied that the baby being birthed out of Ms. Coleman's womb was going to be healthy and do great things for God. It was truly by the grace of God that Ms. Coleman went ahead and gave birth to Liz. Now Liz is faithfully serving God and is called to be an evangelist.

I went in the living room to pray fervently for my best friend:

"Satan, I bind you, in Jesus' Name, that you will not have any place in my friend's life! I pray right now, Lord, that You would open Ms. Coleman's eyes of understanding, that she may see that abortion is wrong and that she will give birth to that baby, that baby whom You have already called, chosen, and appointed to fulfill Your purpose.

I pray that Liz and her mother's relationship is restored, and that Liz will be allowed to come back home so that she can continue to be a Light to her mother, and continue to minister Jesus to her mother by her own actions, words, and deeds. Father, I give you all the Praise, Honor, and Glory and I count all these things done, in Jesus' Name. Amen. Hallelujah!"

I shouted and lifted my hands in order to give thanks and praise to God. Surely, it *shall* come to pass. It had to.

Chapter 23

Decisions

"HOW ARE YOU TONIGHT?" ASKED A FAMILIAR voice on the other end as Sandy lay on her canopy bed drowned in pink satin covers.

Sandy loved to hear Carter talk in his sexy tone of voice. "I'm doing just fine," Sandy responded.

"I didn't ask you how you looked, I asked you how you're doing," Carter said with a slight laugh, remembering when Sandy used the same line on him this morning.

"Oh, you're trying to be funny now?" Sandy said. "Where are you?"

"I'm at home, lying in my bed, thinking about you."

"Oh," Sandy said.

"And where are you?" Carter asked.

"Well, I'm at home, lying in my bed, thinking about you, too." Sandy laughed. She loved messing with Carter.

"Alrighty, then," Carter answered with a chuckle. Suddenly he got serious and almost sinister. "What are you wearing?"

"My pink pajamas that say "princess" on the front."

"Princess?"

"Yeah, princess, is there something wrong with that?" Sandy said with a slight grin.

"No. But why settle for a princess, when you can be the queen?"

Sandy thought about his last comment. "You're right. I should be a queen. But in order to be a queen, I have to have a king, right?"

"Can I be your king?" Carter asked in a voice so sexy that it sent chills down her spine.

"I don't know; can you?"

"I think I can."

"Oh."

"As a matter of fact, I *know* I can."

"And what would you do, as king?"

"I would rule and reign over everything,"

"Oh, really?"

"Including you."

"Oh really," Sandy said with a laugh. "You think so?"

"I know so," Carter said with confidence on the brink of arrogance.

"Oh, okay," Sandy said.

"How is your hair?"

"The same as when you saw it this afternoon," Sandy lied. She didn't want to tell him that it was really brushed around her head and wrapped in a pink satin scarf; she didn't want to ruin his visual image. "And what are *you* wearing?"

"My black satin shorts," Carter said.

"And . . . "

"My black silk tie from work"

"And . . . "

"And . . . that's it."

"Oh." Sandy said.

Why he wore the tie to bed, Sandy wasn't quite sure; however, it sounded good to her.

"Did you have a hard day at work?" Sandy asked, trying to change the direction of the conversation. Sandy got up and turned on the light in her bedroom and lay back in bed.

"Yeah, I had a hard day at work today. I had to stay extra late tonight working on a case."

"Oh, did you win?" Sandy asked as she caressed her white teddy bear, the one Carter gave her.

"No, I wasn't in court today. I just had a hearing and did some research." Carter explained. Then he changed the subject. "I wish you were here next to me," Carter said in a low tone.

"Carter," Sandy said to cut him off. She felt a little uneasy as her own body temperature began to rise. "Do you want to come with me to church Sunday?"

Carter's voice rose two decibels as he proclaimed, "Church? Oh yeah, uh, what church you go to again?"

"Hype for Jesus Church. It's a new church with a lot of young people; it's really good. I mean, the Word is good."

"Oh, okay, we can do that," Carter said.

To Sandy it sounded as if he propped up on his bed in an upright position at the mention of the word "church."

"But first," Carter began, "I want to ask you to come to my place tomorrow night."

Sandy thought that maybe Michelle's assumption about Carter was right; he was starting to move a little too fast.

"I'm having a surprise birthday party for my best friend, Malcolm, tomorrow at my place, and I want you to be with me."

Sandy sighed with relief. *He wants to introduce me to his friends? Praise the Lord!* "What time tomorrow?" Sandy asked.

"I can pick you up around eight-thirty, because I think

my boy plans on having Malcolm at my crib around nine-thirty for the surprise."

"Oh, okay . . . oh, wait, I have church tomorrow." Sandy remembered.

"Oh," Carter stated "I understand then."

"Maybe I can come afterward?"

"What time is it over?"

"Like around nine, but sometimes we go over, though."

"Oh."

There was brief silence on the phone.

"I really wanted to have you with me when I walked in the door, but I know you gotta do the church thing, so that's cool; I can respect that." Sandy thought it was so cute that he really wanted her to be there with him.

"Wait, Carter, that's okay. I'll just miss church tomorrow. That's alright."

"Are you sure?"

"I'm positive, sweetheart, besides, we'll just go to church together on Sunday, right?"

"Right." Carter said.

Chapter 24

Men

LIZ WOKE UP THURSDAY MORNING ON A hard bed with a brown cover, having forgotten that she was in a dingy motel room and not in the comfort of her own bed at home. She flicked on the lamp beside her bed and shut off the alarm, which buzzed loudly to let her know it was 6:30 a.m.

Liz didn't feel like singing this Thursday morning. Just getting up was quite a challenge. After the argument she had with her mother last night, Liz wasn't ready to deal with another day at a school where kids get into fights for no apparent reason, like little Matthew did yesterday.

"Lord, give me strength for another day," Liz groaned as she dragged herself out of bed and headed for the shower.

After she got dressed in a floral romper dress and white closed-toe sandals, Liz knelt to pray.

"Dear Lord, I give this day to You. There is nothing that You can't handle, and without You, I can do nothing. Lord, I need You to open my mother's eyes of understanding, that she may know that she is making a big mistake in considering killing Your child, the one You predestined before he even ended up in my mother's womb. I need You to fix my situation on the job, that there will be no more unnecessary drama or strife. I need You to give me strength to make it through the day."

Liz sat silently with her face in her hands. She wanted to cry, but she refused to allow the devil to steal her joy. She made a decision to go on. She decided not to call in at work today, even though she wanted to. She chose to go to work and be strong for her students. The Lord then spoke to her and said, "I hear your prayer and I will help you. I will be your Comforter, and I will be your Shield. I will be all that you need and more; you'll see. Just follow Me."

Liz rested on the promise of God, drove to work, and arrived in her classroom with a hopeful expectation.

"Okay, God, here goes," Liz muttered as the students began to trickle in one by one. "Stay with me now."

At 8:10 a.m. Liz took attendance and noticed that little Matthew hadn't made it in yet.

"Renita Jones," Liz yelled.

"Here!"

"Joseph Little,"

"Here!"

"Matthew Long,"

"Here," screeched a tiny voice as Matthew came in almost tardy with a backpack full of books on his tiny back.

"Good to see you here today, Matthew," Liz said with a smile as she marked him present in her attendance book. Matthew's peers looked at him as if they were surprised to see that he made it back to school. They were shocked because they thought he would've been suspended for fighting.

Matthew grabbed his normal seat in the back of the room.

"I almost marked you tardy, but you made it just in time," Liz stated.

"Sorry, Miss Coleman, my dad and I were struck in traffic."

"You mean 'stuck' in traffic, Matthew?" Liz corrected him. A few students snickered. After noticing Matthew's obvious embarrassment, Liz replied with a smile, "Okay, then, I'll forgive you this time."

When the recess bell rang at 11:30 a.m., Liz proceeded with her normal routine of lining her students up in a straight line. Matthew dragged his feet as he made it to the end of the line. Liz could tell that he wasn't too thrilled about recess. Matthew held his head low as he got in line behind bubbly little Arnita.

Because Liz was assigned as the lunch monitor for the entire week, she made a special point to really observe what was going on around her to avoid another occurrence like yesterday. She took her normal position on the bench on the playground, but instead of pulling out a good book to read while she ate her lunch, she watched the students intensely as they played.

Several children played on the swings, monkey bars, and slides. Liz scanned the playground in search of Matthew. She didn't see him, so she stood up and placed her hand over her eyes to look for him in the crowd of several students who had finished eating and were playing nearby. She couldn't find him anywhere.

"Maybe he's still eating," Liz thought.

"Miss Coleman." A light voice startled her.

"Mind if I eat with you?" Matthew asked. Liz looked down at him and smiled. Dressed in faded blue jeans and a neatly pressed blue and white polo shirt, which looked like something his father would wear, Matthew really touched her heart.

"Sure, Matthew, you can have lunch with me," Liz assured him. "You didn't want to eat inside?"

"No." Matthew pulled out a peanut butter and jelly sandwich from his green lunch pail.

Liz reached for her smoked turkey and honey mustard sandwich on rye in her lunch bag. She liked the idea of having company for lunch, and it not being another teacher. Besides, now was the perfect opportunity to make sure all was well with little Matthew Long.

"How is your sandwich?" Liz began the small talk.

Matthew nodded vigorously and said, with a mouth full of food, "Good."

"Did you make it yourself, or did someone make it for you?"

"My dad made it."

Liz wanted to remind him not to talk with his mouth full, but she decided not to.

Matthew quickly finished his sandwich and started eating chocolate chip cookies from a small baggie.

"So how are you today, Matthew?"

"Fine," Matthew said quietly. He looked down and twirled his little legs under the bench.

Liz didn't mean to spark up bad memories of yesterday; she just wanted to make sure he was okay. "Feel better?"

Matthew nodded while taking a bite of his cookie.

"I'm glad you were able to come back to school today. I'm glad to have you back."

No response.

Liz really wanted to ask why didn't he get suspended, but she didn't want to pry. He was beat up so badly, the principal probably determined somehow that Matthew wasn't the cause of it. Liz noticed that the older boy, the fourth grader who probably started the fight, wasn't in school today.

"I'm not." Matthew said.

"Not what?"

"Glad to be back."

"Why not?"

"Because I didn't want to come to school today."

"Oh, you didn't?" Liz probed, "Why not?"

"Because, I just didn't," Matthew said, sounding a bit agitated. "Plus, I didn't want to see that water head boy again that tried to beat me up yesterday!" Matthew yelled as if the boy were standing right behind him and Matthew wanted him to hear.

"It's not nice to call people names, Matthew," Liz reminded him.

"He is a water head," Matthew shouted defensively, "and he need to go to hell!"

"Matthew! That's not nice and I want you to apologize right now for saying that about your schoolmate!" Liz was shocked to hear such angry words come from such a little person. She wondered if he picked up that kind of language from his father.

"I won't!" Matthew proclaimed and got up from the bench with his arms folded. "Bad people go to hell and he's a bad person!"

"Matthew, I won't sit here listening to you talk like this," Liz reasoned. "Why are you so angry with this little boy?"

"Because," Matthew said as his bright eyes turned glassy.

"Because why, Matthew?"

"Because he talked about my momma!" Matthew shouted with tears welling up in his eyes.

Liz figured this was just another case of "don't talk about my momma" syndrome. "I'm sorry that Tyrone talked about your mother, Matthew," Liz said in a sweetened tone. "I'm sure he didn't mean it, and he doesn't know your mother like you do."

"My momma dead!" Matthew shouted and burst out in tears.

Liz grabbed little Matthew and held him in her arms. *That explains everything! He misses his mommy!*

Matthew eventually calmed down and cried quietly with his face buried on Liz's shoulder.

Just then a royal blue truck pulled up on the sidewalk in front of the playground fence. A tall, light-skinned figure with a cream three-quarter length jacket and matching cap marched toward the gate, facing Liz and Matthew.

"Dad!" Matthew shouted and ran toward the fence where his father stood on the opposite side, forgetting he had been crying hysterically just minutes before. Matthew's tears dried in the wind as he was ecstatic to see his father on his day off from working on the assembly line at the plant.

"Dad!" Matthew repeated and shook the fence.

"What's up, Champ?" Mr. Long asked his son while rubbing his curly hair through the fence.

Liz slowly walked toward them. She wanted to assure Mr. Long that Matthew was doing a lot better, at least better than yesterday. But she was only fooling herself by pretending that the only reason she moseyed her shapely hips over to the fence was for teacher-student purposes only. *Remember Liz, calm and professional.*

As if his own son seemingly disappeared, Mr. Long suddenly focused his attention on the woman in front of him. A big smile came across his face, one that little Matthew noticed as he turned around to see what his father was looking at.

"Hello, Mr. Long," Liz said, making eye contact.

Liz was glad she decided to wear her zillions down and not in a messy ponytail like she started to do this morning. She even had on a berry-colored lipstick, which she picked up from the dollar store.

She noticed he was again wearing a black polo shirt underneath his cream jacket with black pants. She caught a whiff of his cologne. *So he's widowed, and not divorced. Then again, maybe they were never married in the first place. Most men are afraid of commitment.*

"Hello, Miss Coleman-I mean Liz," said Matthew Sr. "Is he causing any problems out here today?" Matthew Jr. looked up at Liz with a desperate look on his face.

"No, no problems today," Liz said while returning little

Matthew's glance with a smile. "He's doing a lot better today."

Matt Sr. continued to stare at Liz, so much so that little Matthew proclaimed, "Dad . . . Dad . . . DAD!"

"Yeah, son," Matt Sr. finally responded, not taking his eyes off Liz.

Liz felt herself starting to blush. *Remember, he has a child, and he could have issues. Remember, men are not perfect, and most men are dogs.* "Can I go with you, Dad? I want to go home," Matthew whined while shaking the fence as if he was an animal trapped in a cage.

"Are you sure, son?" Matt Sr. finally diverted his attention from Liz and looked down at his own spitting image.

"Yeah, I'm sure. I want to go home with you," Matthew pleaded.

"Okay son, c'mon out and we can go home." Little Matthew's eyes brightened and he leaped for joy. "It's my off day, so why not? I mean, if it's all right with Miss Coleman." Matt Sr. sneaked another glance at Liz.

Liz noticed the cute way his eyebrow arched as he shot another look at her. *Help me, Lord, because this man is fine.*

"It's all right with me," Liz said as little Matthew ran to the playground exit and rushed toward his dad's truck. Matthew didn't even wave good-bye to any of his classmates.

"I'll be there in a minute, son!"

Matt Sr. rested his right hand high on the fence and shifted his body toward Liz. "So, how's he doing?" he asked in all seriousness.

"He's doing well, real well." Liz stated. "I'm sorry to hear about what happened to his mother."

"Oh yeah, his mother, my wife," Matt clarified. "She passed away about a year ago . . . breast cancer."

"I'm sorry to hear that," Liz said sincerely.

"That's okay; she's in a better place now . . . no pain." Mr. Long looked up at the sky.

"You're right; no more suffering."

"Yeah. The Lord's been taking care of us in the midst of

everything," Matthew said. He squinted at Liz as the sun beat down on his moist face.

"He sure has." Liz returned the glance. She didn't mean to flirt. She hoped that their glances weren't generating any unwanted chemistry. She thought about rushing back inside, because she definitely didn't want to end up being the one that this student's father confided in after grieving over his deceased wife.

"Miss Coleman?"

"Yes." *Don't do it. Don't ask me out!*

"I know this may sound kinda forward, but, I believe sometimes the Lord brings people together in the weirdest ways." He chuckled. "My son, amazingly, seems to be taking a liking to you, and . . . "

No, he's not trying to ask me out for his own selfish reasons and then try to put the Lord and his son in the middle of it.

"Are you trying to ask me out, Mr. Long?" Liz stopped him in his tracks. She was starting to admire and respect this man, and now he is suddenly asking her out? His wife was barely a year in the grave! His prior sincere and heartfelt comments now only seemed like an introduction to his ultimate mac move!

"Well, I guess . . . "

"What do you mean, you guess? Are you trying to ask me out or what?" demanded Liz with a sudden ghetto accent. Maybe if she gave him a glimpse of her ghetto side his attraction for her would disappear.

"Well, it's just that I hadn't asked a lady out on a date for a long time. Before Marilyn passed last year, she and I had been married seven years. We were high school sweethearts before then. I almost forgot how to even ask a woman out."

Liz wondered if he was really being sincere. For someone who had been with someone since high school, he sure did get over the grieving process pretty fast. However, the Bible does indicate that after a mate dies, one is free to marry again. But, my goodness, his wife was probably rolling over in her grave!

"I'm flattered, Mr. Long," Liz exaggerated.

"But . . . "

"But I'm going to have to pass on that offer."

"Oh. I'm sorry," Matthew said.

"Don't be."

"No, I really am sorry. You must think I'm some kind of jerk or something."

"No, Mr. Long, I really am flattered. I mean, you're a really nice man. It's just that, your asking me out seems a bit . . . inappropriate."

"I see." Matthew removed his hand from the fence and stood in front of her. "Just thought I'd give it a shot. Life is short, and I never want to live another day knowing that I may have missed out on an opportunity of a lifetime, simply because I was afraid to ask."

Liz looked at him for a moment and finally said, "Good-bye. Mr. Long." She headed toward the playground where students were lining up to go back inside. "Men," she thought.

Chapter 25

Move On

THURSDAY MORNING, I DECIDED TO SKIP
morning prayer service and go to work early so I could
redo my orientation project. I actually had two meetings
scheduled for today, which means my time to work on it
will be limited. But I only have today and tomorrow to
complete it, and I'm about ready to knock this thing out,
even if I have to stay late tonight. My whole reputation as a
dependable employee was at stake. Besides, the project gave
me a good excuse to avoid running into Pierre or Erika.

I took a sip of my caramel latte, and began typing away
on my computer. I was determined to complete the whole
thing by tomorrow. I got so involved in typing that I threw
off my black pumps and kept them hidden underneath my

desk. My feet were starting to hurt, and I didn't want any distractions.

By 9:53 a.m. I had revised the first six pages of my eleven-page project. I put my shoes back on to get ready for the monthly town hall meeting.

I never looked forward to these boring meetings, especially since half of them involved the vice president of the company spouting unrealistic goals that Lazek plans to meet within the next thirty days. I took my normal seat in the back. During the whole thirty-minute meeting, I spent half the time thinking about my own project sitting on my desk. I couldn't wait to get back to it once this was over.

At the close of the town hall meeting, the Vice President of Human Resources, Bob Nash, somehow found his way in front of me as I attempted to scoot my way to the exit door and head back to my desk. Susan, my boss, stopped Mr. Nash since she thought this was the perfect opportunity for him to meet Lazek's brightest human resources rep, yours truly.

"Mr. Nash," Susan said in her most corporate tone, "I want you to meet Michelle Williamson, our newest human resources representative."

Mr. Nash looked at me with beady eyes and a round bald head. He reached out his wrinkled white hand and said, "Oh Hi, Michelle; nice to meet you."

I shook Mr. Nash's hand firmly, but not too vigorously, and stated, "Hello, Mr. Nash; it is my pleasure to meet you," and gave him a nice smile.

"Please, call me Bob," he stated.

"Okay, Bob," I said as he didn't seem to want to let go of my hand.

I wasn't sure if he was a top executive or a pastor at a church; he looked at me with warm eyes and held on to my hand like I needed consoling. I just wanted to snatch it back and march to my desk to finish what I had started. Introductions like this are so unexpected. I was glad I had decided to wear my black and white pinstriped pantsuit; it proved to be appropriate and professional.

"Yes, Michelle has been with our company for a little over a year now, and she is doing a wonderful job," Susan chimed on my behalf. I had a feeling that my boss's compliments were her way of telling me, "You better do good on that project or you will make me and the company look bad and I will never forgive you." She continued to show off her big, bright smile while looking over at me. I knew exactly what Miss Susan was up to.

"Wonderful! Well we're definitely glad to have you here at Lazek!" Bob beamed.

"I'm glad to be here, sir," I said.

"Keep up the good work!" Bob planted a hefty pat on my back that lunged me forward almost an inch. Then he left the room, thank goodness.

"Yeah, keep it up," whispered Susan as she followed Bob. I was relieved to return to my desk. If Susan wanted to make sure I was still on top of things with the project, all she had to do was just ask. But that's just the way it is sometimes in corporate America. Nothing is just stated; everything is implied.

As I deleted and retyped the seventh page of my project, the telephone rang.

I was almost tempted not to answer it, but corporate policy states that the phone has to be answered by the third ring. Besides, it could be a fellow employee with a human resources question.

"This is Michelle Williamson. How may I help you?"

"Hey, gorgeous," said a familiar voice.

Stalker.

"May I ask whom I'm speaking with?" I tried to maintain my professional tone as I grabbed a pencil and felt like breaking it in half.

Why is he harassing me like this?

"This is Pierre, speaking with the lovely Michelle Williamson."

"How may I help you, sir?" I asked through clenched teeth.

I needed to get back to work on my project; I had no time today for Pierre's foolish games.

"Well, you can help me by telling me how you are doing this afternoon, or shall I say this morning."

At that point I was really ready to give Pierre a piece of my educated mind.

"Look, Pierre, I don't have time for playing games with you," I said in a low tone so that neighbors in nearby cubicles wouldn't hear. "I am extremely busy today, and I have to get back to work!"

"Whoa horsey! Watch yo' self."

"And why are you calling me anyway?"

"What, I can't call you anymore?" Pierre whimpered.

"No, and especially not at work; I need to go!"

"It sounds like I caught you at a bad time . . . "

"You did. Anyway, you need to be calling Erika. She's the one you're about to propose to in two days,"

"Who told you . . . "

"Bye, Pierre." I slammed the phone down on the receiver. At that point I didn't care who heard. I wouldn't be surprised if Susan waltzed over here to give me a lecture about how not to handle company property.

I was just so upset that Pierre would even *think* to have the audacity to call me again at work. Why doesn't he just get over it and leave me alone? What kind of games is he playing, anyway? Maybe since he knows that I know he's dating Erika now, he'll leave me well enough alone. He knows that if I tell her what happened between us, it's over for him.

I wonder what Erika would think about her knight in shining armor now if she knew he was harassing me almost every day?

She probably wouldn't believe me. I would probably have to invite her to my apartment and show her my caller ID before she would believe me. Pierre was really starting to get on my nerves. I wondered what I had ever seen in him in the first place.

The sad part about all of this was that I still wasn't sure about how I felt about him, deep down inside. However;

in spite of how I feel, the truth of the matter is he's taken, he's not mine, and I just need to move on. I shook my head fiercely, took a sip of my caramel latte, and tried, once again, to focus on the work on my desk.

Chapter 26

Calm Down

SANDY WAS SO EXCITED ABOUT HER DATE with Carter at the surprise party for his best friend, Malcolm, that she almost called in sick for work. However, her conscience wouldn't let her, so she dressed in her pastel pink, two-piece suit with a lime green rose on the lapel and matching pink shoes and headed for work.

Sandy stared with anticipation at the clock in front of her at her job. She wished the time would fly by quicker. "This *would* be one of the slowest days of the week," Sandy thought while she looked around at the total of two people who were window-shopping inside the store. Sandy and Kellie both stood at their registers, ready to ring someone up, anyone, while knowing that probably neither would make a purchase.

Hoping for a sale, Sandy decided to leave the register and talk to one of the ladies, who was looking around like she was lost.

"May I help you, ma'am?"

The fifty-something black woman wearing a big red hat with a black feather looked Sandy up and down with an accusing glare that said, "Do you know how *short* that skirt is?"

After the glance, Sandy wondered if she had put a slip on.

"May I help you?" Sandy repeated with the same smile, despite the woman's expression.

"Uh, no, I'm just looking. Thank you, dear."

"Well, excuse me," Sandy thought as she waltzed to a rack and pretended to straighten the clothes.

As Sandy combed through the rack, a blonde-haired woman walked in the store with a large, pink teddy bear with red paws. The bear held a helium balloon that read, "Miss You" in red letters. The woman brought it to the register near Kellie.

Sandy's eyes lit up when she saw the adorable bear. She knew it was from Carter, who else would deliver a pink teddy bear?

Sandy skipped behind the register when the delivery woman read the card, "Is there a Miss Sandra A. Moore here?"

"That's me, that's me, that's me!" Sandy sang like a first-grader. Sandy signed for the bear and sent the woman on her merry way, once again without a tip, and immediately opened the card.

"Can't wait to see you tonight," Sandy read, loud enough for Kellie to hear, "Love, Carter."

"Wow," Kellie said. "He's quite the romantic."

"I know, and he's fine, and rich!" Sandy yelped. "Rich, rich, rich!" Sandy was so excited she wanted to dance all around the store.

Geneva heard Sandy's loud screech and came out from the back room with her arms folded. "Sandra, may I remind you that this is still a place of business? This is no place for you to display your personal life with all these frivolous little toys."

Geneva hit a button that time.

Sandy snapped her neck so fast toward Geneva, rolled her eyes, and belted, "Ex - cuse me?"

Geneva positioned her 5' self right in front of Sandy's 5'2" self and stated, "For the past few days, it seems to me that you have been using your place of employment as a display for your little gifts and shenanigans. I'm afraid it has to stop today." Geneva's breath smelled like something terrible. Sandy backed up slightly and grabbed her nose.

"You mean to tell me, I can't accept gifts at my job? It's not my fault my man buys me things. I don't tell him to, he just does."

"Not only that, Miss Moore, but may I remind you that you were thirty-five minutes late coming back from lunch yesterday. That was definitely inappropriate, unacceptable, and uncalled for!"

"But what does *that*, have to do with *this?*" Sandy pointed to today's gift from Carter.

"You know very well what it has to do with it," Geneva stated. "I suggest you limit your 'presents' from this *man of yours* to your own home, and I suggest you get your priorities straight. And can you go home and change into a decent length skirt? This is not a club; this is your job."

Sandy retorted, "And may I suggest you go home and brush your teeth for a change? Your breath smells like boo woo woo!" She'd had enough of Geneva's bossing her around and treating her like a Hebrew slave, expecting her to answer "yes massa, no massa" all the time.

Kellie had been trying to ignore the scene, but now her eyes grew wide. She was afraid the two of them were going to have a fight right there in the store. The one remaining customer quickly found her way to the door as Sandy and Geneva argued. Geneva sternly looked at Sandy and held out her hand, indicating that Sandy hand over her name tag.

"You don't have to fire me, I quit!" Sandy yelled and threw her name tag on the desk, grabbed her purse and gift, and stormed out of the store.

"I can't believe she tried to fire me!" Sandy exclaimed to Carter on her cell phone as she sped away from Donovan's for the last time. Her car made skid marks in the parking lot.

"Who the heck does she think she is?" Sandy was so upset she was shaking. Normally, during times like this, she would call Michelle for sound and rational advice, but instead she wanted to call her man to see what he had to say.

"I didn't get my degree for this!" Sandy yelled in the phone. For all she cared, Sandy was ready to retire from working, marry Carter, let him take care of her financially, and stay barefoot and pregnant.

Sandy was on a mission.

"Wait a minute now, calm down Sandra," Carter said. He sounded more like Sandy's father than her future husband. "Why don't you meet me here at the office, so we can go somewhere and talk about what happened, okay?"

Sandy sighed at his request. She just loved him. What other man that she knew would ever want to take the time to talk about her problems? Besides, Sandy really didn't have anywhere else to go. She didn't want to go home to Madear, who was not working today because she's off on Thursdays and would suspect something if Sandy came home so early. Besides, Sandy didn't want to hear Madear yell at her for quitting her job.

"You just can't keep yo' little butt still," Sandy could almost hear Madear say right about now. Sandy would much rather spend the rest of her day with the one person who really understood what she was going through right now . . . Carter.

"Okay, baby," Sandy said. "Excuse me for yelling; I'm just so mad that I just want to scream! Argh!"

"I understand, sweetheart," Carter sympathized. "Like I said, come on down to my law firm at Maxwell, Wright, and Associates downtown, which is in the glass building on Third. I'm on the eleventh floor. The receptionist will let you in and then she'll buzz me to tell me you're here."

"Oh thank you so much, Boobie," Sandy crooned, using her newly invented nickname.

"You're welcome. I was going to leave early anyway to prepare for Malcolm's surprise party."

"Oh yeah, the party, that's tonight isn't it?" Sandy remembered.

"It's tonight, babe. But, hey, that's okay. I have plenty of time to prepare for it. We can hang out for a few hours, and then I'll just drop your gorgeous self off home so you can get ready to look even more gorgeous for me tonight."

Sandy loved the idea of being the main attraction at a party, especially one filled with lawyers and other men of high prestige.

"Carter better watch himself," Sandy thought with a grin.

"Sandy," Carter said, interrupting her train of thought, "since I'll be with you the rest of the afternoon, I do have some work I still need to finish here, so I'll see you when you get here, okay?"

"Okay, Carter." Sandy said and hung up the phone.

"Did he just try to rush me off the phone? What's *his* problem?"

Sandy circled around the tall glass building on Third three times as she looked for a space downtown to park. She spotted a gentleman waving a flag for her to park in a lot with several other cars, all blocking one another, for six dollars.

"Oh please, I'm not about to park there and flat out give you my car keys so you can drive off with my car," Sandy had never had her car stolen out of one of those lots; she just didn't like the idea of leaving her car keys with some strange man. Sandy just smiled at the Arab man and kept driving.

She finally stumbled across an empty parking spot with a parking meter, grabbed several quarters from her purse, and plopped them in the machine. She put on her pink-shaded sunglasses and walked two blocks to the building, while trying to ignore the whistles from construction workers and honks from cars cruising down Jefferson Avenue.

Inside the building, she smiled at the guard and then sashayed to the elevator that took her to her destination, the eleventh floor.

Admiring all the gold and glass inside the elevator, Sandy thought, "Baby must got some clout. He is on his way to the penthouse."

Sandy got off the elevator, only to be confronted with a glass door directly in front of her and an intercom with a buzzer. She rang the buzzer while peeking through the glass at an attractive black woman with a long, straight black weave who was on the telephone.

"Who are you here to see?" The receptionist asked over the intercom while resting the phone on her shoulder.

"Carter Maxwell is expecting me," Sandy said with confidence. The door buzzed and she opened it.

The receptionist looked Sandy up and down as she waltzed right in with her pastel pink suit. "I'm here for Carter Maxwell." Sandy took off her glasses and leaned over the receptionist's desk as the receptionist continued to talk on the phone.

The receptionist covered the phone and informed Sandy, "He'll be right out shortly, ma'am; you can have a seat," and motioned Sandy toward the brown leather couch in the waiting area.

As Sandy grabbed a seat and waited for Carter, she couldn't help but notice her surroundings. The place was a little dim with its brown walls and oil paintings of cities and black men riding horses.

She noticed two large pictures on opposite sides of each other of African-American men with large gallon cowboy hats riding black horses. "Someone must like horses," Sandy thought.

Sandy sighed, crossed her legs, and picked up the financial newspaper on the glass table in front of her. After a few seconds of being bored with staring at a bunch of words with no pictures in color, Sandy set the paper down and picked up a magazine with an unknown black couple and possibly their son and daughter on the cover. The headline read, "To be Black and Wealthy in America."

"Now that's what I'm talking about," Sandy said out loud.

While Sandy flipped through the pages of the magazine, a dark-skinned man in a black custom made suit flashing a gorgeous smile waltzed right out of another set of glass doors and fixed his dark brown eyes on the angelic figure seated in front of him.

"Miss Sandra A. Moore," Carter said with a huge smile.

"Carter," Sandra sang and plopped the magazine back in its proper place in the middle of the glass table. She arose abruptly and gave Carter a huge hug with her head pointed toward the sky, making sure not to get any of her make-up on his sharp suit.

"Nice office," Sandy said.

"You like?" Carter asked.

"Yeah. Somebody here must really like horses," Sandy commented and looked around at all the pictures on the walls.

"Baby, these are all pictures of Buffalo Soldiers."

"Oh," Sandy replied as if she knew who they were.

"Roxanne, I'm gone for the rest of the afternoon," Carter said to the receptionist who watched Sandy with jealous eyes.

"Okay, Mr. Maxwell; enjoy your afternoon," she said with a fake grin.

Carter led Sandy by the hand through the glass doors and onto the elevator. Sandy thought he looked so good that she wanted to just give him a quick sloppy one in the elevator, just as she'd always seen in the movies. However, since Carter didn't seem to make a move first, she just stood there with her arms folded in front of her.

"Did you find the place okay?" Carter placed his arm around Sandy's tiny waist and edged her closer to him.

"I did," Sandy said with a smile.

"Where'd you park?"

"I couldn't find a space, at first, so I just settled on parking at a meter."

"A meter? You could've just parked behind the building where the employees park."

"Well, I didn't know, Carter," Sandra said innocently.

"You sure look good. Did you do something different to your hair since I last saw you?" Carter said while looking at Sandra's short crop.

"No," Sandy said, wondering what made him think that. "I just parted it a little different and brushed it a different way."

"Oh, well you still look stunning, as usual."

"Thanks, Carter." Her light-skinned cheek turned pink. *He really notices me.*

"So, where are we going?" Sandy asked after Carter opened his car door for her.

Carter plopped in the driver's seat and replied, "My, aren't we anxious."

After Carter's surprise at the upscale restaurant, Sandy was interested to find out where he was taking her this time. However, it was spur of the moment; Sandy realized he didn't have much time to plan anything.

"Have you ever been to the Museum of African American History down here?"

"No, I haven't," Sandy stated as her eyes widened.

Sandy loved art, but she hadn't been to a museum since she was in grade school.

"Well, I think its about time we black folks get to learn a little something about our heritage," Carter said jokingly.

"Wow, handsome, sexy, intelligent, a gentleman, and a

man who knows how to appreciate art," Sandy thought. "This man is all that and then some, and here Michelle is thinking he just wanted to get in my pants. You were *wrong*, sistah girl!"

Chapter 27

Tears Like Rivers

ON HER WAY HOME FROM WORK, LIZ couldn't stop thinking about Matthew Sr. She hadn't had her eye on any man for over two and a half years, to be exact. She was used to living an isolated life filled with just her, God, and daily bouts with her mother.

"My mother," thought Liz as she headed west on 8 mile. She had thought about visiting Ms. Coleman today, if she didn't refuse to open the door.

"I wonder if she made it back to work yet? Oh, God, I hope she didn't go ahead and-" Liz couldn't fathom the idea of her mother killing an unborn child. Liz thought about somehow coming up with an excuse to check on her.

"I know!" Liz concluded as if a light bulb came on in her head. "I'll tell her I'm here to pick up the rest of my things.

It wouldn't really be lying. I really did leave some of my important stuff, like pictures, extra underwear, sweaters . . . I just pray this woman even lets me in the door after the way she treated me yesterday."

Her mother's red car was in the driveway. Liz paused on the porch and whispered, "Okay Lord, I need Your favor with me on this one. Lord, please don't let this woman run me out again. I just want to see how she's doing. Lord, please give me the right words to say, and don't let me fly off the handle."

Liz rang the doorbell.

Even though Liz still had a key, she decided against just waltzing in unannounced. But no one answered.

Liz knocked on the door.

"Who is it?" A gruff-sounding female voice growled.

"It's me, Mom," Liz said, feeling a little scared. "Please open the door, Mom, please-"

"What do you want?" Ms. Coleman shouted, sounding more like an old hag than a concerned mom.

"I, uh, left some of my things and, uh, came to get 'em," Liz said, trying to hold to her story. "Lord, why couldn't I just say, 'I'm here to check on you, Mom, to make sure you're okay?' Oh, because she wouldn't buy that and probably wouldn't open the door."

"Don't you still have your house key?" Ms. Coleman yelled.

"Yeah, but I didn't want to just barge in."

Silence.

"Girl, open the door! I ain't 'bout to get up!"

Liz slowly opened the door and saw her mother sprawled out on the leather couch wearing her dingy white cotton robe and smoking a cigarette.

Liz's mother had quit smoking six months ago. Now she was back at it again. "She shouldn't be smoking while pregnant," Liz thought.

As Liz slowly walked into the living room, not really knowing what to think, Ms. Coleman kept her back to Liz and put out her cigarette. "What you doin' here?"

"I'm just here to pick up the rest of my things." Liz moved closer to see how her mother looked. "Mom!" Liz shouted as she noticed her mother's blood-shot red eyes and dazed expression. "Have you been drinking?"

"Huh?" Ms. Coleman stared at the blank, big-screen T.V. in front of her. "Naw, naw, I ain't been drinking." Ms. Coleman swore with slurred speech as she desperately searched for the remote control.

"Then what's this?" Liz grabbed a small vodka bottle from the floor in front of the couch. Liz also noticed the glass of cola on the glass coffee table. "What's this, Mom?" Liz shook the half-empty bottle in her mom's face.

It had been over a year since Liz remembered her mom having a drink. With prayer and a lot of love and support, and also with the help of *AA* meetings, Ms. Coleman had kicked that old destructive habit.

"Mom, tell me you're not drinking and smoking while pregnant!" Liz pleaded.

"Now here you go again telling me what to do. I know what I'm doing! I don't need your little self-righteous butt telling me what I can and can't do in my own house!"

Liz sat on the opposite end of the couch. "But Mom, there's a baby inside you now. It's not all about you, anymore, Mom."

"How you gon' tell me it's not about me! I knew that when I had *you*. You may be twenty-seven, but I know a bit more about life than you do! I wish *you* would carry this baby. You want this baby, you can have her!" Ms. Coleman swore as she sat up, tied her robe, and took another puff of her cigarette. "Yo' virgin butt won't be able to have a baby no other way, since you ain't never gave it up to nobody. Like you all that. Here, you take this baby, just take her!" Ms. Coleman pulled on her stomach as if to hand the baby over to Liz.

Tears welled up in Liz's eyes. "No, Mom!" she wailed. Then it suddenly dawned on her what her mother just said.

"It's . . . a girl?"

Ms. Coleman stared into her lap.

"It's a girl, mom?" Liz asked again.

"Yeah," Ms. Coleman finally responded. "Another little nappy-headed girl."

Liz began to wipe her tears.

"I had a ultra-thing done this morning and the doctor said, after twelve weeks, it's a 80 percent chance that it's a girl since they saw some lines or something on the whatever-they-called-it." Ms. Coleman sighed. "If you ask me, I just think they say it's a girl 'cuz they didn't see a little pee-pee stickin' out." Ms. Coleman stuck out her pinky finger.

Liz didn't think her mother looked three months pregnant. However, she only gained twelve pounds when she had Liz.

"Oh Mom, a little sister," Liz said and gave her mother a big hug.

"Yeah," Ms. Coleman whispered, "a little sister." She returned her daughter's embrace. "I don't wanna kill anybody, Liz." Tears like rivers flowed from Ms. Coleman's eyes. "I wanna do right." She squeezed her daughter tight.

"You can, Mom," Liz whispered in her mother's ear. "All you have to do is have faith in God, and believe, and He'll see you through." Liz rocked her mother from side to side. "And I promise we'll make it through this thing . . . together."

Chapter 28

Church Time

THE SANCTUARY AT HYPE FOR JESUS CHURCH
was crowded as usual during Thursday night's service.
Michelle rushed inside five minutes before service began.
She had hoped to get there fifteen minutes earlier to save
seats for Liz and Sandy, but it didn't quite work out that way.
She had spent too much extra time in the bathroom getting
dressed and trying to get her flat-ironed hairstyle just right
since she had forgotten to wrap it up the night before. Now
she rushed in, praying the Lord wouldn't let her fall in her
three-inch brown pumps.

An usher Michelle recognized seated her in the fourth
row of the 3,000-seat sanctuary. She placed her black
raincoat in her seat, her small Bible in the seat right next to

her, and her notebook in the next one to hold them while she went back to the lobby to wait for her friends.

"Excuse me," Michelle said to the man and woman next to her as she made her way up the purple-carpeted ramp. By the time Michelle made it back to the lobby, service had just begun and the praise team, which consisted of a group of ten men and women, was leading the song, "Shabach."

Michelle waved to the several people she knew before finally spotting one of her friends. "Hey, Liz, over here!" Michelle yelled and waved at Liz who just entered the lobby from outside. Liz smiled and joined Michelle, giving her a big hug.

"Hey, girl," Michelle said, "you lookin' good tonight," she commented on Liz's black, buttoned-down dress.

"You do, too, girl," Liz said with a smirk. Michelle's brown pantsuit with fitted pinstripe pants complimented her small frame.

"I wish I could wear something like that and get away with it," Liz said.

"Girl, you know whatever you wear you look good in it," Michelle reassured her.

"Guess what?" Liz asked.

"What?"

"Mom's keeping the baby!" Liz proclaimed with a shout.

"Praise God!" Michelle sang and hugged her best friend.

"Yes, God is good." Liz said.

"All the time," Michelle completed the phrase.

"I have to tell you everything else that happened," Liz said, as she noticed Michelle looking around at the front door. "Are you waiting for someone else?"

"Oh, yeah, you know who I'm waiting for . . . "

"Who?" Liz asked.

"Sandy."

"Sandy, oh, she prolly not coming. You know she barely comes to Thursday night service."

"I know, but I just talked to her last night, and she said she was coming."

"Girl, you know that chile can change her mind at the drop of a hat. Remember the last time she said she was coming to Thursday night service? She ended up changing her mind because she had to wash her hair. C'mon now."

"Yeah, but I really wanted her to come tonight. I figured we could all get dessert afterwards and talk. You know how we do it."

"I know how *we* do it, but I don't ever remember Miss Sandra Moore being at any of *our* after church dessert trips." Liz folded her arms.

"C'mon Liz, don't be like that. You and I both know that Sandy definitely needs somebody to talk to right now. Especially with all this crazy stuff with this new man of hers."

"You're right, but I have to talk to you, too, Michelle. The two of us hadn't had a good heart-to-heart in a long time."

"Now I know you not talking, Miss 'Leave-me-alone-while-I-stay-at a-dingy-motel.'"

Liz looked around to make sure no one else heard Michelle's comment. "Look, we'll talk later," she whispered.

The first praise song ended and the second one was about to begin and Sandy was still nowhere to be found.

"Can we go inside now, please?" Liz asked. "If you ask me, she's not coming."

"You're right. I don't see her." Michelle finally gave up after one more search around the faces in the lobby. "Let's go inside."

This time both Michelle and Liz said, "excuse me" to the couple seated in their row as they made it to their seats up front. Michelle and Liz immediately got into the flow of the Spirit as the praise team sang the high-spirited song, "Look What the Lord Has Done."

Some of the church members praised God right out of their seats. Some sang and jumped in the front of the sanctuary. One dark-skinned woman praised God with one hand raised with her long yellow dress and bright yellow hat. Another light-skinned boy was jumping around, dancing, and praising God in the front like he was at a rock-and-roll concert. His curly afro moved as he bobbed his head up and down.

"I got Him in my hands. I got Him in my feet," Liz and Michelle sang loudly along with the praise team and the rest of the congregation. Michelle bounced in her seat while Liz casually praised God with uplifted hands and a huge grin. The sanctuary grew warm as those around them praised God vigorously.

An usher standing in the aisle looked over at Michelle and pointed to the empty seat next to her which she was trying to save for Sandy.

"Is that seat open?" he mouthed. Michelle nodded and removed her notebook from it. She figured since Sandy hadn't made it to church by now, she probably wasn't coming.

"I'll just call her after service," Michelle thought as the usher seated a young man in the once vacant seat. The young man tapped Michelle on her shoulder and she realized it was none other than her friend, David Parker.

"Hey, Michelle!" David sang as the second praise song ended.

"David!" Michelle sang.

Michelle gave her friend a good, church hug. Michelle was glad to be seated next to David because he was always fun to be around, no matter what setting. She hadn't seen him since the other day at early morning prayer when he was telling her and Liz about his trip to see his father in Boston.

All of the congregation remained standing and shifted to a spirit of worship as the praise team led them in the song, "Lord, I Lift Your Name on High."

Michelle closed her eyes and focused on God with uplifted hands. She didn't care about her surroundings; she just began to think about God and how He has been so good to her over the past twenty-five years of her life.

As she sang with her whole heart, tears began to stream

down her already sweaty face. The anointing fell over the whole congregation by the end of the song and everyone began to sing and worship God in tongues and in English.

Women shouted without reservation and people cried out loud in their seats. Michelle noticed David wipe a tear from his eye. The Holy Spirit was heavy in the room, and Michelle was just so thankful to be in His presence and to be worshiping Him among the saints.

Liz also worshiped God with her whole heart. She cried, which she normally didn't do in a church service, and she praised God in the Spirit as she pondered about His Goodness and how He answered her prayers by moving on her mother's heart last night. Not only had Ms. Coleman decided to keep the baby, but she had also listened attentively as Liz ministered to her about the love of God. At 1 a.m., they had prayed together, and Ms. Coleman re-dedicated her life to Christ. Liz praised God for all that He has done, and for all that He will do.

The praise team exited the stage, and Pastor Wilkins walked up to the pulpit and worshiped God even more. "We worship You. We Honor You. We give You all the praise," the pastor sang.

Michelle could sense any burdens she had before she entered church being lifted off of her shoulders. She felt light as a feather as she sensed the warm presence of God all over her.

After a while, everyone simultaneously quieted down. The pastor then spoke in tongues for the next two minutes, and then gave the interpretation of what was said:

"No matter what you may be going through, no matter what it may seem, now is the time to trust in Me. The devil, he thought he had you, but as you tell him 'no,' you will see the victory manifested, for it shall be so. So laugh and dance and shout and sing, because the time is now. No more sorrow or despair, no more wondering how. I have given you victory over all you say and do. And I give you My Authority, so walk in it, too."

After the interpretation, which was given by the pastor for the edification of the church according to 1 Corinthians 14, the entire congregation let out a great big shout of victory and the drummer and organist played fervently while some members of the congregation danced in their seats.

As the music really started to take off, some members dashed from their seats and ran all around the sanctuary while shouting and praising God for the victory. Michelle, Liz, and David stayed and jumped in their seats, still shouting and thanking God.

Once the pastor motioned the organist and drummer to 'cut it,' all the people returned to their seats.

"Praise God!" Pastor Wilkins said enthusiastically.

Everyone continued to stand as the pastor stood contemplating at the pulpit. It was if the Holy Spirit wasn't finished moving yet, and the pastor was waiting to hear from Him as far as what to do next in the service.

Michelle, Liz, and David continued to praise God to themselves with uplifted hands, heads down, and eyes closed. Then the pastor said, "There is someone here who has been contemplating suicide."

The congregation grew silent and looked around.

"I want you to come up front," Pastor Wilkins stated as the congregation continued to look around, but no one stepped forward.

"Whoever you are, I have a word from the Lord for you. You have been allowing the devil to control your thought life for too long. Now make a bold step for God and move forward."

The congregation looked around again as Michelle, Liz, and David prayed in tongues to themselves, supplicating for the person to come forward and receive deliverance. After another two minutes, a young girl in her early twenties with long braids and frail, loose clothing slowly made her way to the front. She came with her head down and her arms folded in front of her.

Pastor Wilkins walked down from the pulpit, stood in

front of the girl, and placed his arm on her shoulder. "The Lord wanted me to tell you that He loves you, and that He will never leave you nor forsake you."

The woman began to cry in her hands.

"He wanted me to tell you that no man can ever love you the way that He can, and that You mean more to him than precious silver or gold."

The girl cried even more as a male usher positioned himself behind her and a female greeter stationed herself nearby with tissue and a lap cloth.

"He also wanted me to tell you that you are beautiful, you are special, and you are truly loved by God."

Michelle, Liz, and David continued to pray while looking at the woman.

"And no devil in hell will ever have you, for you are worth too much to God to die," Pastor Wilkins said and then laid his hand on the woman's head.

The woman's body shook like she received an electric shock and she fell straight back.

The usher caught her and laid her gently on the carpet and the female greeter placed a lap cloth over the girl's chest.

As the girl lay on the floor, Michelle could see a smile on the young woman's face.

The whole congregation praised God.

"God is good," Pastor Wilkins shouted.

"All the time," the congregation responded.

Chapter 29

Butterflies

AFTER SANDY TOOK A NICE, LONG SHOWER, she grabbed her pink robe, wrapped her wet hair in a towel, and tiptoed to her bedroom. She sat on the edge of her bed and grabbed her bright pink nail polish to paint her toenails when she suddenly felt as if she was being watched.

"Going out tonight?" A familiar voice asked from the doorway.

Madear stood in the doorway with her arms folded.

Sandy wished tonight was one of Madear's bridge nights, but that wasn't until Sunday. Sandy just wished that her grandmother wasn't so nosy. She continued to paint her toenails and ignored Madear.

"It's a little late for church, isn't it? Didn't it start at 7:00?"

"Yes, Madear." Sandy didn't look up from her toes. Carter would come to pick her up in the next hour and a half, and Sandy still hadn't figured out what to do about her hair.

"Well, baby, it's going on eight o'clock; you running a little late, aren't ya?" Madear asked in a high pitched, overly concerned tone of voice.

"I know what time it is, Madear. I'm not going to church tonight."

"Oh," Madear said. "You're not?"

Sandy finished polishing her third toe and proclaimed, "No, Madear, I'm not."

"Well, excuse me," Madear said, still with her arms folded. Madear had attended her own church's mid-week Bible study yesterday. She noticed that Sandy had been going to service on Thursday night at least every other week since she got saved, but tonight would make two weeks in a row that Sandy has missed.

"So, where ya goin'?" Madear asked, as if Sandy didn't know that would be her next question.

"I'm going to mind my own business," Sandy hissed underneath her breath. She regretted what she just said immediately and hoped that Madear didn't hear her. She didn't feel like getting into it with her grandmother tonight.

Unfortunately, she must have heard Sandy's comment. Madear unfolded her arms, inched inside Sandy's room, stood over Sandy and asked, "What did you say, young lady?"

"I'm going out, Madear! I'm going out! Is that okay with you?"

"Oh no! You will not raise your voice at me, not while you're in this house!" Madear warned.

Sandy stopped polishing her toes, looked up and said sincerely, "I'm sorry, Madear, I didn't mean to get loud."

Madear sat on the bed beside her grandbaby.

"I mean, sometimes, I just feel like I have to tell you my every move, and to be honest, it can get real annoying."

"I know, baby, I know," Madear said while rubbing Sandy's leg. "I just be concerned about you baby, that's all. I want to make sure you're doing okay. Seeing as how your momma and daddy are no longer here, I want to make sure I'm looking out for you the best way I possibly can."

Sandy smiled. "I know Madear, and you are looking out for me. Momma and Daddy would be proud."

A single tear streamed from Madear's eye as she sprang up from the bed.

"You go on and get dressed, now then, baby. Don't let Madear disturb you."

"Alright, Madear."

"Just make sure you don't stay out too late. I'm going to retire early myself."

"Okay, Madear," Sandy said as her grandmother made her way towards the doorway. "Love you."

"I love you too, baby," the voice in the hallway responded.

Once Sandy finished polishing her toenails, she walked on her heels to the closet and pulled out the dress she was going to wear to the party tonight. Sandy wanted to look extra special for Carter and his friends so she chose her short and tight pink mini dress with criss-cross straps in the back.

Sandy placed her selection on her bed and then went to her vanity to stare at herself in the mirror.

Her skin was pretty clear, for the most part, but she figured a little foundation and light makeup would definitely do the trick to help her look extra fabulous. Sandy ran her fingers in her light-cream colored foundation and began to pat it on her face with her fingertips and rub it in. She put on brown eyeliner and used the kind of mascara that makes her eyelashes look extra long and thick. She even decided to wear blush, which she normally didn't wear. She wore a light pink blush to continue with the soft look she was going for, and she decided not to wear any eye shadow at all.

Sandy unraveled the towel on her head and looked at the wet mess in the mirror in front of her.

"What am I going to do with you?" Sandy said to her hair. She plugged in her blow-dryer, brushed and blow dried it, and added oil to restore its shine.

Sandy stared at her hair for a hot second, looked over at her flat irons and curling irons, then looked to the right and noticed her phony pony on the dresser.

"I can wear my pony tail!" Sandy shouted. "Thank God for fake hair."

She combed out the flipped, curly style, jet black ponytail that matched the color of her own hair perfectly. She brushed her own hair back in a pony tail, added some gel to keep her sides from sticking out, and clipped the pony tail onto the back of her head.

"Voila!" Sandy said as she looked at her new self in the mirror.

Sandy lotioned her legs, sprayed perfume on her neck, and squeezed her body inside the tight dress.

As she zipped it in the back she noticed it was a little tighter up top than usual.

"Oh no, am I gaining weight? Nah, maybe I'm just filling it out a little more." She pushed up her almost nonexistent breasts.

Sandy grabbed her pink, three-inch heel sandals with the toes out and tied the straps around her leg when she noticed that it was now going on nine o'clock.

"I'm right on schedule," Sandy thought as she finished getting ready.

Sandy figured Carter would be pretty pleased with how she looked as she stared at herself in her full-length mirror on the door of her closet.

She turned to the side and frowned as she noticed a little pudge in her stomach.

"Looks like tonight I'ma have to just suck it in," Sandy said out loud.

Sandy grabbed her small pink purse from her closet doorknob and began switching everything from her everyday handbag. As she switched purses, butterflies formed in her stomach. Her stomach was getting so queasy that she almost felt she had to go to the bathroom.

Instead of allowing the butterflies to get the best of her, Sandy took a seat at her desk and pulled out her pink journal, which she writes in from time to time when something exciting is happening in her life. She figured she had a little time before Carter arrived.

Dear Journal,

Well, I'm sitting here about to go out with the man of my dreams! I know I hadn't written in you in a while, journal, but he is definitely a good catch. He and I have been going out for only a few days now and he has treated me like royalty. He always sends me gifts and flowers at work (oh, by the way, journal, I quit my job today, but that's another story) and he even bought me a tennis bracelet! I truly feel he is the one for me, and I know that God has blessed me to be with this man. He is wealthy, successful, intelligent, and the man is Fine! You can't get no better than this, journal. And he even goes to church!

Tonight he is throwing a surprise party for his lawyer best friend at his place, and he wants me to be there with him! I can't believe it, journal, I'm going to be with Carter and meet all of his lawyer friends! This man must be serious. I know for a fact that with a few more of Sandra A. Moore's sweet moves on him, he'll be eating out of the palm of my hand, wanting to marry me tomorrow!

Sandy looked to her left on the dresser and saw the business card on which Carter initially wrote his cell number. "Carter Maxwell," Sandy said as she picked up his card and stared at it while reminiscing about the first day they met in the store. "That's one smooth brotha." She kissed the card and then placed it on top of her journal entry.

Just then the doorbell rang.

Sandy hopped up as she remembered that Madear said she was going to bed. She grabbed her purse, shut off the light, closed the door, and ran downstairs, trying not to trip on the steps in her three-inch high pink sandals.

She opened the front door and once again got a glimpse of what heaven might look like.

Carter stood in front of her with a cream-colored shirt and cream-colored pants and a light pink tie that matched her dress perfectly.

A pink tie! He purposely tried to coordinate with me!

"Wow," Carter said as he took one look at Sandy and licked his lips. "You look absolutely gorgeous." He shook his head and looked her up and down.

"You like?" Sandy asked and twirled around in front of him.

"Do I?" Carter stared at Sandy with hungry eyes. "Does this answer your question?" He grabbed her and gave her a long, passionate kiss.

Sandy's body responded to his kiss as her hands caressed the back of his head. She pulled back when she thought about the possibility of ruining her makeup.

As suspected, Carter's lips were all pink and glossy. She meant to buy the kind of lipstick that doesn't come off, but she just hadn't gotten around to purchasing it yet.

"I'm sorry," Carter immediately said when Sandy pulled away.

Sandy looked deep into Carter's eyes and said, "Don't be," and slowly wiggled herself out of his grasp. "Come inside."

Sandy closed the door behind them and Carter continued, "No Sandy, I'm really sorry." He pulled out his handkerchief and wiped the lipstick off his mouth. "I don't know what got into me."

Sandy decided now would be a perfect time to throw more of her "Miss Sandra A. Moore" moves on him so she purposely got in his face so he could smell her perfume.

"It's okay Carter," she crooned while looking up at his dark brown eyes.

"It's just-you're just so drop-dead gorgeous, sometimes when I see you, I just can't control myself." Carter looked as if he was about to kiss her again. Then Sandy fled from his presence and rushed toward the bathroom.

"That's okay Carter, I understand," she yelled in a cocky way. "I'll be right back, I'm going to the restroom to freshen up my lipstick."

Carter took a seat on the noisy plastic couch and waited six minutes for Sandy to come out. Sandy finally returned and Carter immediately rose.

"C'mon, let's go," Sandy said. She grabbed her purse and a pink wrap for her shoulders and left the house with the man of her dreams.

"For you, my dear," he said as he opened his car door for her with a smile, just like the perfect chauffeur.

"Why thank you."

Inside his ride, Sandy was soothed by the smooth jazz sounds of "Moments in Love."

"I just love this song. Is this on the radio?" Sandy asked.

"No, I got the CD." Carter handed Sandy his case of CDs.

Sandy spotted one of her all-time favorite female vocalists.

"Sade! 'Smooth Operator.' Play that, play that!"

Carter chuckled and said, "Sandy, you're something else, you know that?"

"What do you mean?"

"I mean, just everything about you is so unique. It's like you approach life, like a little kid, viewing every little thing as a new adventure."

"Oh." Sandy wasn't sure whether or not to take that as a compliment.

"Don't get me wrong," Carter explained. "It's a good thing. I mean, it keeps life fresh and exciting."

"Oh!" Sandy perked up.

"Like the way you quit your job today."

Sandy shot Carter a look. She had actually forgotten that she quit her job today. She had no idea what her next move would be.

"I mean, I would *never* do that!" Carter laughed.

"But you," he said, grabbing her left hand and bringing it to his lips and kissing her knuckles, "you just have such audacity, such boldness, such bravery." He continued to kiss her knuckles with his tongue. "You are something else, girl."

To Sandy, his words were sweet and sincere. She just looked at him like he was a newborn baby that she wanted to take home and love forever.

Sandy had always been the one who could have a man eating out of the palm of her hand, but this man had somehow managed to capture her heart, and win her soul. Every word he spoke, he spoke with elegance and charm.

Butterflies formed in Sandy's stomach again. She really wanted to make the best impression she possibly could make on Carter's friends tonight. She wanted him to know that she was worth spending time with . . . for the rest of their lives.

Carter pulled his luxury ride into a long, hilly roadway that seemed to go on forever until it finally led to a three-story, brown brick house on top of a hill. There were tons of trees but no surrounding houses. Sandy wondered if they were out in the country somewhere.

"We're here," Carter sang as he pushed a button on his keys, causing the garage door to lift up so that he could park inside. Sandy noticed a white Beamer in the garage as well.

"This man is filthy rich!" Sandy said to herself as she reached in her purse to touch up her powder. Carter lived in an affluent area in Detroit. Homes there were worth well over half a million dollars.

Carter opened the front door and was immediately

greeted with cheers from a house full of guests including all
shades and sizes of men and women: white, black, Asian,
and Latino.

Sandy's eyes widened as she saw how so many people
smiled at Carter. He strolled around his house, giving
several men hi-fives and several women hugs and kisses
on the cheek, while keeping Sandy tucked neatly under
his arm. Carter introduced Sandy to so many people that
she felt like she was his trophy. However, that night, she
didn't mind. She especially liked the looks she got from the
females, white and black alike, who stared at her with envy
or disbelief and then whispered to their girlfriends.

"Ay, Carter, what's happenin' man?" asked a short, pot-
bellied thirty-something man with a short afro.

As the little man gave Carter a manly hug, Sandy looked
around the room. "Carter sure must love the color cream,"
Sandy thought. There was cream-colored carpet everywhere,
and the dining and living rooms were both filled with cream
furniture with gold overtones. Tan leather couches and a
bearskin rug completed the decor of the living room. Other
rooms were filled with pictures of Egyptian goddesses such
as Nefertitti-like black figures and other black women with
huge chains wrapped around their necks.

"What's happening, Bill?" Carter returned the
enthusiastic greeting.

"Say, uh, whatcha got there?" Bill asked, pointing to
Sandy with one hand and holding a drink in the other.

Sandy shifted her focus to the little man in front of her
who pointed at her like she was a piece of furniture.

"Here? Oh, this here is Miss Sandra A. Moore, my lady-
friend," Carter snickered.

"Yo' lady-friend?" Bill asked in disbelief.

Sandy nodded her head with an assuring look and a
cocky smile.

"Gal, I ain't know they came as fine as you! What you
doin' with this cat over here? You need to come and get
with the real deal, right here," Bill said, pointing toward his

half-drunk self and sticking out his pot belly.

No thanks! Sandy smiled and said nothing to the little man who was almost shorter than she was.

"Naw, naw, Bill, this lady is in good hands . . . mine." Carter said. With that he pulled Sandy closer to him and kissed her on the forehead.

Sandy turned her face toward Carter and softly kissed his lips.

Carter returned the kiss, and the two of them were at it again. Everyone in the room bellowed, "Ooooooo" just like some second graders witnessing two people kiss for the first time.

"Well, excuse me! I get the hint! She ain't going nowhere!" Bill said with a snort. "And you ain't either, buddy!" Bill laughed. "Boy, she must got you whipped!"

"Naw, it ain't even like that, Bill," Carter said while staring longingly into Sandy's eyes. "It ain't even like that."

Sandy loved the way Carter stared at her, as if no one else was in the room. She believed he was falling in love with her, but she wasn't quite sure yet. The true test was to keep him chasing and keep him guessing. So instead of letting him hold her by his side all night long, she wanted to test him to see how he would handle letting her go for a minute.

"Baby, I think I want to grab a bite to eat," Sandy said with a sweet tone.

Carter abruptly let her go. "Oh, no problem; don't let me keep you. Go grab a bite to eat," he insisted. "The kitchen is right around the corner to the left."

"Do you want anything?" Sandy said with a sly smile.

"Oh, no, no. I'm fine, thanks." Bill and Carter nearly drooled as they stared at Sandy's tiny waist and plump behind when she walked away. Sandy figured they would both be checking her out, so she made sure to switch a little more this time as she left the room.

"Daaaaaang!" Bill sang. "That girl gotta *phat* booty!"

"I know," Carter agreed.

Sandy's dress hugged her behind so tight that it really showed off what God had graced her with.

"Carter, I *know* you hit that. Was it good, man?"

"Actually, Bill, I haven't."

"You haven't? Man what's wrong wit' you?"

Carter laughed while still looking in the direction where Sandy left the room. "Nothing, man."

"Look, how long you known the girl?"

"Um, I met her Monday, so what's that, four days now?"

"Four days? Aw, the Carter Maxwell I know woulda don' hit that on the first night!" Bill said with a laugh. "It woulda been like bam! bam! bam! bam!" Bill slapped his hands together.

"Bill, you are too crazy."

"No, you the one crazy. The way she was all over you..."

"Bill . . . "

"Like honey to a bee."

Carter laughed again.

"But seriously, c'mon now Carter, what's the real reason you ain't tapped that yet?"

"There is no reason."

"Don't give me that bull, man. I know you, and I know these fine tricks, I mean fine women you be having on yo' arm."

"I know, I know, but Sandy's different."

Bill looked suspicious. "In what way?"

Carter paused for a moment and replied, "She's a church girl."

"Man, them be the best ones! Them the ones that be horny 'cuz they ain't had none. She might be a virgin!"

"You crazy, man."

"You give her a little piece of what real heaven is like, and she'll be all over you like white on rice!"

"You trippin'."

"You know I'm telling the truth. Now where that girl at, huh? Where she at? I'll show her what real loving is all about, since you ain't." Bill headed toward the kitchen.

"Hey, Sandy," Bill sang, "won't you let me introduce you to my little friend . . . "

Carter placed his hand on his forehead and shook his head.

In the kitchen, Sandy grabbed a small plate and filled it with wing dings, meatballs, macaroni and cheese, and greens. She poured a small cup of punch and sat down on the couch in the living room. She hesitated at first because there were three women already seated, but she saw where there was an open slot and decided to squeeze in.

"Excuse me," she said as she managed to sit down on the leather couch and place her plate and punch on the glass coffee table in front of her. Sounds of Kem blared in the entire room.

As Sandy nibbled on her barbeque wing ding, she felt like she was being watched.

She looked to her right and saw two of the three women on the couch were staring at her while she ate.

"I'm Sandy," she said with a smile in order to break the ice and stop the stares. "I would shake your hand but I don't want to get sauce all . . . " Sandy noticed that the women didn't respond or offer to disclose their own names.

"That's okay," the dark-skinned woman seated next to her said. She had extremely long hair, with silver streaks in it. Sandy thought her hair looked a little spooky, like she was a witch or something.

"Justine," the woman seated next to the witch lady said.

"Nice to meet you, Justine," Sandy said to the seemingly friendly, cute, honey-complexioned woman who had her plate on the table in front of her as well. "That's a sharp dress you have on, Justine." Sandy admired the gold mini-dress and gold high-heeled sandals.

"Thanks." Justine sipped her drink. "So, Sandy, we haven't seen you at any of these parties . . . friend of Malcolm's?"

Sandy just remembered that this was a surprise party for Carter's best friend. Where was Malcolm anyway, Sandy thought. It was going on 10:00. Sandy figured they still must be detaining him a little longer or waiting for more guests to arrive to surprise him. But the house was already pretty full, disproportionately with more women than men, of course.

"No, not exactly. I came with Carter." Sandy made sure to inform the nosy ladies that she came *with* Carter; she was not just another name on the guest list.

"Oh, Carter Maxwell? I know him," Justine replied.

Sandy had hoped she did know him, since she was sittin' in his house.

"He has a lovely place, doesn't he?" Justine looked around.

"Yes, he does." Sandy commented.

The witch lady didn't say a word. She just sat staring at Sandy, until she finally decided to take a sip of her sparkling drink.

"He's also a very successful partner at his law firm," Justine said. "Very successful. But I'm sure you know all of that."

"Yes, I do. I know a lot about him," Sandy exaggerated. "Are you a friend of Malcolm's?"

"Oh, let's just say I have many friends." Justine looked at her girlfriend next to her and they laughed.

"Oh," Sandy said and took a sip of her punch.

"Malcolm, Carter, lets just say I know 'em all!" Justine sang and giggled.

"Oh really? Are you a lawyer as well?"

"No, I'm not a lawyer. But I am a close friend. I met the both of them a couple years ago, and since I met them they just can't seem to get rid of me." She and her girlfriend laughed again. "And you, are you a lawyer? You look a little young to be practicing," Justine concluded.

"No, I'm not a lawyer."

"Then how do you know Carter?"

Nosy wench, Sandy thought. "Well, let's just say one day we met, and since then he can't seem to take his eyes off of me."

The two women looked at each other as if to say, "Who does this woman think she is?"

Tired of sitting with two nosy females, Sandy said, "Excuse me, it was a pleasure meeting the both of you." She grabbed her half-eaten plate and cup and headed toward the dining room.

The two women looked at each other one last time, and Justine's shy friend finally said, "Same here."

Before Sandy reached her destination, she was halted by Bill yelling, "Ay, Sandy, what's up girl!"

Sandy stopped and turned toward the little man in front of her. "Hello Bill. We meet again."

"Sure we do, ah, let me get that for you," Bill said as he grabbed Sandy's plate and put it on top of the mantle. "So, Sandy, you got the hots for my man, Carter?"

Sandy wondered if Carter purposely positioned his FBI interrogation squad all over his house.

"Yes, I do." She was about tired of all these questions. She wished Malcolm would hurry up and arrive to get the show on the road.

"Ay, Butler Man!" Bill screamed in Sandy's ear. She cringed.

A handsome black man in a tuxedo carrying a tray waltzed over to Bill. "Why don't you make this fine lady over here one of your magnisimo drinks!" Bill yelled at the man.

"No thanks," Sandy interjected. "I don't drink."

"You don't drink?" yelled Bill, loud enough for the whole room to hear.

"Oh yeah, I forgot, you one of them church gals. Well even Jesus had a little wine!" Everyone in the room laughed.

"And what about communion? That's all them white folks do in them Catholic churches with them robes on, is drink wine and have communion every day."

He did have a point, Sandy thought.

"Plus, don't the Bible say drinking is okay as long as you

don't get drunk?"

The butler nodded his head.

"I know I read that somewhere," Bill said.

Sandy was starting to think that she read that somewhere, too.

"C'mon now, one little drink won't hurt. I'll make sure my man right here fix it up real light for you. You won't even be able to tell it's liquor."

Sandy thought about it for another second and finally gave in. "Okay, you're right. One drink won't hurt, I guess."

Bill then slipped the butler a large bill and whispered something in his ear as the man departed to mix the drink at the bar.

"So, Bill, are you always this lively?" Sandy asked.

"Yeah, girl! 'Live' is my middle name! Party over here! Party over there!" Bill sang while waving his hands from side to side.

Sandy happened to peek around a corner and noticed three white people and a black couple in a much smaller room surrounding a glass table with white powder on top of it. She also saw a man with a razor blade look as if he was grinding up the powder.

"What's going on in there?" Sandy asked out of curiosity. She wondered why they weren't out in the open with the rest of the party crowd.

"Oh, in there?" Bill laughed. "Ain't nuttin' going on in there." He tried to shift Sandy's focus back to him.

"What are they doing?" Sandy asked again as Bill began to recklessly wave for someone in that room to close the door.

As Sandy returned her glance to Bill, Bill abruptly re-composed himself and said, "Doing? Oh, they ain't doing nuttin'. My man in there, Quincy, uh, he's a doctor! They testing out this new powder medication that they just got in the lab the other day. He just making sure it's okay to give to the patients."

"Oh, a doctor!" Sandy exclaimed. "I should've known."

Doctors and lawyers; she was in here with all the big leagues of the city.

"And you, Bill?"

"Huh?" Bill responded with a nervous twitch as he began to sweat bullets.

"What do you do? How do you know Carter?"

"Me? Oh, me and Carter go way back. We grew up together on the east side. Yeah, we both straight up rags to riches cats. I sell houses and invest in property. Need a house?" Bill asked as he reached in his side pocket to pull out a business card.

"Not yet," Sandy replied.

Just then the attractive butler walked up to Sandy with several bubbly drinks on a tray.

"For you," the butler said as he lowered his tray for Sandy.

Sandy hesitated and then accepted a drink and asked Bill, "You sure this isn't too strong?"

"Watch, you won't even be able to tell it has an ounce of liquor in it." Bill said with a wink to the butler.

Sandy sipped the drink and at first cringed, but then finally enjoyed how the lasting taste simmered slowly and smoothly down her throat. The drink was decorated with cherries and lime, and she loved the taste of any fruity drink. Little did she know that the butler mixed Hypnotic with a shot of *Hennessey.*

"Mmmm," Sandy said, "this *is* good. You sure this is alcohol?"

"I told you it wasn't that much in there. Not even 10 percent," Bill lied.

"This is goooood," Sandy repeated as she took it to the head and finished it off.

Sandy used to drink every weekend before she got saved. She figured this drink was super light, compared to what she used to drink back in the day.

"Say butler, why don't you grab her another round on me!" Bill yelled.

The butler nodded with a wink.

"Matter of fact, make it two more," Bill whispered as he slipped another fifty dollar bill to the butler.

"Sure thing," the butler responded.

"In a larger glass!" Bill yelled as the butler exited. Sandy started to giggle.

She was really beginning to loosen up now, since she just got her drink on. She had forgotten how easily she could get drunk. She couldn't even hold down a wine cooler without getting a little giddy, let alone Hypnotic.

Suddenly the front door flew open and in stepped one of the finest brothas a sistah would ever want to see. The entire house full of people yelled, "SURPRISE!"

Drinks were held high in the air, party favors were blown, and confetti was thrown at the male goddess, as flocks of women headed to his side. Women from all over the place greeted him with hugs and kisses. His light-skinned, chiseled face was covered with different shades of lipstick as he slowly traveled around the room.

His smile lit up the entire room as Sandy, now working on her second drink, wondered who this fine brotha was and how did God manage to create such a being. Sandy saw Justine, the nosy broad, slowly walk up to him and place a long wet one on his thick, juicy lips. The recipient just closed his eyes and received the passionate kiss, and kept his lips poked out as Justine turned around abruptly and switched her little behind back to her seat. The man growled at her like a tiger.

"That must be Malcolm," Sandy thought. At this point, she almost forgot who Carter was as she eyed the tall, burly, super-fine light-skinned man with a bald head heading her way.

Malcolm was stopped short in his advancement toward Sandy as his best friend cut him off.

"Surprise, my man!" Carter said with a hefty pat on Malcolm's shoulder.

"Aw, dawg, you didn't have to do all this for me!"

"What do you mean? We *have* to go all out! At the age of thirty, you hit a milestone, brah!" The two men laughed.

"Man, I can't believe you got me. You got me good, man."

"I know; ain't it funny?"

"Well, hey, any excuse to get our gig on right?" Malcolm said with a bank-head bounce to the left.

"I know that's right," Carter replied.

"And who is this?" Malcolm asked, accepting a drink from a female fan.

"This here," Carter said while grabbing Sandy by the side, "is my lady, Miss Sandra A. Moore."

"Yo' lady?" Malcolm asked in disbelief.

"Yes, my lady," Carter responded as a matter-of-fact.

The two men were used to competing with each other as far as who had the finest woman. Malcolm was single, but he hardly ever spent a weekend in bed alone.

"Pleasure to meet you," Sandy said and held out her sweaty hand. She was starting to feel a little light-headed and horny, and she envisioned planting a hot one on Malcolm's lips. But she had to remember that she already had her lawyer by her side.

"The pleasure is all mine," Malcolm said as he ever so slightly turned Sandy's hand over and kissed her palm, slipping in a little tongue with the soft kiss.

"Ay, ay, ay, now, watch that!" Carter screeched as he watched his lady's reaction from Malcolm's overly kind gesture.

"What you talkin' bout, man? It's all good. Ay, butler man!" Malcolm yelled, "why don't you get this brotha right here a drink! He need to loosen up a bit!"

All three of them laughed.

Chapter 30

Worried

SERVICE ENDED A LITTLE LATER THAN USUAL this Thursday night. Pastor Wilkins laid hands on everyone in the sanctuary that needed healing, and that ran service over about an hour and a half. It didn't matter to Michelle, Liz, and David, though. The three of them, as was their custom, were chatting in the lobby right after service let out.

"So," Michelle said to Liz, "you still want to grab dessert?"

"Yeah, sure, why not?" Liz was down for hanging tonight. Besides, she wanted to tell her best friend about what has been going on in her life between her and her mother and about Mr. Matthew Long.

"Where ya'll going?" David felt left out.

"We're thinking about going to get dessert," Michelle answered.

"Oh, sounds good. I am a little hungry myself," David said, rubbing his stomach.

Liz rolled her eyes. She knew what that meant. If he tagged along with them to get dessert, she really wouldn't be able to tell Michelle hardly anything. Liz respected David, but she preferred to keep her private life, private.

"Hey, why don't I call Sandy and see if she can meet us there?" Michelle suggested.

"Sure, why not, everybody else is going," Liz said, with a grimacing look at David.

David looked at Liz as if to say, "What?"

Michelle stepped outside the church door to use her cell phone so she could get a good reception. After about four rings, she heard a familiar, older woman's voice.

"Hello," answered Madear.

"Hello, Madear?"

"Yes."

"I'm sorry; this is Michelle. Did I wake you?"

"Yes, you did."

"I'm sorry, Madear. Is Sandy home?"

"No she isn't."

"She isn't?"

"Well, she was supposed to be at church tonight," Michelle tattled, "and I was getting a little worried since she didn't show up."

"Well, Sandy went out tonight."

"She went out?"

"Uh huh, I heard a male voice downstairs when she left. I think she went out with that new fella she's been seeing."

"New fella? Carter?"

"I guess that's his name."

Michelle was very disappointed. Sandy forsook coming to church to go out with some man? Did he think he could just show her a nice time and then steal her away from the church? And where did they go, anyway? She hardly knew this guy.

"Do you have any idea where they went?" Michelle probed.

"Well, no," Madear answered. Madear was about ready to hang up the phone so she could go back to sleep.

Michelle suddenly received an unction in her spirit to locate her friend, right now. Michelle recognized that unction. It was the same unction she received moments before Marqueeta got into that serious car accident. Michelle was not about to make the same mistake twice.

"Madear, would you happen to have Carter's phone number?" Michelle asked with a sense of urgency.

"No, I don't."

Michelle couldn't remember Carter's last name; besides, she didn't know what city he lived in to get his number from directory assistance. She didn't want to worry Madear, but she needed to find Sandy.

"Hold on for a second," Madear said as she put the receiver down and crawled out of bed.

"Oh please, Lord, let Madear find the number. I don't want to miss it this time . . . not again." Michelle whispered as she envisioned her sister laid out in the hospital bed as a result of the car accident.

After about five minutes, Madear returned to the phone.

"Okay," Madear said as she returned to the phone in her bedroom, out of breath. "I got the number."

Madear had gone in Sandy's room to look on Sandy's desk and found Carter's business card on top of her journal.

"Praise God, what is it?" Michelle asked.

"It's 313-555-5683." Michelle repeated the number to make sure it was correct.

"Thanks," Michelle said and hung up quickly. She began to dial the number hysterically as David and Liz joined her.

"Is everything okay?" David asked.

"Everything's fine," Michelle said.

The phone rang three times on the other end.

On the fourth ring, a female voice finally picked up.

"Hello!" yelled a giggling voice.

Michelle could hear loud rap music and tons of people in the background.

"Hello!" Michelle screamed over the noise.

"Hello!" the giddy female yelled again.

"May I speak to Carter?"

The female placed the phone to the side of her ear and began to yell, "Carter! Carter! CARTER!"

With each scream her voice grew louder and louder. Michelle heard a gruff male voice yell, "Girl, what you screaming about? You see Carter ain't here!"

"I don't see him," the female said as she returned to the phone.

Michelle knew something was definitely wrong.

What kind of party was Sandy at anyway?

"Oh, no," Michelle said as she hung up the phone. "We gotta get over there."

"What?" Liz asked.

"Sandy, we gotta get to Sandy." Michelle sounded like she was in a trance.

"What's wrong, Michelle?" David asked. He noticed beads of sweat fall from Michelle's forehead.

"I just called over to Carter's, Sandy's boyfriend's, and, I think they're having some kind of party."

"So," Liz stated.

"So, we gotta get over there!" Michelle demanded.

"What?" Liz snapped.

"I'm serious, we gotta get over there now!"

Liz couldn't understand what Michelle was so worried about. Sandy was a grown woman. If she wanted to make mistakes in life with men, let her make her own mistakes and learn from 'em. Liz couldn't see the benefit in always having to baby-sit her, especially since Sandy was going to do whatever she wanted to anyway.

"I got a bad feeling about this," Michelle said.

David, in the two years that he had known Michelle, had never seen her look this worried about anything. "I think we should go," he said.

"What!" Liz shouted. "You too?"

"I mean, if she said she got a bad feeling, she got a bad feeling," David reasoned.

"We don't even know where the man lives!" Liz interjected.

Michelle's face grew disappointed. Liz was right; they didn't know where Carter lived. Michelle didn't think to ask the girl who answered the phone; besides, the girl acted like she wouldn't even know how to spell her own name.

"Call information and do a search-by-number." David suggested.

Michelle's face lit up. "That's right! I can do a search-by-number! They give you the address when you know the phone number!" Michelle gave David a big hug for thinking on his toes.

Chapter 31

Hypnotized

SANDY WAS GETTING TIPSY AS SHE HELD ON
to her third Hypnotic drink. Carter was practically holding
her up with one arm while he held on to his fourth drink
with his free hand. Suddenly, the smooth sounds of Luther
came on in the form of the old school jam, "Always and
Forever."

"Oh, I used to loooove this song," Sandy belted as she
snapped her fingers and moved from side to side. Carter
bobbed his head from side to side while following Sandy's
body movements with each beat of the song.

"Care to dance?" Carter asked.

Sandy didn't say a word, but instead grabbed Carter's
pink tie and pulled him out into the middle of the living

room.

As soon as the two of them began dancing, four other couples joined them. The guys were all excited as they held their women close, because they knew that Luther could always be counted on to get their ladies in the mood.

Carter held Sandy tight in his arms and rocked her from side to side like a baby. Sandy loved the feel of Carter's rugged, masculine hands wrapped around her. She allowed him to hold and caress her while she wrapped one arm around his neck and held her drink with the other hand.

"Mmmmmm," Sandy moaned with a smile.

"Mmmmmm," Carter moaned in return.

"You are so beautiful tonight," Carter whispered. "Your perfume smells so good, and your body, it feels so soft." His hands roamed up and down Sandy's back, finding their way to the behind that Carter so admired. Carter rolled his hand around Sandy's behind and pressed her warm body against his.

Sandy moaned even more as her body gave in to Carter's advances. She threw her neck back and took a swig of her drink. She forgot how much fun she thought she had when she used to drink, how it made her feel so sexy and so alive. She liked the way Carter's body felt against hers.

As Sandy finished her drink, some of it dribbled off the side of her mouth. Carter licked it off and then kissed her, softly at first, then wildly as Luther continued to sing.

Sandy forgot she was out in public; she felt like she and Carter were the only two people in the world.

The two were kissing recklessly when Sandy noticed that Carter was moving her toward the steps. She laughed as she noticed jealous stares glaring at her from the two females she had talked to earlier. She was so caught up in the moment that she helped Carter lead her upstairs as they kissed like they were ready to tear each other apart.

In the upstairs hallway, he flung his bedroom door open like a madman.

Carter was all over Sandy like she was water and he was

a man who had been away in a desert for years. He didn't even make it to the bed; he pressed Sandy against the desk and pulled off the straps of her dress, kissing her neck and shoulders wildly.

After he failed to unsnap Sandra's bra, Carter pulled her bra straps down and let the bra remain wrapped around her waist. Sandy moaned with pleasure as he lifted her dress.

She was so tipsy and horny. She could tell this man knew what he was doing; he knew how to make a woman feel good.

Carter plopped Sandy on top of the desk and began to undo his pants.

In the midst of her high, Sandy suddenly felt confused. *What am I doing?* She was dazed, almost hypnotized. She kept kissing Carter passionately, but shifted her body so that he didn't have easy access.

"No, baby . . . " Sandy whispered in his ear. Carter kept kissing her hungrily.

"Noooo . . . " Sandy moaned a little louder this time.

Carter wasn't buying it. His body pushed Sandy's body farther back on the desk. "C'mon now," he begged. "You know you want it." Carter whispered in Sandy's ear while nibbling on the tip of it. "It wants you, too."

Sandy somehow felt like she had heard Carter's last line before. She couldn't exactly remember, at first, but then it dawned on her that those were the exact words that Mark said to her when he tried to have sex with her a few days ago.

"No!" Sandy screamed in Carter's ear and startled him. She used the little strength she had to push Carter's football-like frame away from her.

Astonished and now angry, Carter jumped on top of her, pinning her to the desk. "C'mon now, Sandy, don't gimme that!" Carter growled as he kissed her neck. "You think a brotha like me would invest all his free time and money in someone like you for nothing?"

Trickles of tears streamed down Sandy's face. What

happened to the kind, sweet man she met in the store the other day? She felt like she was in the middle of a nightmare.

"I see how you look at me all the time," Carter continued, "with those short, tight dresses you wear, just screaming my name." Carter was about to force himself inside her when Sandy kicked Carter in the stomach with her three-inch heeled sandals.

"I said no!" Carter flew three feet this time and tripped and fell backward.

Shaking, Sandy pulled up her bra and dress straps as Carter glared at her from the floor near the bed. The man she thought would one day be her lifelong partner looked at her like he was Satan himself.

Afraid and half-dressed, Sandy headed for the door.

Before she could make it, Carter bolted up and slapped her so hard that she fell against the side of the desk. With a loud thud, she was sprawled out on the floor, unconscious; trickles of blood oozed from her temple.

Carter savagely pounced on top of Sandy and raised his hand high to smack the living daylights out of her, but suddenly the bedroom door flew open and someone yanked him away.

A short man punched Carter in the face until blood shot out of his mouth. David punched Carter so many times that Carter's pretty-boy chocolate face turned black and blue.

Liz rushed to the telephone on the nightstand and dialed 911. Michelle rushed to Sandy's side and held her, crying with fear. Sandy's eyes were half closed. Michelle followed the trail of blood and noticed a huge bump on her head. Michelle took off her suit jacket and wrapped Sandy in it while rocking her.

"Oh God, no!" Michelle yelled.

David left Carter practically unconscious and joined Liz at the desk. As she slammed down the phone, a short, loud-mouthed figure rushed inside the room to see what was happening.

"What's going on in here?" Bill demanded as he saw Michelle rocking Sandy, and his best friend half-naked, beaten, and bloody in the corner by the bed. "Carter? What ya'll do to him?"

"What did we do to him? More like what did he do to her?" Liz retorted and pointed to Sandy. "I just called the police, so I suggest you get out of here, unless you want to go to jail with your friend over there." Liz had seen enough evidence downstairs to know people were doing drugs downstairs.

"The police?" Bill yelled. "I gotta get out of here!" He ran downstairs and announced to everyone that the police were on their way.

Within minutes, everyone from the party gathered all of their belongings and rushed to leave the house, including Bill.

Chapter 32

Waiting

THE EMS TRUCK CAME MOMENTS LATER AND
hauled Sandy out on a stretcher. Michelle, crying silently,
climbed into the ambulance with Sandy.

Neighbors in the upscale neighborhood came out of
their homes to see what all the ruckus was about. Three
policemen escorted Carter Maxwell in handcuffs to a police
car. Two other policemen rushed inside to search the
house. The prominent black lawyer, who was on the rise as
a possible mover and shaker for the city of Detroit, was now
beaten up, bruised, and going to jail.

As Michelle sat beside Sandy, her cell phone vibrated
on her hip. "Oh shoot," Michelle thought, embarrassed, "I

forgot to turn this thing off." Who could be calling at 2 a.m. anyway? The caller ID had Sandy's number on it.

"Madear!" Michelle exclaimed. She dreaded having to tell Sandy's grandmother what had happened to her grandbaby.

"Liz, call Madear for me!" Michelle said to Liz who was standing outside as the EMS truck lowered. Liz nodded.

Liz proceeded to call Sandy's grandmother on her cell. "Lord, I hope she doesn't have a heart attack."

Madear answered after the first ring. "Hello."

"Madear?"

"Yes, who is this?"

"This is Liz, Sandy's friend."

"Where is Sandy?"

"She-she's-on her way somewhere."

"Where? She betta be on her way home. Her little butt got me up worrying all night for her; I can't sleep."

"She's on her way to the hospital."

"To the hospital? What do you mean? What happened?"

Ever since Michelle had called and asked for Carter's number, Madear had a funny feeling that something was wrong. Madear knew that there was something sneaky looking about that man just by the way he came in their house, showing off his expensive suit and his expensive car.

"What did he do to my baby?" Madear yelled.

Liz was surprised at Madear's keen insight. Then again, grandmothers always seem to know when something's wrong. "Madear, I'm going to send someone to pick you up, so you can go see Sandy."

Madear dropped the phone, clasped her hands together and screamed, "Dear God in heaven, No! What did he do to my baby?"

Liz could hear Madear screaming in the background and felt two tears stream from her eyes. Instead of giving in to her emotions, Liz wiped her tears, hung up the phone, and looked around for David.

"Where is he when you need him?" The EMS truck pulled off, blasting its siren. She hadn't seen David since he was inside the house. Liz noticed that there were still two police cars at the scene, even after the one drove off with Carter inside.

Liz rushed back in the house to find two police officers standing over David, questioning him while he sat helpless in a chair.

"I'm telling you the truth, officers, I didn't even know who Carter Maxwell was until tonight." David said. "When I came over and went inside the room, I just saw Carter on top of Sandy, about to attack her, so I grabbed him and started fighting him so that he wouldn't do any more damage. He probably raped her, for God's sake!"

"He's telling the truth, officers," Liz chimed in. "David didn't act alone. He, Michelle, and I all came to this house looking for our friend, Sandy. Someone told us that they had seen her go upstairs with Carter. We found Carter on top of Sandy. David just grabbed Carter to get him off of her. My friend Michelle went to console Sandy, and I-I'm the one who called the police."

David was relieved to see Liz come to his rescue. He was determined not to even give the policemen Michelle and Liz's names if it meant that they might be called in for questioning. David couldn't believe this was happening to him.

"You're the one who called the police?" the female officer asked.

"Yes. My name is Elizabeth Coleman." The two officers looked at each other. "I don't mean to be rude," Liz continued, " but my friend is now in an EMS truck on the way to the hospital, and my best friend is riding with her, and I was wondering if David could pick up Sandy's grandmother and bring her to the hospital. She's really worried about her."

"Sandy's grandmother?" The policeman asked.

"Yes, Sandy was raised by her grandmother. Her parents died in a car accident when she was six."

"Oh."

"And I told Madear, I mean, Sandy's grandmother, that someone would pick her up and bring her to the hospital, since she can't see that well at night."

David looked up at the two officers to see if they would release him from being questioned.

The white male police officer finally gave in and said, "Oh, well in that case, you're free to go."

"Yes!" David screeched.

"Let me just get some basic information from you both, and I may have to call you and your other friend to the station to answer a few more questions, so we can get to the bottom of this," the male officer said.

"Sure, no problem." Liz and David gave the female officer general information that she jotted down on her note pad, and then the two of them made their way out of the house.

"Thank you," David said and kissed Liz on the cheek once they headed toward his Durango.

"Yuck." Liz said and grinned.

David opened the door to his ride for Liz and gave her a hand to help her inside. Once inside himself, David sped away so fast that Liz nearly got whiplash.

"Where to?"

"David, why are you driving so fast? You don't even know where you're going?" Liz retorted.

"So tell me, where are we going?"

Still disturbed by David's speed, Liz stated, "She lives on the east side. Just go south on the Lodge freeway, and I'll tell you where to come up."

Liz wished she had driven to the hospital by herself, but then David might have scared Madear with his driving. She buckled her seatbelt as David got on the freeway and increased his speed to 90 mph.

"If we get a ticket, it would be all your fault and it would just waste more time," Liz warned.

David ignored her and turned the latest Fred Hammond CD up real loud.

"And don't think you're going to be driving this fast with

Madear in the car; she would probably have a heart attack!"

"You know what?" David finally spoke up. "I have about had it up to here with your little snide remarks. Do you ever say anything good about anyone to anybody?"

"Good? You're driving like a maniac!"

"Fine," David said as he slowed to 75 mph. He hated backseat drivers with bad attitudes.

Except for giving directions to Madear's house, Liz remained silent for the rest of the ride. When they pulled into the driveway, Madear immediately opened the door and came out with a duffle bag.

David placed the bag in the backseat and then opened the door to help Madear into the front while Liz moved to the back.

Madear sat silently as David drove. Finally, he broke the ice.

"Hi, uh, Madear. I'm David, Michelle and Sandy's friend."

"Pleasure to meet you, David," Madear said. "Now can somebody please tell me what happened to my baby?"

Liz scooted forward, placed her hand on Madear's left shoulder, and asked, "Are you ready for this?"

Madear swallowed, folded her hands in front of her, and replied, "Please, be straight with me."

"Madear, Sandy is about to be admitted to the hospital."

"What for?" Madear asked, expecting the worst.

"Well, Sandy went out with Carter tonight, and he-there is a possibility that he may have tried to-or maybe did-rape her."

"Rape? Oh, God, no!!" Madear screamed as her hands flew over her face and tears welled up in her eyes. "Oh no, not my baby! Not my baby!" She fumbled around in her big black purse.

Liz wasn't sure if she should tell Madear the rest. She didn't want the old lady to have a fit, but she took a deep breath and finished the story. "And somewhere along the line, when he was trying to do you-know-what to Sandy, she got a bump on her head."

"That little punk done attacked my baby!" Madear shouted as she popped two nerve pills into her mouth. "I should've known that man was up to no good! I should've known with him coming all up in my house, all 'high and mighty' looking. Oh, God. Oh, Lord, please place Your healing hands on my baby right now. Watch her! Protect her right now from all evil! Forgive her, Lord, if she missed it in any way."

Liz bowed her head but kept her hand on Madear's shoulder. Madear continued, "Keep her Lord, under the shadow of Your wings. Heal her Lord, heal her body, and heal her mind. May your angels surround her during this time. For she is the one that you have entrusted to my care." Madear's voice broke and she bawled like a little baby. "Forgive me, Lord, for not being there for her. Forgive me for not being there for my baby!"

"It's not your fault, Madear. It's going to be okay." Liz reassured her as she rubbed Madear's shoulder. "It may not be as bad as you think."

Liz sure hoped it wasn't.

———◆———

David walked briskly inside the emergency area of the hospital as Madear and Liz slowly trailed behind him. He questioned the nurse at the front desk and learned that Sandy had already been admitted to a room in the intensive care unit area.

"Room 189!" David whispered loudly to Madear and Liz. "She's in room 189, down the hall to the right, on the end here." David pointed.

"Only immediate family members can be allowed in rooms within ICU," the nurse at the desk stated.

Dejected, David and Liz looked at one another.

"What about a good friend?" Liz asked. The nurse

sympathetically shook her head and said, "No, sorry."
Disappointed, Liz and David headed toward the waiting
room and perked up once they saw Michelle there.

Inside the ICU, Madear slowly opened Sandy's hospital
room door, afraid of what she might see. Sandy had a
huge black and purple bruise on the side of her face and a
bump on her head the size of a golf ball. Sandy's eyes were
slightly opened, and she looked rather dazed and confused.
Madear, with her hand clutched to her mouth, walked
to Sandy's bed and reached for her hand. To Madear's
surprise, Sandy snatched her hand away quickly and looked
at Madear as if she had no idea who she was. Tears flowed
from Madear's eyes as she felt helpless. Her only grandchild
looked totally defeated and worn-out.

A nurse with a brown tablet entered the room and asked
Madear, "Are you her mother?"

"No," Madear said quietly, "her grandmother."

"Oh," the nurse said and placed the tablet in front of
Sandy's bed. "I'm sorry that you have to see your granddaughter this way. Don't worry; we'll take good care of her
here."

"Thank you."

"As a matter of fact, I'm going to ask that you allow me to
get Sandy ready for some tests."

"Tests?" Madear asked.

"Yes. The doctor has to test the severity of any damage
which may have been done to the brain."

"The brain?" Madear asked in shock.

"Yes, her head was hit really hard."

Madear gasped and clutched her mouth.

"I know it's devastating, but I'm going to ask that you
wait out in the lobby; the doctor will be out with you
shortly," assured the nurse.

It seemed to take forever as Michelle, Liz, David, and

Madear waited in the waiting room. All of the gloomy faces around them, including two people who were asleep, didn't help the atmosphere either. David soon got tired of reading boring magazines, so he hopped up and started pacing the floor.

"Why are you pacing like that?" Liz asked as she opened her small Bible in her lap. "You're making us all nervous."

"I'm sorry," David admitted, "It's just . . . I don't know."

"But he was wounded for our transgressions," Michelle read out loud from her own small Bible. "He was bruised for our iniquities, the chastisement of our peace was upon him; and with his stripes, we are healed. Isaiah 53:5." Trying to remain calm, Michelle looked up and assured David, "Everything is going to be fine."

"I know." David sat down. "I know," he repeated while rubbing his hands together.

"Ms. Moore?" A handsome black gentleman in a white coat walked in with a writing tablet. "May I speak with you for a moment?"

Madear reached for her purse and rose from her seat.

"May I be allowed to come with her?" Michelle asked the doctor.

"I want to give Ms. Moore Sandy's test results. Are you family?"

"Yeah, I guess. I mean, she's my sister in Christ."

"Well, I'm sorry; I can only disclose this information to family members of the patient."

"It's alright," Madear interrupted, "she is family to me." Madear grabbed Michelle by her arm. "C'mon, Michelle, I need you to help me listen to this stuff so I can understand what's going on." Michelle followed Madear. "I need her wit' me," Madear told the doctor, "so I'm giving her permission to come."

Inside a small office with blue walls, the doctor sat in a large chair as Madear and Michelle were seated in front of him.

The doctor began, "First, I want to give you the not-so-good news." Michelle and Madear looked worried.

"We've just completed a series of neuroradiological tests on Miss Moore. CAT scans, MRI-"

"And?" Michelle asked.

"And unfortunately, we did find the presence of intra cranial hematoma."

"Intra wha'?" Michelle asked.

"Some bleeding inside the brain." Madear shut her eyes.

"Intra cranial hematoma is common, though, in most head injuries. Her brain was damaged, but right now the tests are not indicating the severity of the damage, only the presence of blood."

"Bleeding in the brain?" Michelle repeated quietly with disbelief. "So what does this mean, doctor? Is she going to be mentally ill now or something?"

"No, not necessarily."

"Then what?"

"Well, we're going to have to keep her overnight for more testing, to see if we need to perform neurosurgery. In its mildest case, it could be determined that she has suffered from a slight concussion which can be treated with therapy, lots of rest, patience, and TLC."

"And the worst case?" Michelle asked as a spokesperson for Madear, who was busy holding back tears and keeping herself from having a nervous breakdown.

"In the worst case, she could suffer heavy bleeding in the brain overnight, which could cause a blood clot to crowd the brain against the skull and she could-"

"What, she could what?" Michelle asked in anticipation.

"She could die."

"Oh, God!" Michelle gasped and grabbed Madear as they both cried. Madear closed her eyes and rocked in her chair.

"However, that is only the *worst* case scenario. The good news is she has been in and out of consciousness since she's been here, which is definitely a good sign. Once more tests are done, I am sure tomorrow we will have the proper diagnosis."

"How is she doing now?" Michelle whispered.

"She's resting," the doctor reassured them. "She's still a little shaken up, but rest is good for her right now. The nurses will be checking on her periodically throughout the night. We are doing everything possible to make sure Sandy pulls through. Don't give up; there is still hope."

"And hope maketh not ashamed," Michelle whispered as she continued to hold Madear.

David and Liz didn't know what to think when they saw Michelle and Madear return with such fearful looks on their faces.

"Well?" Liz asked.

"They have to keep her overnight, for more tests," Michelle said and took a seat. "You guys have been great by being here, and I really appreciate it, but you can go home now. I know you have to work in the morning. I'll stay here with Madear."

"You sure?" Liz asked, concerned.

"I'm positive. We'll be alright. I'll call you in the morning and let you know how everything turns out. Just pray."

Liz gave Michelle a huge hug. She also hugged Madear, who didn't return the embrace; she just sat there stiff as a board with a blank look on her face.

"You sure now, cause I can stay all night," David insisted. "I really don't want to just leave you here like this."

Michelle forced a slight smile. She knew David really cared. "I"ll be alright," she said with a nudge. "I'll be fine."

"Well, can we pray now together, before we go?" Liz asked.

"Sure," Michelle said. They all formed a circle and prayed, though Madear remained seated.

"David," Michelle said. Shocked, David realized she wanted him to lead the prayer.

"Dear Father God in Heaven, we come together right now giving You all Praise and Glory. Lord, You said that where two or three are gathered together in Your Name, that You are in the midst of them. So we thank You and praise You right now that You are in the midst of this situation. We thank You that your Healing Hands are at work right now, that Your ministering angels are comforting our Sandra Moore, and we thank You that your Word says that by the stripes of Jesus she is already healed. We thank You that when Jesus died on the cross, that He died not only for our sins, but for sickness as well." David's voice shook with emotion.

"Lord, You said in Your Word that the prayer of faith will save the sick, and that You, Lord, will raise him up. So we join our faith together, right now, in the Name of Jesus, believing Your Word to be true. Jesus is the same yesterday, today, and forever. So, if You were a Healer yesterday, then You are a Healer today. We will not believe in a bad report from any doctor; we will only believe in the report of the Lord. Oh yes, Lord, we are believing for a miracle on today. What Satan meant for evil, God will turn it for good. We thank You, and we praise You that you are a God of a turn-a-round, and that You can and will turn things around right now in the Name of Jesus, and by Your precious blood, Amen."

"Amen" the ladies repeated, included Madear, whose face was now drenched with even more tears.

Everyone in the waiting room looked in awe at the young man who just prayed with such fervor and conviction. David's prayer instilled a sense of hope for everyone. "Thank you," Madear said as her brown wrinkled hands grabbed David's hand and looked at him with glassy eyes. "Thank you."

Forty-five minutes went by as Michelle and Madear still

sat patiently in the waiting room. Tired from reading the small print on her Bible, Michelle closed her eyes as she sat in her chair. Eventually, someone sat down next to her and nudged her shoulder. Michelle opened her eyes to see what rude person would interrupt her attempted snooze.

"David!" Michelle shouted, loud enough for the person that was sleeping across from her to pop up and look around.

"David," Michelle repeated, quieter this time. "What are you doing here? I thought you went home."

"I know. I was going to go home, at first. I dropped Liz off, then I decided to come back." "You didn't have to do that." Michelle said.

"I know. I just didn't want to leave you two ladies down here so late by yourselves." David looked over at Madear, whose eyes were closed as she sat upright in her chair.

"Don't you have to work tomorrow?" Michelle asked.

"Aw, I'll call in. You know I work at the plant. I can call in whenever I want. Besides, this is an emergency. If they got something to say about it, they can talk to my Union rep!" David said with a grin.

Michelle returned the smile. She couldn't believe that he would come all the way back to the hospital to wait with her and Madear. He barely knew Sandy.

"David, this is really, really, sweet of you, but I didn't expect you to come all the way back. You *really* didn't have to do this."

"I wanted to. I wanted to be here." He looked intensely into Michelle's eyes.

Michelle had never seen this look before. She was used to his playful tone and boyish gestures.

"So," Michelle attempted to change to a lighter tone, "what in the world came over you when you threw Carter off of Sandy and started beating the crap out of him?"

David laughed out loud. "I don't know, man. It's like, this strength came on me out of no where! I felt like I was David from the Bible and Carter was Goliath."

Michelle smiled. She was certainly glad that David returned to the hospital to wait with her and Madear. She would never have believed, in her wildest dreams, that he would do such a thing. The person she always considered as simply her brother in Christ was starting to become someone very special and dear to her heart. Even though he wasn't Michelle's type, per sé, she was beginning to see past his exterior and was growing fond of the man of God within. Only, Michelle would never tell David that; she didn't want to ruin their friendship.

Michelle briefly returned David's glance and then looked back down in her lap.

"So, any word yet?" David asked as he sat back in his chair.

"No word yet. I believe they're still testing and letting her rest and stuff."

"They're not letting you all go in there yet?"

"No, not yet," Michelle said, with her eyes still looking down. She almost wished David hadn't come back. He was beginning to make her feel uneasy because she was starting to like him. David wasn't the most handsome brotha out there, but he definitely had a heart of gold.

They were silent for a few minutes. Michelle closed her eyes and retreated to resting.

"And how are you doing?" a comforting voice asked.

Michelle opened her eyes and saw David looking at her with his face inches away from hers.

"Huh?"

"How are you doing, through all of this?" David repeated, staring intensely.

"I'm okay, I guess." Michelle felt a bit nervous. This all seemed too unreal.

"No," David probed and lifted Michelle's chin ever so lightly with his finger. "How are you *really* doing?"

"Really doing? Well, really-I'm okay. I'm fine," Michelle attempted to convince herself.

"C'mon Michelle, you don't have to put on any front

with me. I've known you for, how long, two years now? And in the two years I've known you, I can tell that you are an honest, caring, beautiful, virtuous woman of God."

Michelle smiled.

"So c'mon," David continued, "you can be real with me."

Michelle finally gave in and said, "Since you put it that way, you really want to know the good and honest truth?"

"Yes, the good and honest truth."

Michelle looked at David with a slight pause, as if she was testing whether or not he could be trusted with her deepest thoughts and secret fears. She had been hiding her fears, trying to remain strong for everyone else. She didn't want anyone to know that she could be weak.

With a deep breath and glassy eyes, Michelle finally admitted, "I'm scared, David." Michelle's tears flowed uncontrollably down her brown face and dripped onto her chest. "I'm scared." By simply admitting her true feelings, Michelle felt like a huge weight was lifted off her shoulders.

David reached over and cradled Michelle in his arms; she rested her head on his shoulder.

"It'll be alright, Michelle," David said and rocked Michelle ever so slowly, like a mother would cradle a newborn baby. "Everything is going to be fine."

Michelle closed her eyes.

Chapter 33

If It's Meant to Be . . .

LIZ DIDN'T WANT TO WORK FRIDAY, BUT
it was too late to call in. Besides, she didn't want to
inconvenience the staff who would have to find a substitute
teacher at the last minute. Since she had spent Thursday
night praying for Sandy instead of sleeping, the Lord would
have to give her enough strength to deal with the energetic
second graders at the academy.

After Liz led the students through their normal morning
exercises, which included singing praise and worship songs,
reciting the pledge of allegiance, and reading the scripture
for the day, Liz assigned the students to work in groups on
a picture project. She was relieved as she walked toward her

desk to rest for a minute.

Liz was about to sit down until she noticed a dozen yellow roses neatly wrapped in green paper lying across her chair. *Who could have sent those?* She looked around and saw little Matthew playing nicely with the little boy and girl beside him. *Some people just never give up.*

Liz must admit, she was flattered. The card read, "Beautiful roses for a virtuous woman. Much Love in Christ, Minister Matthew Long." *Minister?*

"Hmm," Liz said, and then was startled as she looked up and saw Matthew Jr. standing right in front of her.

"Miss Coleman, do you like the flowers?"

"I do like the flowers. Are they from you?"

"No, they're from my daddy."

"Your daddy?" Liz pretended to be shocked.

"Yup, but I picked them out though," Matthew said with a wide grin.

"You did?" Liz exclaimed. "Well, you come here and give me a big hug!"

Little Matthew skipped around the desk and gave his teacher a hug.

"Matthew, is your daddy a pastor?" Liz asked.

"No, my daddy's not a pastor, but he helps out a lot at the church, though."

"He does? What church do you attend?" Liz couldn't believe she was interrogating the little boy, but she was curious.

"We go to Faith in Christ Church downtown. Daddy's a minstra there. I think that's what they call him." Little Matthew scratched his head.

"Oh, a minister?"

"Yeah. A min-is-ter!"

"Are you proud that your daddy's a minister?"

"I sure am, and he's a good one, too!"

"Oh really, now what makes a good minister?"

"My daddy just like Jesus!" Matthew proclaimed.

Liz was impressed. Most little kids don't lie about how

their parents behave when no one else is looking.

And here Liz was thinking she had this man all figured out. She assumed he was just like all the other losers she ever went out with, but instead he was a man of God with a ministry call on his life.

"You tell your daddy I said thank you very much for the flowers, okay?"

"I will," Matthew sang as he skipped back to his desk with his two classmates.

Liz felt so small.

She didn't even let the man give her his phone number, so there was no way she could call to thank him for the flowers. Besides, how would it look now if she just all of a sudden became interested because she found out he was a minister? Liz figured she had too much stuff going on in her own life now, anyway. Her mother was pregnant at forty-five, and now one of her friends was in the hospital with a possible brain injury.

As Liz thought about all of the things going on in her own life, she concluded that now wouldn't even be a good time to pursue any type of relationship.

"I'm okay," Liz convinced herself. "Besides, if it was meant to be, it'll be." Even though one day she would like to settle down and have kids of her own. "If not . . . oh, well." Liz set her roses aside on her desk.

"Okay, class, let's see whatcha got!" Liz proclaimed to her second graders.

Chapter 34

Not Again

I WOKE UP IN THE HOSPITAL WAITING ROOM, glanced at my watch, and saw that it was 5 a.m. Half the people who had been waiting with us were now gone and replaced with new faces.

Madear was still asleep in her chair, but I also noticed that the chair next to me, where David had sat, was empty.

He must have left.

Or maybe he never came back in the first place, and it was all some sort of a dream.

Just then David entered the waiting room with bags of food and hot drinks in trays.

"Good morning," David sang. "Good to see you finally managed to wake up." He placed the bags and drinks on the table in front of me and began to sort out everything.

David had bought doughnuts and hot chocolate for the three of us.

I stared at him with adoration as he sorted everything out so neatly. He even remembered to bring extra napkins.

I cracked a smile. "You are so sweet, David."

"I figured you guys would be hungry," he said as he looked over and saw that Madear was still asleep. He then sat in the chair next to me as I munched on a glazed doughnut.

"Michelle?" he asked.

"Hmmmm?" I responded, unable to talk with a mouthful of food.

"You know how I told you, once I dropped Liz off at home, that I had every intention of going home myself, but was led to come back?"

"Mmmm hmmmm." I looked up at him with bright eyes.

"Well, I was led to come back . . . for you."

What?

"Michelle, while I was visiting my dad in Boston last week, he asked me if I was seeing anyone, and I said no. Then he asked me why, and I didn't know the answer." David took a deep breath. "I didn't know the answer, because I *was* interested in someone, but I just didn't know how to tell her because I was afraid of her response."

David rubbed his hands together and looked down at his lap. "Then my father went on to say, 'life is short, son, and if you see something you want, you just have to go for it. You have to be a man and take the risk." David leaned his body closer to me, grabbed my hand, looked deep into my eyes, and said, "It's time for me to be a man, Michelle."

"Ms. Moore!" The doctor announced as he entered the waiting area and looked around for Madear or me.

Startled, I hopped out of my seat and left David leaning over the chair.

"Good morning," the doctor greeted me as I found my

way over to him with a confused look on my face.

"Good morning," I responded.

"Can you and Ms. Moore follow me to my office?"

"Sure," I said and rushed to wake Madear. David sat back in his chair and grabbed a powdered doughnut.

"I have some good news," the doctor began inside his office.

"Is she going to be okay?" I asked.

"She is going to be just fine."

"Praise God!" I shouted. Madear cracked a smile.

"After further testing, including certain behavioral testing and more neurological tests that Miss Moore underwent earlier this morning, it has been determined that she has only suffered a slight concussion."

"A concussion? What is that?" I had heard of football players getting concussions, but I never quite knew what it was. It sounded pretty serious.

"A concussion is a closed head injury which is a result of slight bleeding in the brain. The hemorrhaging miraculously did eventually stop, which means she does not have to undergo any type of brain surgery."

"Thank you, Jesus!" Madear belted with joy and clapped her hands together.

"She did exceptionally well on the behavioral and cognitive tests. Sandy was a real trooper and demonstrated the ability to move her limbs and eyes, and she was even able to carry on conversations with the nurse."

"Look at God!" I shouted.

"However, I do want to advise you, there may be a long road ahead."

"What do you mean? I thought you said she was doing fine?" I asked.

"She is . . . right now. However, in the very early stages of a closed head injury, it is impossible to predict the road ahead. You just have to keep having faith."

Madear looked confused. I was a bit confused myself. "Can you elaborate on that, please?"

"You see, recovering from a head injury is like running a marathon. A marathon is 26 miles long, and you can't just sprint 26 miles. You have to pace yourself for the long race ahead." Madear and I looked at each other. He added, "Just make sure to keep a positive attitude along the way, for Sandy's sake."

"Oh, we will doctor," I assured him. "So can we see her now?" We had been waiting long enough.

"Yes, she's in a room in our step-down unit now so you are free to see her. No more than two visitors at a time," the doctor said. "We also would like to keep her here for another 24 hours for close observation."

The doctor rose from his seat and opened his office door for us. "Just remember that she has just gone through a lot, and she may seem a bit confused. She may not remember right off hand who you are. Don't be alarmed; it's normal recovery for one getting over a closed head injury. With time, it will get better. The brain will spontaneously heal itself. Any additional treatment can also be accomplished through therapy, if necessary."

"Thanks doctor," I said with a slight smile.

"You're welcome." I couldn't fathom the idea of Sandy not recognizing me. Forget what that doctor just said, she would recognize me. Everything was going to work out just fine and Sandy would be able to just put all this behind her.

Madear and I slowly entered Sandy's room. I had stopped in the hospital gift shop earlier to pick up a half dozen pink roses. I knew Sandy would love them.

As soon as Sandy saw the roses, as I predicted, her face lit up like a kid looking at a fully lit Christmas tree.

"For me?" Sandy gasped as I placed the roses in her lap.

"Yes, for you," I said.

"Thank you so much!" Sandy beamed.

"You're so welcome," I said.

Sandy stared at the roses in awe, without looking up or acknowledging me or anyone else in the room. I wanted to make sure what the doctor said about her did not prove to be true. I wanted to make sure Sandy knew who I was and that I was right concerning my faith confession about Sandy's instantaneous recovery.

"Do you know who they're from?" I asked in an attempt to divert Sandy's attention from the roses. It was as if she was lost in them.

Sandy looked up at me as if I interrupted her moment.

"No, who are they from?" Sandy looked puzzled and searched around the room.

"Me!" I exclaimed. *Don't you know who I am?*

"Oh, you! Thanks. That was very thoughtful of you." Sandy continued to stare at the roses.

Madear and I exchanged glances. Maybe the doctor was right. Maybe the brain injury totally jolted her memory. Maybe she doesn't even remember that I am one of her closest friends.

I hesitated and then asked, "Do you know who I am, Sandy?"

"Sure, I do, you're . . . " Sandy said as she placed her finger on her chin and began to ponder.

The room fell silent.

I looked at Sandy and then at Madear in desperation. The Lord had placed Sandy in my life so I could help her grow spiritually, but now she didn't remember me. Once again, in response to God's unction to keep a loved one from harm's way, I moved too slowly and missed it.

Once again, I was too late.

If only we had found Sandy before she received the terrible blow to her head from Carter, then maybe she wouldn't be in the predicament she was in now.

I couldn't take any more of the agony of knowing that I missed it yet again, as the young woman in front of me who was once so vibrant now looked aimlessly around the room. I rushed toward the door in tears.

"Mickey!" Sandy shouted. I stopped in my tracks and turned toward my friend who sat up in the hospital bed.

"Mickey, where are you going?"

I raced to Sandy's bedside and gave her a hug and kiss on the cheek.

"I always knew you were a fighter." I said with tears streaming down my face. "I always knew you had it in you."

"What do you mean?" Sandy looked perplexed. I wondered if Sandy was even aware of all she had just gone through.

Madear walked up to Sandy and cupped Sandy's face with both of her wrinkled hands and stared intensely at her. Madear was so glad to see her grandbaby in front of her, a survivor. Unlike Sandy's parents, who failed to survive the horrendous car accident, this child made it.

"Momma?" Sandy asked. Madear shed a tear and gave Sandy a huge kiss on the cheek. "Momma?" she asked again.

"No baby," Madear said this time. "It's Madear."

Sandy reached her arms out and embraced her grandmother who raised her for the past seventeen years.

Chapter 35

A New Beginning?

LIZ WOKE UP SATURDAY MORNING AT 8 A.M. with a new attitude and a renewed faith in God. She had spent most of last night shouting and praising God after Michelle called to say that Sandy had recovered from the head injury and was soon on her way home.

Ms. Coleman, as little as she could move while pregnant, praised God right along with Liz. Sandy's recovery was now a testimony to all of God's Faithfulness.

Liz had purposed in her heart last night that she would wake up early Saturday morning, pray, and then take herself to the gym. Even though her mother had stopped picking on her about her weight, Liz had decided to do something about it herself, instead of just talking about it.

———————◆———————

Inside the gym, Liz looked around at all the different equipment. Bikes, treadmills, cruncher-looking-type things—Liz didn't know where to start.

Everyone else seemed to know which machines to use and how to use them. There were the muscular men with the tank tops and huge belts. Then there were the little women wearing leotards and biking shorts.

Sometimes Liz wondered if gyms were for overweight people; it seemed like whenever she went, she would just see people who were already in shape. Liz decided to hop on a stair-stepper treadmill and walk for a good hour. She made sure to bring her thermos of cold water and her headphones so she could listen to her Hezekiah Walker CD as she stepped.

Liz felt sweat forming on her neck after only twenty-five minutes. She made sure to hold onto the poles beside her, which moved back and forth, so she could get a good workout on her arms as well. She was getting so tired, though, already, that she wondered if she could make it for the full hour. She didn't want to seem like a treadmill hog either, as she looked around and saw that all the other ones were also taken.

"Maybe I'll just do forty-five minutes on this thing," Liz concluded.

Liz got off the treadmill after forty-five minutes and looked around to see what she would try next. She was determined to work more on her arms, which had always been too flabby for her to feel comfortable wearing a strapless dress or even a sleeveless shirt.

She saw a machine that looked like she could sit down while lifting the weights on either side. The only thing, though, when she sat down, she had a hard time trying to position her arms correctly to get a good grip on the thing.

She didn't know how to maneuver it.

"Let me help you," a familiar male voice said.

The man placed the metal bar on both sides of the mechanism in a lowered position, so Liz wouldn't have to lift so much weight. He positioned the mechanism for her so her arms could be comfortable and well adjusted to her height.

Liz finally caught a glimpse of her savior; it was none other than Matthew Long, Sr.

"Mr. Long!" Liz exclaimed. "What a surprise to see you here."

Liz couldn't believe that out of all of the places to run into him again, she would see him here, in a gym, when she looked "tore up from the floor up" after forty-five minutes on the stair-stepper.

Her braids were in a sloppy ponytail, and she wore a gray jogging suit, which now showed a ton of sweat on her back and underneath her arms. Liz also didn't have any makeup on because she didn't expect to see anybody worth being concerned about in the gym.

"Oh, are you surprised to see me in the gym?" Mr. Long said and laughed.

"No, I didn't mean it like that . . . "

"I try and come here at least three times a week, to keep up my physique." Mr. Long said with a proud pat to his hard chest.

Liz couldn't help but notice that all he had on was a white tank top and navy blue shorts, showing off his muscles and track-star like legs.

"Did you get the flowers I sent you?" Matthew asked.

Liz had almost forgotten about those; she was so embarrassed about her appearance.

"You sent me those? I thought they were from your son." Liz said with a smile.

"Oh, is that what he told you?"

"No, I'm just kidding. I knew they were from you . . . thank you, they were beautiful."

"You're more than welcome." Mr. Long looked longingly into Liz's eyes.

"I didn't know that you were a minister."

"Miss Coleman, there are a lot of things about me that you don't know."

"Well, ex-cuse me," she responded with an attitude.

"You probably also didn't know that I received my law degree from Howard University, and that I enjoy scuba diving as a hobby."

"No, I didn't know that," Liz admitted.

"Well, there's more to know about me than that, Miss Coleman, but in order for that to happen, you would have to agree to go out with me, now wouldn't you?"

Liz couldn't believe this man was still trying to ask her out on a date, with her looking like she is looking now. She wondered if he needed glasses and just didn't wear them today or something.

"I'm flattered, Mr. Long, but right now I'm looking a total mess, and you're kinda catching me off guard here."

"How am I catching you off guard?" Mr. Long asked, "I think you look beautiful right now."

"You what?" She didn't mean to say what she was thinking out loud; it just came out of her mouth.

"I said." Mr. Long leaned in closer toward her. "I think you look beautiful right now."

"Oh, thanks," Liz said. She wasn't buying that.

"You do," Mr. Long continued. "From the first day that I met you at the school, you carried a certain radiance, a certain confidence that initially attracted me to you. And even now, as I stand before you, and here you are looking all cute with your jogging suit and ponytail . . ."

Liz had to crack a smile. This man was serious.

"And I still think you're as gorgeous as the first day I met you."

Liz was deeply flattered. No man has ever said anything as sweet as that to her. She never had a man tell her she was simply beautiful just the way she was.

Liz was speechless.

"So can I call you sometime, and maybe we can go out on a date?" Mr. Long said like a ninth grader asking a girl out for the first time.

Liz hadn't heard that word in a long time, "date." She had given up on men, and felt they had no place in her life right now. She didn't want to have to deal with all the drama, and besides, she had her own drama to deal with.

"I don't know, Mr. Long," Liz began.

"Please, call me Matthew. And you're right, Liz, you don't know, until you give it a try."

Does he mean give love a try, or give men a try? What was he getting at? Liz had to admit, the man was persistent. Maybe his running into her here at the gym was somewhat divine. She thought she would never see him again, at least not for a long time, after the way she turned him down at the school.

"Oh, alright."

Matthew quickly whipped out his cell phone to add Liz's number.

"It's 313-555-4521." *Getting picked up at the gym.* Liz had to laugh at herself. *Maybe it's a set up for a new beginning.*

"Got it," Matthew said with a boyish grin.

Liz looked up at Matthew Long and smiled in return.

Chapter 36

Finally

I WOKE UP SATURDAY MORNING, SHOWERED, threw on some blue jeans and a T-shirt, prayed, and rushed to the phone to call the Moore residence to see how Sandy was doing.

"Hello," answered Madear.

"Hi, Madear, this is Michelle."

"Well hello, Michelle, how are you?" She sounded chipper.

"I'm fine. How is Sandy?"

"Oh, she's doing fine. She's sleeping now, though. The doctor said she would be tired a lot, and that a lot of rest would be good for her."

"How did she do last night, through the night and all?"

"Oh, she did just fine. Slept like a baby. I got up and checked on her at least four or five times last night. She was sleeping so hard, I believe she was snoring."

"Praise God, I'm glad to hear that."

"Thanks for calling to check up on her, Michelle."

"Oh, it's the least I can do. Madear, you think it'll be alright if I stop by tonight, and maybe spend the night?"

"That's fine, Michelle."

"Thanks, I'll see you tonight then."

"Okay, baby. Bye, bye."

I was glad to hear that Sandy got a lot of rest last night. After all she's been through in the course of one week, she was in desperate need of relaxation. I figured by spending some quality time with her tonight, I could pinpoint whether or not she had healed not only physically but also emotionally from her traumatic relationship with Carter.

I walked to the kitchen, grabbed some bacon and eggs out of the frig, and was about to make breakfast when my intercom buzzer buzzed.

Who in the world could that be at 10 a.m.?

"Who is it?" I yelled.

"It's me." It sounded like . . . no, it couldn't be . . .

"Me, who?"

"Pierre."

"Will you leave me alone!"

"Michelle, please. I'll be brief. I promise."

I folded my arms and didn't respond.

"Michelle. Please let me inside."

I let him in the complex but refused to open my apartment door right away.

He knocked lightly and I slowly answered.

Pierre gave me a huge grin, stretched his arms out wide and sang, "Michelle!"

I shut the door in his face. I don't have time for games. I know that probably wasn't the most Christian-like thing to do, but Pierre was really starting to irk me. What was he trying to do anyway, calling and harassing me, and now just popping up at my place unannounced, knowing he's about to propose to Erika? Did he come here just to rub it in even more that he's about to get married and I'm not? Hopefully he got the hint and high-tailed his self right back down the hallway.

To my dismay, he knocked again.

Not today Lord, not today.

I opened the door again.

"Why did you slam the door in my face?" Pierre asked in an unusually calm manner.

"Why are you here?" I asked with an attitude.

"It's like that, now?" Pierre asked.

"It's like that." I coldly folded my arms.

"I needed to talk to you, if you must know," Pierre confessed.

"We already talked, remember?"

"No, we didn't."

What exactly is this brotha talking about now?

Finally, I stepped into the hallway with my cherry-red toenails and closed the door behind me.

"What is it, Pierre?"

C'mon, spit it out. Obviously something is on this man's mind.

"As I told you earlier this week, today, I had planned on proposing to," Pierre let out a huge sigh and said, "Erika Richardson."

"And?"

"Well, since that night we met at *Starbucks*, I couldn't stop thinking about . . . you."

"What are you trying to say, Pierre?" I asked with squinted eyes.

I was tired of his beating around the bush. If he had something to say, then why didn't he just say it, for goodness' sake?

"What I'm trying to say is . . . " Pierre paused and looked down at his feet. "What I really been trying to say all this time is . . . "

I had never seen Pierre look this nervous before. He was usually so suave, so confident.

"Spit it out!" I shouted with a laugh in an attempt to break the tension.

"I love you, Michelle."

I stopped laughing.

The words rolled off of his tongue like music to my ears. Until today I had never, ever, heard a man, besides my natural father and God, tell me that he loved me. I never knew what it felt like to be loved by any man. I used to wonder when Pierre and I were together for those six months, if he had ever loved me.

I just wished he had told me back then, and not now.

Then again, wait a minute. Maybe this is some sort of trap. Who does Pierre think he is, anyway? I need to just get my head out of the clouds, and stay focused on the matter at hand. I have to stay determined not to let my measly emotions get the best of me.

I thought Pierre was a good catch at the time, a great catch, but now he's no longer with me. He's with her; he's about to marry *her*. I am out of the picture. Pierre blew his chance with me when he walked out on me, period. Anything he has to say does not change the fact that he hurt me. And I hate getting my heart broken.

"Don't say that," I said to Pierre.

It never ceased to amaze me how some men use the word "love" so loosely. Though he sounded sincere, I didn't believe him. I didn't want to believe him.

"Why not? You told me to say what I had to say, and I said it. I love you, Michelle," Pierre repeated.

I wasn't buying it. I must admit, though, hearing him say those words did sound kinda nice.

Nope. I must not give in.

"But how could you say that after you walked out on me? And then stopped calling me ever since?"

Pierre looked down at his feet again.

Figures.

"And now you come here out of the blue talking about you love me? You don't love me, Pierre. You don't know what love is."

"You're right, Michelle. I don't know what love is," Pierre agreed. "At least I didn't know before, while I was with you. But now, since you've been out of my life, I know what it's like to think about someone else every waking hour of the day, wondering what she's doing or how she feels. I know what it's like to want to be with someone so bad, that you do stupid things like try and be with someone else who somehow reminds you of the one you truly want to be with, by the certain ways that she acts and talks, only to find out that she's not you."

Pierre grabbed my right hand. "I know what it's like to long to have that someone you lost back in your arms so bad, that you can't think straight, and you can't talk straight, and you feel like you're about to go crazy. I know what it's like to be compelled to pray for someone all the time, to pray for God's best for her life, even though she has no idea you're even praying for her. I know what it's like to go to bed every night, praying to God that maybe, somehow, the one you gave up because of your own foolish pride would find it in her heart to forgive you for all the mistakes you've made in the past, and how stupid you were to let her get away."

Looking at Pierre closely, I thought I saw his hazel eyes grow glassy.

"It may have taken a long time, Michelle, and it may even be too late," Pierre said and suddenly dropped down to one knee while still holding my hand. He reached into his pocket and pulled out a small gray ring box. He opened it and I was almost blinded by the 2-karat gold, princess-cut diamond ring that just "bling-blinged" right in my face.

"This engagement ring always had your name on it." Pierre showed me that the ring was engraved with the words, "Meant for Michelle."

"And I don't want to risk losing you again."

My heart raced 100 miles a minute. All of the previous accusations I placed on Pierre were so untrue. He must really love me. The ring was so huge and so shiny. What do I do now? I needed some time to think. I had always wanted to get married around this age. But was Pierre the one God had ordained me to be with? Had Pierre been "The One" all along?

"I choose you, Michelle," Pierre said, looking desperately into my eyes, still waiting for my response.

Finally, I was chosen.

Finally, I was face to face with a man who chose to love me, not because I was born into his family, and not because I was even a child of His, the way God loves me, but because he loved me for who I am. Out of every woman in the world, and even in spite of Erika, Pierre Dupree had chosen to spend the rest of his life with me.

Caught up in the moment, captivated by the ring that shone right in front of me, I forgot all about the one part of the equation that makes this whole scenario not so ideal.

Erika.

And then there's David. I gave him my cell number when I left the hospital. I'm sure he plans on using it any day now. My feelings for David were starting to grow, and now Pierre here was sending my emotions on yet another roller coaster ride.

In response to Pierre's proposal, the only thing that came out of my mouth was what I knew, in my heart of hearts, that I had to say.

With watering eyes and in a voice as soft as can be, I replied, "I'm sorry Pierre, but . . . I don't . . . choose . . . you." I stepped back inside my apartment and closed the door behind me. Tears streamed down my face as I waited to see if he would knock again.

He didn't.

I closed my eyes as what I just did finally hit me.

Though I truly cared for Pierre, and probably even loved him at some point, I just didn't feel he was the one that God wanted me to be with. Besides, he had too much control over my emotions, and one thing I hate to give up is control. He could go on and give the ring to Erika, and I could now go on with my life.

I made my way back to the kitchen and sighed in relief. I wiped away my tears and cracked two eggs in a bowl. I placed two bacon strips on the heated frying pan. "Well Lord, there goes that one." I placed two pieces of bread in the toaster. God, I hope I did the right thing.

"He did what?" Liz asked late Saturday afternoon as she sat on my living room couch.

I was preparing a tray of tea and cookies for the both of us.

"Girl, he proposed!" I repeated.

"You've got to be kidding?"

"No, I'm not. I kinda wish I was kidding, though." I nibbled one of the store-bought sugar cookies from the tray.

"I'm sure you let him know exactly what was on your mind!"

"I did, I guess. But, Liz, you should've heard the long speech he gave me, about how much he looooved me all along, and how he didn't realize that he really loved me until I was gone."

"They all say that," Liz said as she made herself more comfortable on the couch. "He wasn't too slow about going to get himself another girlfriend. And didn't he try to talk to Erika when he was still dating you?"

"Oh, yeah," I said. I had forgotten that part. There's nothing like a good best friend to bring things all into proper perspective for you. "I guess you're right."

"Don't worry girl, you did the right thing by telling him no."

"Did I tell you, he even had the words, 'Meant for

Michelle' engraved on the ring?"

"What?" Liz exclaimed. "You've got to be kidding."

"No, I'm not."

"These men are something else. They kick you to the curb, then they try and come back into your life just like nothing happened. Like they just didn't put a sistah through hell on earth by leaving her and then making her spend the rest of her days trying to figure out where *she* went wrong in the relationship."

"Amen to that," I said, sipping my orange tea.

"Enough of talking about him. What's been going on with you, Miss Lady?" I changed the subject. Liz and I hadn't talked one-on-one in a long time, and I really needed to catch up on what was happening in her life. "How's your mom?"

"Girl, it's a miracle! Total 180-degree turnaround! I told you she decided to keep the baby, right?"

"Oh yeah, praise God!" I shouted. "Do you know what it's going to be?"

"Well, the doctor says there's a good chance of it being a girl."

"Aw, another little mama to run the house," I teased.

Liz laughed and said, "And the best part about it, this morning, Mom even asked me about going to church with me in the morning!"

"Praise God, gimme some!" I said while throwing my hand in the air to give a high five.

Of course, Liz didn't leave me hanging; we slapped hands and then I grabbed another sugar cookie from the tray.

"Yeah, and I haven't found one liquor bottle in the frig, or laying around the house; she probably poured them all out."

"That's wonderful!"

"Yeah, God is good, ain't He?"

"All the time."

We both took another sip of tea.

"So," I continued, "what else is going on with you?

How's work?"

"Oh," Liz said while shifting her body more toward me, "funny you'd ask about work."

"What do you mean?" This sounded like it could be interesting.

"Well, there's a student in my class, I call him little Matthew, and he's as sweet as can be."

"Uh huh."

"And, his father, nice man, would always pick him up everyday, after he came home from work and all . . . "

"Uh huh."

"Well, his father kinda asked me out," Liz said with a sneaky smile.

"What?" I knew there was juice involved. I was growing more interested in this conversation by the minute.

"Twice."

"Twice? When did I miss all this?" Liz sure knew how to keep secrets from me. And I'm supposed to be her best friend.

"Well, Michelle, you know how I am."

"Oh yeah, I know."

"You know how I can be sometimes with men . . . "

"Don't I? You don't even give 'em a chance."

"Well, this time, it was different."

"What do you mean? You're going to go out with him?"

"Maybe."

I couldn't believe it. Liz Coleman, going out with a man? The father of one of her students? What was the world coming to?

"Who is this guy?" I asked, wondering who had finally opened the door to Liz's once pad-locked heart.

"Well, he works at the plant, but he serves at his church as a minister."

"A minister!" I shouted.

I should have known. The only way that Liz would agree to go out with any man was that he had to be heavily involved in the church, which is fair since she is called to be an evangelist. But I never thought she would agree to go out with any man who already had a child. She always talked about having a family of her own, with no baby-momma-drama.

"Yeah, and he was married before, which is where Matthew Jr. came in, but his wife passed away a year ago."

That explains it.

"A year ago, huh? That's not that long ago. He's ready to go out again already? What does his son think?"

"Well, his son just adores me, and I adore him, too." Liz beamed.

"Unbelievable."

Liz must really like this man. I couldn't wait to meet him.

"I'm little Matthew's favorite teacher," Liz said with a proud smile.

"So when are you guys going out?"

"I don't know. I just gave him my number when I saw him this morning at the gym."

"*You* went to the gym?"

Okay Lord, where is the real Elizabeth Coleman, and what did you do with her? Liz *never* goes to the gym. She thinks it's just a meat market.

I guess Sandy's accident made all of us change a lot of things.

"Yeah, how ironic, because just yesterday at school he had a dozen yellow roses sent to my class."

"Fo' real?" I was starting to like this guy already.

"Yeah, little Matthew had put them on my seat. The card read something like, 'flowers for a virtuous woman,' from Minister Long."

"Wow, talk about a divine hook up."

"I guess." Liz took another sip of her tea.

"Wait a minute now," I said. I had to break it down and make sure I had everything right. "You mean, you gave a man your phone number at the gym?"

"Right, but this just wasn't just any man, this was . . . "

". . . the father of one of your students," I completed her sentence, "who had been trying to holla at you but you kept turning him down."

"Yup," Liz said as a matter-of-fact with a grin.

"What's come over you, Liz?"

"What do you mean?"

"It just doesn't sound like you." I shook my head.

"I know it doesn't. But that's the best thing about it. The Lord has shown me, in prayer, that because of my past bad experiences with men, and because of seeing my mom get entangled with such losers every other week, that I had forgotten how to trust men."

"You're right about that," I said with a hint of sarcasm.

"But I believe that God brought Matthew into my life to give me an opportunity to trust again."

"Praise God! Soooo," I said with a sly grin, "do you like him?"

"I like him a lot," Liz admitted as she folded her legs on the couch. "I was attracted to him the minute he first stepped foot into my classroom. Oh, and the way he treats his son! It's such a turn-on."

A turn-on? I didn't think Liz could ever get turned-on.

"Well, good for you." I smiled and said, "He sounds like a good catch."

"I sure hope so."

Just then my cell phone rang. I looked on the caller ID and smiled. "Excuse me, girl; this is David."

"David?" Liz asked in shock.

I answered the phone, covered the receiver with my hand, and whispered to Liz, "That's another story."

Chapter 37

Single . . . Again

"SANDY, YOU DON'T HAVE TO DO ALL THAT.
I can fix it myself!" Michelle yelled from the plastic covered
couch in the living room as Sandy fooled around the
kitchen trying to fix something to drink for Michelle and Liz.

Liz and Michelle were surprised by how energetic and
full of life Sandy was behaving. Ever since they arrived at
Sandy's house Saturday evening to spend the night, she just
couldn't sit down.

"That's okay, I got it!" Sandy yelled back. "What would
you like, pink lemonade, or red pop?"

"I'll have the pink lemonade," Michelle responded.

"And you, Liz?" She was seated in the plastic covered
chair next to the couch.

"I'll just have water, thanks," Liz replied.

"Now, where did I put those cans of lemonade?" Sandy whispered. She thought she at least put one of them in the frig so it could get cold, but she finally found them on the floor beside the refrigerator.

"Here you go," Sandy said as she brought out pink lemonade and water.

Michelle asked, "Uh, can I have some ice?"

"Oh, yeah, ice. Sure. What was I thinking? I forgot to get the ice."

Sandy retreated to the kitchen with Liz's drink as well.

Liz and Michelle exchanged concerned looks.

Sandy finally came back, handed them their drinks, and plopped on the floor near Michelle.

"You don't want to sit on the couch?" Michelle asked.

"Oh, naw, I'm alright," Sandy said. "Thanks though."

"So, how ya been feeling?" Liz asked.

"Fine, real fine."

"That's good." Liz said.

"Been getting a lot of rest?" Michelle asked.

"Have I?" Sandy looked up to her friend. "Girl, that's all I been doing since I been out of the hospital. Rest, rest, rest."

"That's good," Liz said with a sip of her water.

"As a matter of fact, being up with you guys now is the first time I been out of the bed all day. I may just have you ladies up all night!"

Michelle and Liz laughed.

"That's real good then. The doctor said that a lot of rest would help you heal," Michelle said.

"What do you mean, help me heal?" Sandy said defensively. "I'm already healed, praise the Lord."

Michelle was happy to hear Sandy using her old phrases again.

"That doctor ain't got nuttin' on Miss Sandra A. Moore. I'm fully recovered!" Sandy proclaimed with a wave of her hand.

Michelle and Liz just looked at each other again and shook their heads.

"Okay. Well, I can see you're doing well physically, but how are you doing otherwise?" Michelle asked, wanting to get down to the nitty gritty. She had learned from Madear that Carter had not raped Sandy; he only tried to. But Michelle wondered how her friend was faring emotionally after all the drama.

"What do you mean?" Sandy asked.

"Well, Sandy, you been through a whole lot this past week," Michelle said.

"I know," Sandy admitted while looking down. "I made a lot of mistakes, that's all."

"Are you going to press charges against Carter?" Michelle asked.

"Press charges? I haven't even thought about that."

"He sexually assaulted you and tried to rape you, for goodness' sakes; you should press charges!" Liz stated loudly.

"I guess." Sandy said. She didn't sound convinced.

"Yeah, Sandy, don't let him get away with this. No telling what other innocent woman like you would be his next victim," Michelle said.

"I guess you're right," Sandy said.

"Look, no matter what you decide to do, just know that we're here for you, and that we'll be right by your side every step of the way," Michelle assured her friend.

"Thanks," Sandy said in a low tone.

"What's wrong, Sandy?" Michelle asked.

"Nothing. I guess."

"C'mon now, Sandy, you're not fooling me," Michelle said.

"I guess, it's just that I'm tired of getting myself in these situations. No matter how hard I try, I keep making these foolish mistakes with men," Sandy whined.

"We all make mistakes, Sandy," Liz stated.

"But why am I always the target for these stupid men to

run games on? I thought Carter was different. I mean, he said he was saved, and I really believed him! But he just turned out to be like all the rest!"

"Sandy, you don't mean that," Michelle said.

"Yes, I do!" Sandy shouted. "All men are just dogs, whether they in church or not!"

Liz could think of a few dogs herself.

"That's not true, Sandy," Michelle said, although before this morning she, too, was about to believe it herself.

"Look at Mike Turner, from our church. He goes with our youth minister, Minister Leslie Davis. He's definitely a man of God," Michelle said in defense of her Christian brothas.

"Man of God, huh? He tried to talk to me two weeks ago," Sandy said.

"You're kidding?" Liz said.

"No, I'm not. I saw him at the mall and he stopped me and asked me for my phone number. He must didn't know I went to Hype or something."

"Oh well, there goes that example," Liz said and laughed.

"But still, Sandy, that's just one example," Michelle said in defense.

"One example!" Sandy shouted. "Look at Carter! Look at Mark! And even look at the guy you went out with, Pierre. He dumped you out of nowhere 'cuz you wouldn't give him none, and he supposed to be *in* the church! Dogs, just dogs."

"Ruff!" Liz barked with a laugh.

Michelle looked at Liz with desperate eyes, begging her to be serious.

"Sandy, I know where you're coming from," Liz empathized. "I used to feel the same way about men." Michelle gave Liz an accusing glare. "Okay maybe I still do, a little," Liz concluded, "but I'm getting better. I'm just now realizing, through prayer, that a lot of my problem has to do with the fact that I've never even met my father. And since all I've heard growing up is my mother bad-mouth him, I started to believe that all men were like him. I hated-excuse the harsh tone-but I really hated the man for walking out on my mom and me, leaving us to fend for ourselves."

Sandy listened intently as Liz spoke.

"But Sandy, the Lord has shown me in my prayer closet that I have to forgive him. I *have* to, if I want to move on with my life. Because if I don't forgive him, I could never forgive any man."

"So you forgave him?" Sandy asked.

"I'm still working on it. I have forgiven him, by faith. The Word of God says in Mark 11:24 that if I can't forgive him, then God won't forgive me. And if God doesn't forgive me, then my prayers about anything won't even be heard or answered by God. So I have to forgive my father for myself, if for no other reason."

"But why would God be that way? Why would He make you forgive someone that didn't even give you a chance-that didn't even *try* to love you?" Sandy asked sincerely.

Liz shed a single tear and wiped it before Sandy even noticed. "Well, because God forgave us, while we weren't even trying to love Him. We weren't even thinking about Him when we were out there in the world, doing our own thing, and He loved and forgave us anyway. He sent His own Son down from heaven, His own flesh and blood, to die for us, while we acted like He wasn't there. So God figures if He can do that, which was the ultimate sacrifice, then we can forgive each other."

"Oh," Sandy said, "it's just not fair." Sandy said, pouting.

"Life's not always fair," Liz said, "but God is always fair and just."

"It just seems like men can get away with anything these days," Sandy said.

"Why do you say that?" Michelle asked.

"I mean, it seems like all these men want is sex. It's hard to forgive that! If these men supposed to be saved, then why are they pressuring us to have sex?" Sandy screamed in desperation. "It's like people all holy and sanctified in the church, but soon as they step outside, they get all fake and freaky acting."

"You're right, Sandy. A lot of men are just fake and just want sex," Michelle said, "but then there are some out there who aren't. I believe there are some men out there who sincerely do want to live holy, Christian lives and are willing to wait for the one that God has ordained them to be with, their one wife, before they have sex."

"Well, if there are, I sure hadn't met any of them," Sandy said with a sigh.

"Trust me, they're out there," Michelle said. "The thing is, Sandy, you have to be content where you are right now."

"Here we go again," Sandy said. "Here comes the 'wait on the Lord' speech."

"More than that," Michelle continued. "You have to be satisfied with yourself while you're single. You have to be happy with yourself while you're not dating. In the long run, it's not all about them anyway, Sandy; it's about you. You have to be fulfilled in your singleness, and know that you don't need a man right now to make you happy."

"I guess you're right. But, to be honest, Michelle, I think I do need a man to be happy. I mean, without a man in my life, I get kinda lonely."

"I know, Sandy," Michelle said, "and that's why we're here. We all can hang out, and sometimes we even hang out in groups, men and women."

"I know, but it's just not the same. I like it when a man tells me 'you're fine' or tells me that he loves me and that he wants to be with me all the time."

"But the thing is, Sandy," Liz chimed in, "God wants that very same relationship that you crave in a man. He wants for it to be the way you feel about Him."

Sandy looked at Liz strangely.

"God wants to be with you all the time. He wants you to seek His face every day and every night so He can tell you how fine and beautiful you are to Him. He wants to tell you He loves you over, and over, and over again. God wants to be your lover, your best friend, your everything," Liz concluded.

"I never looked at it like that," Sandy said.

"If we could only come to understand how much God truly loves us, then we would really be able to trust Him with our lives. He will give us the desires of our heart, but He wants us to desire Him, first," Michelle added.

Sandy looked down at her freshly painted pink toes.

"You know, Liz, and Michelle, you're both absolutely right," Sandy said with a renewed smile. "It's not even about them anymore, it's about me. I have to be happy with who I am and where I am right now, and I have to seek God, and trust in the Lord."

"You got it." Michelle raised her glass of lemonade to salute her friend.

Sandy got up from the floor and gave her friends a group hug. "I love you guys."

Chapter 38

Surprise!

Six Months Later

"HEY, MICKEY, DID I TELL YOU CARTER'S SUPPOSED to be getting married?" asked Sandy. She was sprawled out on her bed with her feet propped up on this brisk Sunday afternoon in October, talking to Michelle on her cell.

"No!" Michelle screeched.

"Yup. I heard he's getting married to some woman who bailed him out of jail."

"You're kidding."

"Nope. I think his bond posted for $5,000, or something like that, and she got him out and now they're getting married. I think next week."

"Who told you all this?" Michelle wondered how Sandy could find out just about anything about anybody.

"Madear told me."

"Madear?"

"Yup. Madear was at Nell's Beauty Salon, and Carter's best friend's sister-in-law's cousin Shaniqua, work there, and she told her."

Michelle burst out laughing and said, "Girl, you something else." Michelle shifted gears and asked, "Do you have a court date, yet?" After much coaxing from Madear, Michelle, and Liz, Sandy eventually had decided to press charges against Carter.

"They're supposed to let me know. But the crazy thing about it, it may be another four to six months before I can even appear in court."

"That's crazy. But, Amen, we all know you're going to win the case, and God's child will be vindicated!"

"Praise the Lord!" Sandy shouted.

"So how do you like the choir?" Michelle asked on a lighter note.

"Oh, it's going great! I made my first rehearsal last week. The best part about it is that I have favor with my new job as a manager in training at Braxton's Department Store. They let me leave at 6:00 on Tuesdays so I can make it to choir rehearsal on time!"

"Praise God! Look at God! Favor!"

"Yeah, praise the Lord, Mickey. I love it! We learn a new song every week, and I love the choir director, Minister Brown; she's the best."

"I'm glad you like it."

"Oh, and guess what."

"What?"

"Guess who's in the choir with me."

"Who?"

"Dustin!" Sandy retorted.

"Dustin?" Michelle couldn't recall any Dustin.

"The guy we met at that fancy restaurant downtown,

back in April? Ya'll ministered to him and he got saved?
Remember?"

"Oh, Dustin! Him? He's in the choir?"

"Yeah! I guess he took you and Liz up on your offer and
came to our church that Sunday. He's now a full-fledged
member, and I just saw him in the choir last Tuesday!"

"Get out of here!"

"Yup."

"Did you speak to him?"

"Not really. I was way over in the soprano section. But I
did catch a glimpse of him. I smiled at him and he liked to
fell out of his seat!"

Michelle cracked up. She was glad to hear her friend
back to her old chipper, over-confident self again.

"Alright now Sandy, now don't get all excited and worked
up about-"

"I know, I know," Sandy said, imitating her good friend
and spiritual guide, "be patient, trust in the Lord, let the
brotha mature spiritually, ya dah ya dah ya dah." Michelle
laughed.

"But fine is fine!" Sandy shouted.

Michelle's phone beeped indicating she had another call.

"Hold on, girl," Michelle said with a laugh. "Hello."

"Hey, Michelle!" Liz chimed.

"Hey Liz!" Michelle squealed. She hadn't heard from
her friend during the past week while her mom was in the
hospital recovering from the delivery.

"Mom and baby are home!" Liz exclaimed.

"They are? Praise God! Is everything okay?"

"Everything is wonderful! Mom gave birth to a super
healthy, 7 lb, 8 oz baby boy!"

"Baby boy? I thought she was having a girl?" Michelle
asked.

"I know. We all thought she was having a girl. I think
little Joshua even had the doctors fooled."

"A boy! Praise God. Finally, a man of the house!" They
both laughed. "When can I see him?"

"You can come see him now if you like."

"Are you sure?" Michelle asked. She figured that Ms. Coleman wanted to be alone with the baby and get some rest.

"Sure, I'm sure. Mom's been home a few days now, and besides, there's other people here visiting right now."

"Really?" Michelle asked. "Who?"

Liz looked over at the couch at the two heads, one big and one small, that were content watching the television. "Matthew and little Matthew are here," Liz said.

Michelle should have known Matthew Long and his son would be there. He and Liz had been dating consistently for the past six months. When Michelle met him six months ago, she knew instantly that Liz and Matt were made for each other.

"Hold on," Michelle said, remembering she had Sandy on the other line.

"Sandy?" Michelle said.

"Yeeees." Sandy sounded like she had been waiting for eternity.

"Liz's mom is home with the baby!"

"Fo' real? Praise the Lord!" Sandy shouted.

"Hold on," Michelle said and clicked back over to Liz.

"Can Sandy come, too?" Michelle asked Liz.

"You can bring whomever you want," Liz said, "as long as you all wash your hands before you hold the baby."

"Yes, momma Liz," Michelle said with a laugh. "Okay then, I'll see you in a bit."

"Bye," Liz said and Michelle clicked back over.

"Okay, Sandy?"

"Um hmm."

"We're about to go and see the baby, if you wanna come. I'm so excited!"

"I would love to come!"

"Oh, and she had a boy."

"A boy? I thought it was supposed to be a girl?" Sandy asked.

"I know."

Just then Michelle's line beeped again.

"Hotline," Sandy said.

"Who could this be now?" Michelle said.

"I know who it is," Sandy said with a sly grin.

Michelle clicked over. "Hello."

"Hey, sweetheart."

"David!" Michelle sang. Her anxiety calmed as she heard her man's voice. They had been dating for the past five months. Michelle was always ready to talk to him.

"How are ya, babe?" David asked.

"I'm wonderful!"

"What's up with all the excitement?"

"Liz's mom is now home the baby!"

"Really?"

"Yup, she's been home a few days now."

"That is something to be excited about."

"Hey, Sandy and I were about to go and visit the baby."

"This soon?" David asked.

"Liz said it was okay. Besides, she already got people over there already anyway," Michelle said, referring to Matthew and his son. "Do you think you can scoop up me and Sandy so we can all ride over there together?"

"Sure," David said. Any excuse to be with his lady.

"Great. Hold on a minute." Michelle clicked over to the other line.

"Sandy?"

"Um hmmm."

"This is David on the other line."

"You're kidding?" Sandy said with a laugh.

"He's going to pick us up."

"Sweet."

"So be ready in about a half hour." Knowing how Sandy would spend extra time in the mirror getting prim and prissy, Michelle added, "I'm serious, Sandy."

"Okay, okay. I heard you the first time. I'll be ready."

"Okay."

"Tootles." Sandy said and hung up.

Michelle clicked back over to her boo.

"Okay," Michelle said. "Oh, and thanks for agreeing to pick us up, sweetheart."

"No problem."

"I told Sandy to be ready in a half hour."

"Sounds good to me."

"Oh, and Ms. Coleman had a boy."

"A boy? I thought she was having a girl?"

"I know."

Chapter 39

God's Greatest Gift

"SURPRISE!" DAVID, SANDY, AND I SANG AS WE entered the Coleman residence. David carried large bags of toys and other items for the baby, I carried several balloons that read "Congrats!" and "Way to go!" and Sandy carried in a half sheet cake decorated with blue and green icing that read, "Welcome, Baby Joshua."

Ms. Coleman had insisted on not having an official baby shower because she felt she was "too old for such a fuss," so I figured a welcoming party for baby Joshua was more than appropriate.

Liz was astonished as she saw us bombard her living room with so many items. She hadn't expected this type of a welcome for her baby brother, but, then again, Liz never knew what to expect from the three of us.

Matthew Long saw the three familiar faces and immediately hopped off the couch. Little Matthew followed right beside his father, with his eyes popping as he eyed all the large bags.

"Hello everybody!" Matthew greeted everyone and gave dap and a brotherly hug to David. Little Matthew also hugged us, and David rubbed his curly head and gave him a high five. I really like this Matthew Long fella. Every time I see him, he is always so friendly and full of life. Just perfect for Liz.

"Let me grab that for you," Matthew Sr. said, taking the cake from Sandy.

Such a gentleman, I thought.

Then I glanced over at my man, David, who was busy laying all the items from the bags out neatly on the couch so Liz and Ms. Coleman could see them. It was David's idea to pick up the gifts on our way to the house; he even charged them on his credit card that he pays in full every month.

On the couch were brown and blue teddy bears, a bouncer, four newborn baby outfits, baby shoes, and plenty of bottles, bibs, and diapers. Little Matthew immediately grabbed one of the brown teddy bears.

Matthew Sr. eyed his son as if to say, "That's not yours; put it back."

"That's okay," David said as he kneeled down to little Matthew. "That one's for you." Though we had forgotten to get something for little Matthew, David saved the day. I looked adoringly at my man as he rubbed the child's head and little Matthew smiled.

"You guys are too much!" Liz proclaimed as she eyed the many items. "Mom is going to just scream!"

"Hey, where is she anyway?" Sandy asked. "Enough of the hoopla," Sandy placed her hands on her hips and rolled her neck, "it's time to see the baby!"

"They're in the bedroom. C'mon," Liz said quietly.

David, Sandy and I all followed Liz, Matthew, and little

Matthew to Ms. Coleman's bedroom door.

"Shhhh," Liz said as she quietly opened the bedroom door. Little Matthew mocked her and said, "Shhh," as well.

Once inside, we all were taken aback by the beautiful sight of a mother holding her newborn baby and reading the Bible to him. Baby Joshua was wrapped in a baby blue blanket. Ms. Coleman was reading from the book of Proverbs in the Bible that Liz bought her on the day Ms. Coleman was baptized last May. Ever since that day, she had turned her life around. She stopped chasing men and started focusing more on her upcoming life with little Joshua. Her relationship with Liz had been totally restored, and they now regularly attend church together.

I eased closer to the baby and squealed, "Awwww," as I witnessed the tiny little pink creature with his eyes half open in his mother's arms.

"Wanna hold him?" Ms. Coleman asked sweetly, placing the Bible on the other side of the bed and smiling. I wasn't sure about holding such a tiny little creature. He looked so fragile, so miniature; I didn't want to break him.

 Ms. Coleman placed the little bundle in my arms. I cradled him in my arms and placed my right hand underneath his tiny head for support.

I was awestruck by the joyous sight I beheld in my arms: a newborn baby, almost fresh from the mother's womb. A new creature brought to this earth to experience life, true happiness, and love. I believe that any new life brought into the world is truly God's greatest gift.

Holding the baby reminded me that I, too, one day will get married and then have the privilege of bringing life into the world. I carefully examined the baby's bright pink face, tiny hands, and teeny toes, until I was joined by a familiar person who rightfully took his place beside me.

David stared at the baby with longing eyes as he placed his hands on my shoulders. For some reason, I knew that he, too, believed that the gift of life is God's greatest miracle. As I looked deeply into Baby Joshua's squinting eyes, I whispered ever so softly to the baby, "God is good."

And David whispered in agreement, "All the time."

An Invitation From the Author

If you have never received Jesus Christ as your personal Lord and Savior, I would like to invite you to make the best decision you could ever make in your entire life.

Romans 10:9-10 states:

That if thou shalt confess with thy mouth the Lord Jesus, and shalt believe in thine heart that God hath raised him from the dead, thou shalt be saved. For with the heart man believeth unto righteousness; and with the mouth confession is made unto salvation.

Recite this prayer:

Father, God, I believe that Jesus Christ is the Son of God. I believe He died for me, carried my sins for me, and that He arose, and is alive right now. Lord, Jesus, come into my heart, and save me now. I repent of sin, and I turn toward You. I receive You as my Savior, and I confess You as my Lord. I thank You, Lord, that according to Your Word, I am born again. In Jesus' name, Amen.

Praise God, you are saved! Though you look the same on the outside, on the inside you are a new creature in Christ (2 Corinthians 5:17). If you do not have a church home, I encourage you to join one that teaches the Word of God.

Today marks a day of new beginnings for you!

Sign and date below as a way to remember this day forever.

Signature _____

Date _____

About the Author

Kimberley Brooks has her BA in English from Michigan State University, and is a graduate of Word of Faith Bible Training Center. Kim is a member of American Christian Writers/Detroit. Her articles have appeared in *Soul Source* magazine and *The Michigan Front Page*.

To contact the author for book signings, speaking engagements, or to order more copies of this book visit:

www.kimontheweb.com

or send correspondence to:

Driven Enterprises
P.O. Box 231133
Detroit, MI 48223-1133